A KISS IN THE SHADOWS

Lily DANES · Eve KINCAID

A LOST COAST HARBOR NOVEL

Dark & Stormy Books

Cover Designed by Najla Qamber Designs
www.najlaqamberdesigns.com

Publisher's Note:
This book is a work of fiction. Names, characters, places, and incidents are products of the author's imagination or are used fictitiously. Resemblances to actual locales or events or persons living or dead is coincidental.

ISBN 978-1-944506-03-2

To Mona.
She knows why.

CHAPTER ONE

"Erin, your *boyfriend* is looking for you in the waiting room."

Her coworker's singsong tone sounded cheery as she leaned into the break room, where Erin Grady was attempting to convince the vending machine to part with a diet soda. But under Joan's chirpy voice, Erin could hear a mocking contempt for the guy sitting in the waiting area, probably shivering with delirium tremens.

"Yeah, I'll be right there," Erin said, almost keeping the impatience and exhaustion from leaking into her own voice. She knew who the man in the waiting room was and why he was here.

She abandoned her seventy-five cents to the soda machine and walked down the hall to the emergency room waiting area. Only thirty more minutes and she could go home. Take a shower. Go to sleep. And then in a few hours, come back to Lost Coast Harbor Medical Center for another twelve-hour shift. Such was the glamorous life of an emergency room nurse.

At least after Sunday night, she would be free from the

three-month stretch of weekend, overnight shifts. It played hell with a girl's love life. Not that she had much of one to start with, but it would be nice to give that another try.

As she expected, Rob Katri was shaking so hard that he was nearly vibrating out of his chair. He was tall and lanky, his right foot tapping violently against the linoleum. There was no trace of the former high school all-star baseball player whom Erin had known since kindergarten. His dark hair was cut short, probably by the jail's in-house barber before his last release.

"Hey, Rob, you all right?" Erin sat in the chair next to him and looked him in the eye.

"Nah, not doing so good. Had an accident. My back. It's all messed up." His gaze darted away as soon as she made eye contact and he blinked quickly. He smelled like dirt, and she suspected that he'd been camping out, sleeping in the woods because his wife wouldn't let him come home until he cleaned up. Rob's problems went beyond his addiction, though.

"Have you seen Dr. Kozak lately?" It was a two-hour drive to the psychiatrist who could prescribe Rob with the lithium that would address his schizoaffective disorder. He sort of shrugged, jerking his head to one side in an action that might indicate a no.

"Can't get there right now. Can you help me out?"

Of course he couldn't get there. Rob was only barely employed, working odd jobs when the weather permitted. But she couldn't give him the opiates that would calm his jittery nerves and help him get through the next few days. It wasn't just the psychological benefits that he craved. Rob had been self-medicating since shortly after high school and was a full-blown addict.

"You want Dr. Ashette to take a look at your back?"

She glanced up at the counter and saw Joan shake her head slightly. Erin frowned. If Rob really had hurt himself, she wasn't about to run him off just because he was also an addict. It was tricky, trying to balance pain management with a known addiction, but that's why the doctors made twice her salary.

Rob stood up, shoving his hands in the pockets of his coat. He watched a man, similarly dressed and ungroomed, walk quickly out from the intake area and then into the parking lot. The two made eye contact and Rob started toward the door.

"Rob, wait." Erin followed him to the glass doors, which slid open and let in a blast of damp morning air that penetrated her scrubs. "Are you sure you don't need to see the doctor?"

He shook his head, his eyes downcast. "No, thanks, Erin."

He bolted through the door and into the parking lot, walking fast in the direction that the other man had gone. It looked like he'd get a few pills to tide him over.

"Who was that guy?" Dr. Ashette asked, joining her near the ER counter.

Erin watched Rob hurry to catch his friend. "My prom date."

"Lucky girl," Dr. Ashette said with a short laugh.

"He's bipolar and has schizophrenic hallucinations when he's really manic. Because we don't have a psych doc on hand, his mental illness is largely untreated."

"So get him in with Kozak," Dr. Ashette said.

Erin glared at the glib response. "He can't get there for regular visits. He needs a doctor here. Or at least somewhere his family could drive him on a regular basis."

Dr. Ashette shrugged. "Tough break."

Logan Ashette was a young and inexperienced doctor, and he was new to Lost Coast Harbor. Erin had been trying to cut him some slack as he got to know the hospital's procedures, because with a little more maturity, he'd be a good doctor. As soon as he figured out that the nurses were his partners, and could teach him a lot. But she was running low on patience. He was too young to be this callous.

And she was also exhausted and knew her own temper. It was time for her to walk away. She checked the clock—ten minutes left on her shift. Surely she could find a task away from the flippant young physician until seven o'clock arrived. She started down the hall, but only made it a few feet before Dr. Ashette called her name.

"Do me a favor and don't hand off the junkies to me, okay?" he said.

Erin turned so fast her ponytail whipped around and hit her in the face.

"Oh, of course, Dr. Ashette. I'll make sure you only get the healthiest of patients in the ER," Erin said. "Get over yourself. It's a fucking emergency room."

The doctor's head jerked back like she'd slapped him. Which she would love to do. As it was, in her burst of sarcasm, she'd nearly called him Dr. Asshat—her secret nickname for the arrogant jerk. Either action would probably cost her at least a demotion to a less desirable shift. Though she couldn't imagine a worse assignment than the weekend overnight shifts in the emergency room.

"Who are you—Florence Fucking Nightingale?" he snapped.

Erin stalked back to the break room, grabbed her soda from the tray where it had finally dropped, and headed to the locker room to change out of her scrubs and into running gear. A run would do her good. Just get out and clear her head and get Dr. Asshat and Rob Katri out of there. She clocked out and finished her soda on the way to her car.

After dropping her scrubs in the washing machine, Erin stepped out of her back door, let herself through the gate, and began her run up the hill, her shoes barely making a sound on the thick carpet of redwood needles.

The Redwood Park Trail ran along the north side of the town of Lost Coast Harbor, starting at the beach and ending three miles inland. It ran behind Erin's neighborhood, and she could walk out her backyard and step onto the trail. Minutes later she'd be taking the stairs down to the beach, or be running up the hill on a soft dirt path that wound through the tall trees.

Usually by the time she neared the cemetery, she'd have found her stride and her mind would be clear and focused on the sounds of the wind through the branches. But this morning her mind was filled with images of Rob Katri shivering in the emergency room. His family blamed his problems on drugs, but Rob's diagnosis wasn't that simple. It wasn't possible to separate the two threads of addiction and mental illness—not while he was in the throes of both. He needed help that wasn't available in Lost Coast Harbor.

At least, not yet. Erin was working to get a mental health clinic in Lost Coast Harbor. After two years of begging for support and donations from the medical community, she'd been close. But a couple of weeks ago, her plans hit yet another hurdle and she worried that she would be starting over.

Erin hit the bend after the cemetery, breathing hard and no closer to that elusive runner's high. She rounded a curve and saw the row of wooden fences that marked the beginning of the neighborhood where she lived as a child.

As always, she kept her gaze straight ahead as she ran and didn't look at the weathered barrier that separated the large house on the end from the public trail. She hadn't even meant to run all the way to the park and her legs shook slightly as she stopped at the entrance to turn around. The high-pitched sound of children laughing filtered across the park from the direction of the soccer field and Erin realized that it was Saturday morning and the crowds would be growing. She wasn't feeling particularly social, and she needed to get some sleep before she had to report back to LCH Med Center for the Saturday overnight shift, so she slapped the top of the post marking the entrance to the park, turned, and started back down the trail.

This time, she let herself look at the familiar wooden fence. The gate was as she remembered it from when she was nine, before her parents divorced. Her mom had run a string up and over the top of the gate so she could easily get back into the yard from the park, since she couldn't reach over the top and unhook the latch.

Every time she passed by the back of the house, she wondered why she and her mother had moved to a run-down duplex across town and why Jerry Grady remained in the large house next to the park, a perfect place for a child to grow up. Instead, she had had a small backyard that was mostly a cracked cement patio. Good for hopscotch, but not much else.

She shook herself out of her reminiscence and started back down the trail, taking her time with a slower pace. The slight downhill slope was a nice cool-down after her two-mile run. A few yards down the hill the path narrowed, a steep hill to her right and the fences to the left, creating a tunnel effect for about fifty yards. The geography and trees muted the sounds of the park and she could only hear the birds and the rustle of the branches overhead.

It was the peace she'd been hoping to find.

Until the rustle in the woods grew louder, and escalated into crashing and snapping branches.

And a man crashed through the brush and onto the trail, just yards in front of her.

Chapter Two

From the moment his front tire hit the rock in its path, Will Patton knew it wasn't going to end well. He gripped the handlebars and tried to guide the bike back onto the path that dozens or hundreds of previous mountain bikers had carved in the soft dirt.

No deal. His momentum was too great and he and the bike were launched beyond the edge of the path, over a fallen tree, its branches reaching up and scraping Will's skin. He stuck one leg out to slow his descent down a steep grade, but this just changed his trajectory, and his tumble into the ravine continued. A thick branch filled his view and he ducked, narrowly missing having his head taken off. His limbs tangled with the bike, and as one, they slid, rolled, and bounced through a patch of thick bushes and came to rest on a bed of redwood needles.

Will didn't move for a long moment, his heart racing and his body screaming. He ran through an anatomical inventory and confirmed that everything hurt. He opened his eyes at the sound of footsteps and tried to move but found his legs immobile—but from the bike or some other reason, he couldn't tell. A bubble of panic started to rise in his gut, threatening to choke him.

"Don't move."

He blinked and tried to twist his head to see who was talking to him, but a hand firmly held his head in place by pinning his helmet to the ground.

"Do not move."

It was a woman, a bossy one, but whoever she was would remain a mystery. With his head on the ground, his only view was of the dirt and leaves and brush that he'd just mowed through. Cool hands pressed against his neck and shoulders as the scent of decomposing pine needles filled his nose.

"Can you move your fingers?"

He wiggled them experimentally. At least he'd still be able to type. His boss would be thrilled.

She blew out a relieved breath and he assumed it was good news. She moved to his feet, her capable hands probing around his ankles. Trying not to move his head, which was throbbing from the impact with the ground, he caught a glimpse of her in his peripheral vision and his breath quickened.

Holy God, she was pretty. Long hair, the color of honey, pulled back into a ponytail. Her eyes were downcast as she focused on looking for any injuries, and thick black eyelashes rested against creamy skin. She was wearing running clothes. She disconnected her earbuds from her phone and dialed. She looked up at him and caught his eye, giving him a reassuring smile that quickly faded as the call connected.

"I need a medical assist, on the Park Trail. Got a biker down, possible broken shoulder, maybe a concussion. Unsure if there's neck or spinal trauma. I'm near the top of the trail."

Will could hear the 911 dispatcher's response, but it was muffled. The woman looked around the wooded area, her forehead furrowed. "If the ambulance goes to the parking lot at the city park, they're going to have to walk about a half-mile to the trailhead. The fastest way is through Chief Grady's backyard. We're about seventy-five yards west of his gate."

More indecipherable mumbling from the dispatcher. His rescuer moved his sock around to check his ankle and he jerked in response.

"Don't move."

"Your hands are cold."

Her serious expression softened a bit with a hint of a smile. "That's good news."

He relaxed a bit at her diagnosis. He wasn't paralyzed.

"Patient can feel cold in extremities and can move his fingers," she said, all business again, answering questions from the dispatcher.

She ran her hands up his leg, feeling for broken bones, and he momentarily forgot the pain. Her hands were capable and professional, but it had been a while since a beautiful woman had knelt in front of him for any reason. He swallowed hard and tried to focus on the pain in his shoulder.

"No apparent fractures."

Another pause in the conversation.

"Yes, this is Erin Grady." She looked up at him with wide gray-blue eyes. "What's your name?"

He swallowed, staring into the stormy depth of her eyes and trying to remember even the most basic information she had asked for. He may have landed harder than he originally thought. He'd never had trouble talking to women. Yet here he was, stammering and struggling to respond to her.

She leaned forward, her worried expression growing, and he forced himself to focus over the sharp jab of pain in his temple.

"Will Patton," he said.

"Where do you live?"

"516 Sand Piper Court."

"You're local?"

"Sort of."

She relayed the information to the dispatcher, then turned back to him with additional questions designed to check for brain damage—the year, the name of the president, the current date.

"Is there anyone I can call to meet you at the hospital?"

Will paused a second before answering that. "No."

Not a soul cared that he'd just tossed himself off a cliff. His parents lived seven hundred miles south in San Diego, but were on a cruise in the Greek Isles. A few friends from law school, now scattered across the state, would probably piss themselves laughing. There were a couple of friends who lived a two-hour drive away in Ukiah, where he'd lived before he was transferred to Lost Coast Harbor. In the four months he'd lived in Lost Coast Harbor, he'd immersed himself in his job and had met very few people who weren't his coworkers. He didn't plan on staying long, so there was no need to put down roots.

"I hear them," Erin said into the phone, then she thanked the dispatcher and disconnected the call. She waved up the trail and the sound of footsteps grew. Then a cloud passed over his rescuer's face as the paramedics grew closer.

"Erin, what the hell do you think you're doing?" The angry man approaching knew his rescuer, and didn't seem at all happy to see her.

"It's going to be easier to get Mr. Patton off the trail if we can use your backyard. But if you're going to be an ass about it, I'm sure one of your neighbors will do the right thing and let us cross through their property."

From behind him, Will heard the deep, frustrated huff from the man.

"No, of course they can." The man walked to where Erin still knelt in the dirt and redwood needles. He placed a hand awkwardly on her shoulder, which she ignored. "Good to see you."

She bit her lip. "Yeah, you, too."

Erin Grady was a terrible liar. The man behind her knew it. He had a short, silver military-style haircut and a deep scowl and he was familiar to Will—Lost Coast Harbor Chief of Police Jerry Grady.

"Hey, Chief."

"Patton," Chief Grady said with a nod. "What happened here?"

"You two know each other?" Erin asked, eyeing Will with suspicion. "Are you a cop?"

"He's with the district attorney's office," Grady said.

"Ah," Erin said, smirking and looking away, very much not impressed.

The paramedics had him strapped to the board in short order with Erin's help. No one seemed to think he had sustained any damage to his spinal column, but until they could get an X-ray, they weren't taking any chances. His arm was bound across his chest with a strap to minimize movement of his shoulder, where a sharp pain told him he had probably broken something. Erin followed them up the trail and through a wooden gate. Chief Grady carried Will's bike and set it on the back deck of the two-story bungalow.

"You can come by and pick it up later," he said, as Will was loaded into the ambulance parked in the chief's driveway.

Will had met Chief Grady several times in the last few months since he was transferred to the Lost Coast Harbor office of the Mendocino County District Attorney's office, but those meetings had been brief, professional. Will hadn't learned much about the man from their face-to-face talks. But Will had read enough reports from the LCH Police Department officers to get a better idea about Grady's long reign as chief. The department had problems, and the chief either didn't care about sloppy police work, excessive force, and other questionable practices, or he was as incompetent as his officers.

But recently, the town was rocked by the arrest of Peter Hastings—wealthy local businessman and the most prominent citizen of Lost Coast Harbor. Hastings, now residing in lockup in Oakland, was facing multiple federal charges for gun running, accused of using his shipping company to transport illegal weapons.

This gave Will an opportunity to exit this small town at the literal edge of the world. The federal agents were investigating and prosecuting Hastings. But Hastings' scheme couldn't have operated without help—and Will was willing to bet that the local cops had helped the man evade law enforcement.

Erin climbed in beside him, adjusting the straps on the gurney and helping one of the medics get it secured.

"You're coming with me?"

"I work at the ER," she said.

"A doctor?"

"I'm a nurse."

"You're in good hands," the chief said, and then looked at Erin. "Come by for dinner."

It didn't sound like an invitation, more like an order. She bristled at the command, but gave a quick nod. "I work nights."

"Not all of them," Grady growled, then slammed the door shut.

Erin ignored the outburst and kept her focus on Will. "He's my father," she said.

He studied her, tried to see any resemblance to the chief. She must have taken after her mother because he wouldn't have guessed that she was related to Chief Grady. Some of her light-brown hair had escaped her ponytail and fell around a pretty face with gray eyes and fair skin that turned pink when she realized he was looking at her.

"You don't take after your father," he said.

"No, I don't," she said, looking away quickly and tugging a blood pressure cuff into place on his free arm. She dictated his vitals to the EMT. There wasn't time to do much more than that before the ambulance parked in front of the emergency room doors and Will was extracted and rolled into the

ER, Erin Grady jogging along at the side of the gurney.

"Weren't you just here?" A woman in her forties asked, joining Erin. From her scrubs and badge, he figured the dark-haired woman was also a nurse.

"Missed you guys too much," Erin said, flashing a smile at the nurse.

A doctor who was so young he looked like he was playing dress-up bent over him and checked Will's eyes with a penlight, then did the same Q&A that Erin had already done on the trail, but with less concern.

"I'm Dr. Logan Ashette. We're going to get you into X-ray. Looks like your shoulder took the brunt of your fall. You may have broken your collarbone."

He pushed himself back and snapped his fingers at one of the nurses. "Hey, get his helmet off."

The dark-haired nurse gently unbuckled Will's chinstrap, giving him an apologetic smile.

Erin Grady had disappeared from Will's view, but she hadn't gone far. As more people joined in to transfer him to a different gurney, she rattled off her findings—his blood pressure, notable contusions, and which bones to check for fractures. His helmet was removed and he heard a low whistle as someone examined it.

"Lucky guy," Erin said, coming back into his view with a warm smile. "If you weren't wearing that helmet, you wouldn't be dealing with Dr. Asshat."

"Erin, honestly," the other nurse said with an exasperated laugh.

"You mean I could have gotten someone with a better bedside manner?" Will asked.

"No. You'd be dealing with Dr. McCormick, the medical examiner."

"I guess I prefer Dr. Asshat."

She grinned, revealing deep dimples, then patted his arm. The warm touch made his skin tingle. "Try and stay on the trail next time."

She disappeared again and the gurney started rolling away.

"Wait—"

"Is there anyone I can call for you?" the dark-haired nurse asked, as she pushed the gurney down the wide hall. "A wife, or a girlfriend?"

She looked at him with such open curiosity, Will briefly considered lying. "No."

"Boyfriend?"

"No."

She looked even more curious. "How about family? Friends?"

"No. I just moved here."

"Oh, really? How long have you been in Lost Coast Harbor?"

"About four months."

"And no friends, huh?"

Where was this X-ray room, a neighboring county? Will thought.

"I've been working a lot."

He'd been throwing himself into his job in order to avoid dealing with the fact that he'd been shipped off against his will to this small town on the edge of California, and trying to find a way to get back to civilization. There was no telling how long his sentence to this "promotion" was, but if he could find a few high-profile cases to send back to his boss, that could earn him some time off for good behavior.

"What do you do?"

"I'm a deputy district attorney." His actual title, supervising assistant district attorney, implied some authority or importance, when in truth he managed two other lawyers and oversaw misdemeanor prosecutions, while all the big cases were sent to the main office, where he used to work, to be taken to trial.

"A lawyer, huh?"

The foot of the gurney hit a set of double doors which he hoped meant that Nurse Busybody would stop asking questions.

A couple of hours later, his ribs were taped, his arm was in a sling, and his legs and arms were slathered in antibiotic cream where they'd been sliced from the branches. While he had wrenched his shoulder, it wasn't broken, and neither was his collarbone, but he was going to be sore for a few days.

The helmet had done its job and spared him from death or permanent brain injury. But the few blows he had taken had resulted in a slight concussion and a killer headache—and without someone at home to take care of him, Dr. Ashette refused to release him.

"We'll take good care of you," Nurse Busybody said, as she helped him into the regular hospital bed.

If he was going to be stuck in the hospital overnight with nothing but basic cable, he might as well make the most of it. Fate had dropped Erin Grady into his life at the best possible time. He wasn't going to let that opportunity pass. Especially when the chief's daughter turned out to have interesting gray eyes, dimples, and a quick wit.

Will checked the badge pinned to the nurse's dark blue scrubs.

"So, Joan," he said with a warm smile. "What's the story with Erin Grady?"

CHAPTER THREE

Erin walked through the empty waiting area and toward the employee lounge, ready for whatever trauma the Saturday night shift would throw her way.

By morning, she expected that she and her coworkers would have patched up several wounds from bar brawls. There'd be the usual alcohol poisonings, drug overdoses, domestic violence fall-outs, car accidents, and maybe even a gunshot. Those were growing more common, as battles over marijuana grow sites heated up along the Lost Coast.

No matter what came her way in the next twelve hours, she'd tackle it knowing she was now only two shifts away from ending a three-month rotation on weekend overnight shifts.

Her coworker Joan, coming off the day shift, followed her into the lounge, carrying a small stack of patient files to hand off to Erin. "Thank you, my dear, for your delivery this morning. Any time you want to bring us a gorgeous, charming lawyer, you feel free to do that. Will Patton has certainly improved the view around here today."

"Well, I saw him lying on the ground and I just couldn't

resist," Erin said with a grin. "But why is he still here? I thought his injuries were superficial."

"Dr. Ashette kept him overnight because he has a slight concussion," Joan said. Her voice dropped in volume. "He's single. No one at home to care for him."

She gave Erin a knowing nod.

"Thanks for the tip. Maybe I'll get lucky on my break," Erin said, stuffing her duffel bag into a locker.

"You're terrible," Joan laughed. "The good Lord throws a man at you, you don't ignore that."

"You're saying God threw a man off a cliff at me?"

Joan shrugged. "It could be a sign."

Erin gave her coworker a skeptical look. In truth, though, she was secretly pleased that she might be able to see Will Patton again. He had been on her mind since the brief encounter that morning. Who was he and why was he in Lost Coast Harbor?

"He was asking about you."

Her stomach did an unfamiliar flip at Joan's words, but she shook her head and gave her coworker a dismissive wave. "Go home. Get out of here and have a social life. Do it for those of us stuck on the night shifts."

She grabbed the files from Joan and returned to the main nursing station to start her shift, but stopped at the intake counter when she saw a familiar pair checking in—her friend Maddie Palmer and Maddie's new boyfriend Gabriel Reyes.

"Hey guys, is everything okay?" she asked.

Maddie smiled and nodded toward Gabe. "Just here to get his stitches removed."

Erin took the clipboard from the clerk. "I can handle that.

Come with me."

She led them through the swinging doors into the triage area, past the usual pre-shift-change chaos, and to a quiet corner. Gabe sat on the edge of the bed and Maddie perched on a plastic chair at the side. He kept Maddie's hand in his as Erin cleaned up and brought out a tray of tools and supplies.

Erin pulled up a stool and sat next the bed, then rolled up the short sleeve of Gabe's T-shirt and studied the crooked line of stitches across his skin.

"This has healed up well, Gabe. You probably won't even have a scar."

She wiped down the area with antiseptic and got to work. It had been a week since Gabe and Maddie had been caught up in the arrest of Peter Hastings on gun-running charges. The gash on Gabe's arm brought home how lucky the couple was that this was the extent of their physical damage.

Erin smeared some antibiotic cream over the pink healing skin, then taped a gauze pad over the wound and pulled his sleeve back into place. She removed her gloves and pushed the tray away.

"Do you have a minute to talk?" Maddie asked.

The ER was busy, but not yet chaotic, so Erin led them through the back of the triage area to a hall that led to the general admission area where it was quieter. She pulled them around a corner, near an empty room, where they wouldn't be disturbed.

"What's going on?" Erin asked.

"We met with that attorney, the one from San Francisco. He's going to represent us, in case Hastings' attorneys try and harass us. Gabe kind of pissed the man off." Maddie smiled at her new boyfriend, and Gabe returned it. For just a moment, the two were lost in their own world.

Erin's heart squeezed at her friend's happiness. Her own thirtieth birthday had just come and gone and she was no closer to finding that sort of happiness herself. Maddie's love gave Erin hope that it wasn't impossible to find someone, even in Lost Coast Harbor.

"I'm really happy for you. For both of you," she said. "Did your lawyer have any news on the case?"

"We discussed how Hastings could have gotten away with this for so many years," Gabe said. "He didn't think it was a federal agent who was tipping off Hastings. He says it's more likely someone in local law enforcement. Like the police or the district attorney's office."

Maddie shot a worried glance at Erin. "Could you talk to your father? Maybe he'd know if someone on his force—"

Erin shook her head, her stomach churning at the thought. "No. I can't talk to him about this. I can't talk to him about anything, but especially not whether he's hired dirty cops."

She understood Maddie's worries. There could be loose ends, unknown conspirators, or partners who wanted to hide evidence of their involvement with the businessman-turned-criminal mastermind.

"Jerry Grady is not going to open up to me," Erin said. "But if there's anything else I can do, please call, okay?"

"I will," Maddie said. "How are the plans for the clinic coming along?"

Erin groaned. "Well, you guys busted my biggest donor, so I may lose that fifty-thousand-dollar pledge. But it was probably dirty money anyway."

Despite the many hours of work she'd put toward the goal of providing mental health services for the small town, she felt no closer to accomplishing it. She'd gotten many small donations, some larger ones, and had even talked a local attorney into helping her set up a nonprofit organization and handle the licensing paperwork. But her attorney warned her that Hastings' arrest meant she might never see his donation.

"Sorry, Erin," Maddie said, with a sympathetic smile. "You'll make it up, I'm sure."

Erin wasn't at all sure she'd be able to find another donor willing to part with fifty thousand dollars. Hastings was the wealthiest man in Lost Coast Harbor. The thought of having to cobble together enough money to cover that loss made her a little sick to her stomach.

She pointed Maddie and Gabe toward the main entrance so they wouldn't have to go back through the emergency room, then turned to return to the ER. As she started toward the door that would lead her back into the Saturday night madness, she caught a glimpse of a familiar name on a door.

She paused in the doorway and knocked, and Will Patton looked up from the bed.

Good God. Her breath caught in her chest at the sight. When the man had fallen into her path, she'd noticed his strong jaw, his broad shoulders, and especially those thighs, thick and muscled. She wasn't blind. It hadn't been easy to stay focused, but her medical training had kicked in and she didn't have enough time to appreciate those features. Now she took it all in—his eyes that were not quite brown or green but something in between, the way his muscular chest and arms managed to look sexy even in a hospital gown. His short, dark hair that was slightly damp from a shower.

He waved her into the room with a smile that made her heart skip. He looked relaxed as he watched a college basketball game on the small, wall-mounted TV. If it hadn't been for the hospital gown and the navy blue sling that kept his shoulder immobile, he could be any other sports fan enjoying a game.

"Hello, Erin Grady," he said, motioning to the chair by the bed.

Several deep red scratches marred his forearms, but those would fade to nothing in a week or so. His face was untouched by the tumble through the trees. It was a nice face, too. His eyes were fringed with long eyelashes, and the overhead fluorescent lights that made most people look even more sickly managed to highlight his cheekbones.

Erin smiled at his greeting, but remained standing by his bed. "Will Patton. How are you feeling?"

He tilted his head and studied her. "Still have a headache, but otherwise, I'm fine."

Erin glanced at the gilt-edge China plate on his tray table, where remnants of his dinner remained. "Funny, I don't think I've ever seen pot roast served to our patients here. Are those roasted carrots?"

Will laughed and the deep sound sent a shiver into her stomach.

"My neighbors brought me dinner. Barb was worried that the food here wouldn't be any good."

"I'm glad you found some friends," she said, then poked another small plate on the tray. "And the cheesecake?"

"Nurse Brenda brought that for me. She seems nice."

Erin snorted. "You must have really turned on the charm because Brenda Portofino has never brought me cheesecake in the five years I've worked with her."

"I guess she likes me."

His smile, confident and warm, nearly took her breath away. *Damn.* A smile like that could get a girl in trouble. Composing herself, Erin raised an eyebrow. "Be careful. Brenda has three unmarried daughters in their early twenties."

Brenda wasn't subtle about her desire to get her girls married off and producing grandchildren for her, but this might have been a new low—trawling the hospital for potential suitors.

Will's face blanched beneath the slight scruff of beard. "She didn't mention that."

"Did she invite you to dinner yet?"

His face paled even more. "Should I have said no?"

Erin smiled. "Guess it depends on how much you like that cheesecake."

She picked up his chart, noted his diagnoses, and that his nurses were checking in on time or early on their rounds. She couldn't blame them for stopping to chat with the good-looking newcomer to Lost Coast Harbor. After all, she didn't even work in this department and yet here she was, standing next to his bed trying not to stare.

"Looks like you'll be out in time for your neighbors to make you breakfast," she said, setting the chart back in the plastic bin next to his bed.

"I don't usually get so spoiled. I may have to fall off my bike more often," he said, his smile growing.

He shifted and tried to pull up the pillow behind his injured shoulder and Erin automatically stepped forward to help. It was a simple task, one she'd done countless times since becoming a nurse. But when her hand brushed against the skin at the back of his neck it sent a delicious tremor throughout her body.

She stepped back quickly, her heart beating a little faster. "I should get back to work. I just wanted to make sure you were okay."

"Thanks for coming by. I never really got a chance to say thank you. In fact—"

Brenda Portofino stuck her head into the room, interrupting Will. Her smile faded as she saw Erin.

"Oh, Erin, what are you doing here?"

"She saved me on the trail," Will said and Erin stifled a laugh at his overblown description of what she'd done.

"Oh, that was you? How nice," Brenda said. Her smile was forced and her voice as tight as the permed curls that encircled her round face. "Well, I'm sure you're very busy. The ER is always so exciting on the weekends."

"Right, yes, I should be going," Erin said, turning back to Will. "Glad to see you're feeling better. Take care."

She started to the door, and Brenda moved to one side to let her out.

"Maybe you can talk with my daughter, Evelyn, about the nursing program at San Francisco State. She's going to be stopping by later," Brenda said. Erin glanced back at Will, who now looked trapped in the bed.

"I didn't know Evelyn was interested in nursing, but I'd be happy to talk to her," Erin said, then gave Will a pitying look. "Good luck, Will."

"I'll see you tomorrow night," he said.

"Wait, what?" Erin asked.

"Huh?" Brenda said, her brow furrowing.

"Erin is going to let me buy her dinner, so I can pay her back for taking such good care of me," Will said.

Erin raised an eyebrow in Will's direction, and he flashed that smile at her again, sending a flutter through her stomach.

"She's working tomorrow night, right, Erin?" Brenda's desperation shone through the question and Erin bit her lip to keep from smirking.

"Yes, that's right. He meant Monday night," Erin said, tapping her own head. "It's the blow to the head. You should keep an eye on that."

She slipped out the door, throwing a wink to Will, who smiled gratefully.

He wasn't serious about dinner, but she was happy to help anyone escape Brenda's matchmaking clutches. Brenda's loser son had finally gotten married, so at least she had stopped eyeing Erin and her child-bearing hips.

And it wouldn't hurt to have a friendly contact inside the district attorney's office with so many loose ends still in the Hastings case. Gabe and Maddie were right to be worried about others who helped Hastings evade arrest for so many years. If that was someone in the police or district attorney's office, Will might know who it was, or how to find them.

Erin returned to her department, and back to the regularly scheduled chaos of a small town emergency room. It wasn't until nearly dawn when Erin found time to sit down at the nurses' station and take a few minutes to catch up on paperwork.

A brisk knock on the counter made her jump and she looked up, expecting to find Dr. Asshat with another demand that he could easily handle himself. Instead, she found herself looking at her father.

Not Jerry Grady, chief of police for the town of Lost Coast Harbor. But the man she considered her real dad, the one who raised her since she was eleven, who taught her to ride a bike, drive a car, and land a punch should she ever need to defend herself. Alan White, though technically a stepfather, had earned her devotion.

"Hey, Alan," she said with a smile at the surprise visit. Then her mind went to the reasons for a surprise visit to an emergency room. "Is everyone okay?"

Alan nodded, but his eyes were tired. The overhead fluorescent lights picked up the strands of silver threaded through his dark hair, which usually made him look distinguished, but tonight made him look older than his sixty-two years.

"Your mom. She's having a tough spell. I'm driving her to Santa Rosa this morning. Her doctor called in a prescription to pick up here before we go."

Erin stood, the adrenaline overriding the effects of a twelve-hour overnight shift. "Is she here? What are her symptoms?"

"She's meeting with Dr. Ashette to get the prescription filled," Alan said, putting a hand on Erin's arm. "And she's going to be okay. She's just been up all night. It's been going on a few days. Trust me, Leanne knows she needs to do this."

Her mother's bipolar disorder was carefully managed, but

the swings between depression and mania still happened. They just didn't come as often, and weren't as wild, as before.

"How long will you be gone?"

"Let's see how it goes," Alan said. "In the meantime, can you keep an eye on the kids?"

"Of course. They know what's going on?"

He nodded. "They've been watching her in the past couple of weeks and we've talked about this."

"Not with me," Erin said.

"I didn't want to worry you," he said, and Erin frowned. If anyone knew the difficulty of living with someone, of loving someone, with bipolar disorder, it was the two of them. She often thought of herself and Alan as a team, the two people with the most experience managing Leanne's mental health.

"I should have called sooner. I thought I'd see you next week and we could talk about it then. But this morning, she told me she hadn't been sleeping for several nights, and… well, I guess it was worse than I realized," Alan said.

Erin nodded. "It's okay. What can I do to help?"

"June's going to stay at the house with Colin and Hayley," Alan said.

Erin nodded. If anyone could wrangle the two teenagers, it was their Aunt June, a retired schoolteacher.

"Colin has an early class, so Hayley may need a ride to school in the morning," Alan said.

"I thought she was taking her driving test Friday," Erin said. Her sister had been dreaming of the freedom that comes with a driver's license since she was ten years old. Her first two attempts at passing the driving test hadn't gone well.

Alan shook his head and looked down with a small smile.

"You probably don't want to bring that up with her. Maybe you could take her out driving. She could use some practice."

"Oh, hell, no," Erin said. "Anything else I should know?"

He shook his head. "I'll be home as soon as I can."

The implication was that Leanne would need to stay longer at the hospital's psychiatric ward. Erin followed Alan's gaze down the hall toward a private consulting room, where the door was closed. She hurried to the door, knocked and let herself in. Her mother sat rigid on a chair, one foot rapidly tapping the floor. Dr. Ashette had pulled up a stool and held Leanne's hand. Her eyes were wide and damp with tears.

"You're going to be fine, Mrs. White," he said. "You've got a great family to care for you. We'll get this under control."

Leanne gave a jerky nod, and then she saw Erin and smiled with trembling lips.

"Mom," Erin said, rushing forward to embrace her mother.

Love and worry twisted her insides. Three years ago, during Leanne's last episode, she'd taken her easel and oils and disappeared for two days, caught up in the euphoria of her manic episode. Erin still got frantic when she remembered the hours spent searching the coastline for her mother's body.

"Oh, sweetheart, I'm so sorry," Leanne said, returning the hug. Erin closed her eyes and breathed in the familiar scent of her mother's favorite perfume, mixed with a hint of oil paint and linseed oil from her art studio.

"It's not your fault. It's going to be okay," she said.

"I spoke with admitting and they're waiting for you in Santa Rosa. Everything's ready for you. It's time to get well, to take care of yourself," Dr. Ashette said, his voice gentle and soothing.

Erin walked her parents out of the ER and into the still-dark parking lot where the inky sky was starting to lift. The street lamps were ringed with halos, as the light reflected off the fog that blanketed the coast in the early morning.

"Be careful," she said, as Alan hugged her. "It's thick out there. Don't drive too fast."

"Hey, who's the parent here?" He gave her an affectionate squeeze at his joke, but they both knew the answer to that. For too many years, Erin was the one responsible for making sure her mother went to work, went to a doctor, or made meals.

She kissed her mom and closed the passenger door, then waved as the car pulled away.

When she turned to walk back into the hospital, Dr. Ashette was standing by the entrance waiting for her.

"She's going to be okay," he said.

Erin pressed her lips together. "Yeah. I know."

"I'm not just saying that, Erin. I've seen a lot of patients with your mother's diagnosis. She sought the help out herself, she recognized her symptoms. She didn't try and rationalize them away until she was in psychosis," he said. "Your mother's illness can be managed and she knows that. And she wants to manage it. That there is more than half the battle."

Erin felt the pinprick of tears behind her eyes and looked away toward the empty parking lot.

"Thank you," she whispered, as she felt the rush of air from the sliding doors open behind her.

She looked over her shoulder. She was alone in front of

the doors.

Damn it. She might have to stop calling him Dr. Asshat

CHAPTER FOUR

Will shifted his weight, unable to get comfortable in the hard metal folding chair. It wasn't just the sling keeping his arm pinned to his chest, which he still wasn't used to a couple of days after his brief hospital stay. Nor was it the literal pain in his neck where the muscles were still healing from the fall. He could head back to the hospital for a checkup, just as soon as Erin Grady was working again. But that wasn't until later in the week, according to her gossipy coworker. He'd just have to find some other excuse to see her.

Since he'd met her, he found himself increasingly distracted by thoughts of her—her smile, the take-charge way she'd handled the EMTs and his transport to the hospital, the way her scrubs managed to hint at the sexy curves underneath. That thought made him wonder what she was wearing under the simple uniform. Something sporty, he figured. She was a runner, so he could far too easily imagine her in something simple, that just cupped her curves.

Barely suppressing a frustrated sigh, he dragged his thoughts to the problem in front of him—the metaphorical pain in the neck sitting across from him in the small interview room.

"Mr. Acuff, why would the police want to set you up? What motive would they have to frame you?" Will asked, glancing up from the empty legal pad to study the scrawny kid in orange jail garb. Bad haircut, pockmarked sallow skin. Far too young to look that worn out. At the kid's side was his harried public defender, Melissa Murphy.

Bobby Acuff looked away, his brow furrowed. "I don't know, man. But they did it. I swear."

Melissa nudged her client with her elbow. "Tell him, Bobby. We're here to get a deal. You don't get a deal unless Mr. Patton knows what you know."

He shrugged. "Yeah."

There was a long pause, as the young man screwed up the courage to keep talking. Will could tell it was fear that was keeping him from talking. He'd read Bobby Acuff's priors and he wasn't the quiet type. Most of the 22-year-old's prior run-ins with the law had started with him shooting his mouth off and ended with him in a fight.

"What's going on, Bobby?" Will asked, setting his pen down on the legal pad and rested his elbows on the table.

"I know I've done some stupid things, but I swear, Mr. Patton, I didn't do this," he said, his sunken eyes meeting Will's. "I didn't have nothing in my car when they pulled me over. It wasn't my meth."

Always with the dirty cop routine. There wasn't a criminal out there who hadn't tried that line at some point. Will squinted at the young man, going over the details of Bobby's case. It hadn't stood out among the typical, run-of-the-mill arrests he saw weekly in Lost Coast Harbor. He had rolled through a stop sign, the officer pulled him over, and saw a pipe in the kid's center console. Upon a search of the vehicle, the officer found a bag of meth big enough to make the case for distribution, though it was still only charged as possession at this point.

"So, what do you want me to do here, Bobby?"

"Come on, Will. Just listen to him, okay? There may be a Hastings connection," Melissa said.

As soon as she mentioned Hastings, Will was listening. In fact, he was trying not to appear too eager for the information. It might not be worth the time Melissa had asked for. But if Bobby Acuff actually knew something about dirty cops that were connected to Hastings, then Will wanted that information more than Melissa could ever know.

"Don't disappoint me, Bobby," he said.

Bobby sat up straighter in his chair. "Okay, see, I used to drive for Hastings, make deliveries. Nothing big. I mean, just short trips by car."

Will tilted his head, but didn't say anything.

"And I know the back roads, so I used to meet up with someone on 101, then I'd drive back. It was pretty easy money and I never got caught. I thought that was sort of strange, you know. I mean, they bust a lot of people around here and I'm driving around with a trunk full of the best weed in the county."

"Wait—weed?" Hastings had been selling illegal weapons, likely to Mexican drug cartels, offloading the goods in international waters. But there hadn't been any talk about adding drug trafficking to the long list of charges Peter Hastings was facing.

"Yeah. Weed. And lots of it."

"Okay, and you personally dealt with Hastings for these trips?"

Bobby frowned and shook his head. "No, man. It's just that now when I think about it, it must have been him, right?"

Will started to stand. He had a stack of case files on his desk to review before court and had heard enough of Bobby's conspiracy theories.

"Wait, man," Bobby said, his voice desperate. "Look, there's something else, but I don't want anyone to know that I told you this."

Will sat down, but tapped his watch.

"Okay, so, I picked up a load and brought it back to this barn off old Coast Trail. You know, up north about five miles or so."

Will nodded, but didn't say anything.

"Well, I drove through Lost Coast Harbor, just on the edge of town and I got pulled over and I thought, that's it, I'm dead. I was driving a mini-Winnebago and it was packed with like, a crap-ton of weed, man. It was in coolers and it was shrink-wrapped, but if the officer brought in a drug dog, I would be so busted," he said, his voice growing more animated as if the adrenaline from the event were still coursing through his veins.

"The officer asked me a bunch of questions about what was in the back and I could tell she was suspicious," he said. "I heard her call it in. She thought I was hauling a load of pot, and she wanted backup, but she got connected with someone who told her to let me go. She fought with them.

I could only hear what she was saying and not all of it, but she was pissed."

That was slightly more interesting, but still not a smoking gun. "What happened after that?"

"Nothing. I made my delivery. But I stopped driving for them like three months ago. I got a job, I was totally legit. Then my kid got sick and my hours got cut at the mill. So I took a job driving for some other people."

"Who?"

Bobby looked down and Melissa coughed softly. "Not today."

Will nodded. "Okay."

"On my first trip for them, I got busted. But the thing is, I was on my way back. I wasn't carrying anything. I offloaded everything. And I don't do meth. You check my blood work, man. I wasn't using that pipe they found. That wasn't mine."

Unbelievable. The kid's defense against a possession charge was that he was trafficking. Will glanced over at Melissa, nodded and stood.

"Okay, thanks, Bobby. I'll look into it and I'll let your lawyer know if it's something we can use," Will said.

He walked out, leaving Bobby in the holding cell with his lawyer, but waited in the hall for Melissa, who emerged a few minutes later.

"Not sure what you think I can do with this," he said.

She shook her head. "I know, it's nothing solid, but that's why you get the big bucks, Patton."

"It's about as solid as smoke. He *thinks* he was working for Hastings because a cop pulled him over and didn't arrest him?" Will asked, pressing the button for the elevator.

"There's something else."

"There better be," he said with a laugh, allowing Melissa to enter the elevator before him.

She waited for Will to join her in the elevator and for the doors to close before continuing. "I think this bust was dirty."

"The report's clean. A tip from a known informant, reliable, pointed to Bobby. Cops got corroborating evidence. Warrant is solid. Search was legal. Drugs were plentiful," Will said.

Melissa nodded. "I would agree, but in this case, something's not right."

The elevator doors opened and they walked out into the jail lobby, then out the front doors to the street. Their offices were in buildings that faced each other, around the corner from the courthouse, and they walked down the block in that direction.

"He just confessed to trafficking a Winnebago full of pot," Will pointed out.

Melissa stopped at the corner.

"Look, I get it. If I had a dollar for every time one of my clients said he was set up by the cops, well, I'd double my salary," she said with a wry smile. "But on this one, there's something that doesn't sit well."

The light turned green, but Will didn't step into the crosswalk. "What would you like me to do with this, Mel?"

She smiled. "You could start by questioning the cop who pulled him over."

"The unnamed cop?"

"The female officer. There's only one."

She had a good point. The Lost Coast Harbor Police Department was small and decades behind in gender equity efforts, which did make it easy for him to figure out which officer stopped Bobby Acuff last year.

"I will see what Valerie Childs has to say."

"Thanks, Will. You're not as bad as the rest of them," she said with a grin, then turned toward the Public Defender's office.

He waited for a break in traffic, then jaywalked across the street to his office. Will doubted anything would come of Bobby's allegations, but he could at least cross it off his list with minimal effort.

He worked through lunch to prepare for the arraignment calendar, where a half-dozen defendants were charged with crimes ranging from drunk in public to felony assault. The more serious cases were sent up to the main court in Ukiah, but the misdemeanors were prosecuted locally. Several of his coworkers had wanted this position—a promotion to assistant district attorney, a bump up from the regular title of deputy district attorney, and in a gorgeous small town on the edge of the Pacific Ocean. There had been two attorneys with more experience who saw it as a good half-step toward retirement. It was an easy gig. Few trials, and those were misdemeanors. He should be enjoying the job, the regular hours, the low stress. Will was not.

There were plenty of outdoor sports to do in Lost Coast Harbor—hiking, surfing, and biking, when he could manage to stay on the trail. It had also rained nearly every day since he'd arrived four months earlier and the near-constant cloud cover was starting to wear on him. He had moved only the barest essentials into his rental house, keeping most of his furniture in storage and ready for the next move. And there would be another move. Hopefully, soon.

His secretary took the stack of files from him as he returned from court and gave him a short list of phone calls to return. There wasn't anything urgent, so he flipped through Bobby Acuff's file again. The bust was handled by Detective Todd Butler, who did most of the drug investigations. That made sense, because Butler would have the confidential informants. He was in his mid-forties, a career police officer with a solid record in the local office.

Valerie Childs, on the other hand, was new to the town and to the job. She was young, in her early thirties, and only recently promoted to detective. Before last month, she had been on patrol. She stood out on the force, not just because she was the only woman. She was also very attractive—on the petite side, with long black hair, and brown eyes with a slight tilt that hinted at her Asian heritage.

He had considered asking her out. They were about the same age, in the same field, and both were new to Lost Coast Harbor. But Will got no hint that Valerie was at all interested in him. She was cordial and professional, and he felt absolutely no spark with her, and almost immediately forgot that he had ever wanted to pursue her. Plus, he'd recently discovered that his type leaned toward a certain gray-eyed nurse. He just needed to figure out how to find Erin Grady when she wasn't working.

Since Valerie was no longer on patrol, she would probably be in the office if he walked two blocks to the other side of the courthouse and stopped in to see her. In his experience, it was best to surprise someone with an in-person interview if you wanted honest answers.

He found Valerie in the corner of an open office, hunched over her desk and typing on an aged computer. He knocked on the desk and she looked up, her expression annoyed. That faded in an instant when she recognized him.

"Hi, Will. What are you doing here?" She motioned to the chair at the side of the desk and he took it.

"Had a question for you about a case and I needed to come over here anyway."

Valerie gave him a nod, so he continued. "You pulled Bobby Acuff over about eight months ago on Cold Creek Road?"

She sat up and glanced quickly around the office, which was empty but for an officer at the counter on the other side of the room.

"I did. How did you know about that?" Her eyes narrowed and her expression hardened.

"I just spoke with Bobby and his attorney this morning. He mentioned it. He says he was hauling, in his words, a 'crap-ton' of weed," Will said. "Can I ask why you didn't call for a drug dog or backup?"

Valerie's mouth tightened into a frown. "I tried."

"What happened?"

"Why?"

"Just curious."

She raised an eyebrow. "You have time to be curious about people who *weren't* arrested?"

"He was arrested last week, but claims it was a set-up," Will said.

Valerie looked around again, this time alarmed. "What?"

"I'm not buying it, don't worry. And your name isn't on the report, so it's not your problem, anyway."

She stood up as a door in the back of the office opened and Chief Grady walked out of his office and through the desks. Grady gave a slight double take at Will's presence, then headed to Valerie's desk. Will stood and greeted the chief, still trying to discern any resemblance between Jerry Grady and his daughter. They shared the same eyes, but that was where the similarities ended. And even then, Erin's eyes were a soft gray that lit up when she laughed with him, while Chief Grady's eyes were hard as flint.

"How ya feeling, Patton?" the chief asked.

"Better, thanks," he said, shaking hands with Grady.

"Didn't expect to see you here," Grady said. "Can I help you with anything?"

"He needs to see the evidence in the McIntosh case. It's going to a preliminary hearing," Valerie said.

Grady nodded and started to walk off, but Will called him back.

"I wanted to thank Erin for her help on Saturday," he said. "Can you give me a tip on something she'd like? Her favorite flowers or restaurant?"

From behind him, Valerie cleared her throat and Will instantly regretted the question. Grady's ruddy face darkened and he shook his head. "I'm sure she'll like whatever you get her."

His steps quickened his exit from the main office.

"Why did you ask him that?" Valerie hissed.

"Why did you lie to him?" Will returned.

"Come on," she said, leading him down a hall in the opposite direction of the chief's destination.

"Where are we going?"

She didn't answer, just waved to a clerk who sat at a desk in front of the door marked "Evidence" and signed into a clipboard. He signed his name to the list under hers and noted the time.

The evidence locker was a long, windowless storage room with rows of shelves, upon which bags and boxes were arranged with labels facing outward. Valerie led him to the back, then pulled a box from the depths of the bottom row.

"Here's the Acuff evidence," she said.

"I didn't ask for this," Will said.

"I know," she said, fixing him with a steady gaze. "By the way, don't ask the chief about his daughter. It won't go well."

"They don't get along?"

"I doubt they speak to each other," she said.

"Why not?"

She shrugged. "This is just what I've observed."

He'd seen them speak Saturday morning, but it was not with any sort of affection. In fact, it had been a rather chilly interaction. Erin had shown no more affection toward the chief than she had toward the two EMTs who arrived with him.

Valerie shoved the Acuff box at him and nodded toward a desk in the corner of the room. "You can look at everything in here, but you can't take it with you. And if you need a cross-reference, try this case."

She pulled another box off the shelf with a tag reading "Katri, R." and a case number from the prior year.

He hadn't asked for any of this. She was clearly trying to lead him to something, but didn't want to say what.

"I'll take a look at it," he said slowly and she nodded. "And if I have any questions—"

"You don't ask them here."

She turned and started for the door.

"Wait, Valerie."

She stopped at the door and turned back.

"If I do this, you have to do something for me."

Valerie didn't respond, but stared at him, her eyes boring into him.

"Can you get me Erin Grady's phone and address?"

She paused, and then shook her head with a short laugh. "Stop by my desk on your way out."

She hurried from the room and he was left holding the two boxes that he didn't want. But he had time, so maybe it was worth trying to figure out the detective's cryptic clues.

He opened the Acuff box and peered in.

CHAPTER FIVE

"You're not my cat," Erin said to the skinny black cat that was winding around her legs.

She held out a piece of tuna and the cat stood on its hind legs to take it, purring loudly as he ate the treat from her fingers.

"You probably have a home."

The cat meowed for more food and looked up with startling green eyes. Erin set the dish on the patio and the slinky creature dove into the food. That's what she needed—to be single, living alone, and start adopting cats. But since her single status didn't show signs of ending anytime soon, maybe she should just throw in the towel and start collecting stray animals.

She emptied the water dish and refilled it and tried to tell herself that, all evidence to the contrary, she didn't have a cat.

"I'm not naming you."

The black cat showed up about a month earlier, thin and ragged, and out of pity, Erin had set out some tuna. Now that was a daily occurrence. She was even buying cat food for him, but had forgotten to stock up, so the unnamed feline was getting some of her dinner.

She stepped back into the house and closed the sliding glass door behind her, keeping the damp air out. She didn't know where the cat went when he wasn't sleeping on her patio furniture. He didn't seem to want to come inside and she wasn't sure she wanted him there.

She'd never had a pet before. Her mother had had enough trouble trying to keep track of a child. Even then, Erin knew it would be asking too much of her mother to make her responsible for yet another living creature. Leanne hadn't been diagnosed with bipolar disorder until Erin was about seven years old, but the symptoms had shown up years earlier. They were still living with Jerry then, but her parents' marriage was rocky on a good day.

When things were good, her mother's bright and sunny personality lit up Erin's life. Those times were rare. Leanne's good moods eventually would grow into a caricature of happiness, a frenzy of painting and talking and impulsive shopping and travel. Then in the crash that followed, Leanne could spend days or weeks on the couch, with the curtains pulled, barely able to get herself dressed.

It couldn't have been easy being married to her, but when her mother finally got some treatment, instead of being supportive, Jerry had backed away.

It had been a huge relief to finally move into their own place. Leanne was marginally more stable, but Erin knew that she couldn't be relied on for things that her friends' mothers did. She never held it against her mother, though. Leanne was fun and funny, beautiful and artistic. She loved adventures and Erin had lots of happy memories of spontaneous weekend trips.

Erin poured herself a glass of merlot and slipped her shoes off, padding to the living room. She had finished three months of overnight, weekend shifts—a punitive schedule that was the result of her quick temper. She would have had the next ten days off before starting daylight shifts, but had stupidly volunteered to cover someone's shift next Saturday night. At least Saturday nights went by fast in the ER, and it wasn't like she was giving up a social life.

The schedule gave her time to drive to Santa Rosa as soon as Alan let her know that her mom was up for visitors. That could be a few days, though. They'd been through this before.

She'd tried to roust Maddie or their friend, Bree Rogers, to meet her for a drink, but Bree was working and Maddie had plans with her new love, Gabe. Naked plans, probably, Erin thought as she sipped her wine.

Not that she wasn't happy for her friend. But Maddie's new relationship was a reminder that Erin hadn't exactly been putting herself out there to meet anyone. Not that there was an abundance of single men to choose from in Lost Coast Harbor. But one had nearly fallen into her lap. Maybe she should figure out how to run into Will Patton again.

The ancient doorbell rang just as she sat down. Keeping her wine in hand, she walked to the front door. She stood on her toes to look out the peephole and saw a familiar figure on her porch. She set the glass down on the side table in the foyer and opened the door, saying a silent good-bye to her peaceful evening as her teenage sister burst through the door.

"Oh my God, Erin! You have to come now! Colin's in trouble!"

Hayley stopped her animated rant to take a breath and Erin grabbed her shoulders. Her sister's eyes were wide, her hair windblown as if she'd ridden her bike the mile across town to get to her.

"Is Colin okay? Where is he?" Not now. Not with her mom in the hospital, with Alan out of town. "Where's Aunt June?"

Hayley gasped for breath. "At the police station."

"Oh, fuck," Erin said, running to the living room to grab her shoes. She hopped, trying to jam her feet into the boots, while simultaneously searching through her purse for her keys.

"What happened?"

"There was a party and everyone got taken to the police station! And he was there. And I didn't know what to do!"

Erin managed to shove her feet into the boots and grabbed Hayley's arm, pulling her through the door and locking it behind her.

"What was Colin doing at a party? He doesn't go to parties."

"I don't know! I never told him about it. I don't know how he even knew about it."

"Oh, for Christ's sake, Hayley. *You* were at the party?" Erin jumped into the driver's seat and slammed the door shut behind her.

"It's not a big deal," Hayley said, sliding down in the passenger seat.

"How come you're not at the police station?"

Hayley looked down, her long hair obscuring her face. "Because a bunch of us ran away and they didn't catch us."

Erin blew out a frustrated breath. Her siblings were good kids. Colin was eighteen and about to graduate from high school. He was smart and smart-mouthed, and she'd adored him from the moment she'd seen his squalling red newborn face, topped with black curls. Her sixteen-year-old sister, Hayley, had inherited the same light brown hair as Erin, but with their mother's blue eyes. Even with that difference, it was like looking at a younger version of herself.

But Erin couldn't remember ever getting in as much trouble as Hayley found. She had been too busy trying to keep her grades up so she could escape Lost Coast Harbor. She'd had friends, boyfriends, and fun—but never got in trouble. Having a stepfather who was also her high school principal had helped keep her in line, too. Though it sure wasn't slowing Hayley down.

Erin parked her Jeep at the end of a long line of minivans in front of the police department downtown. She hauled Hayley into the small lobby, where a dozen parents were either yelling at the harried police department employees or at their children. June was leaning over the counter, arguing with a young officer who was shaking his head. The retired elementary school teacher pointed a finger in the man's face, just as Erin fought her way to the front of the crowd.

"Look here, Sean Hollis, I don't care that you're a sworn police officer now. I've known you since you were in fourth grade and picked your nose for a living. Now go get me my nephew," June said.

"I'm sorry, Ms. White, you'll need to talk to the chief." Sean Hollis was sweating under the glare of his former teacher. His clean-shaven jaw tensed and his gaze darted around the room, as if he could summon backup.

Erin pulled June away. "I'll take care of it, June. Maybe you should take Hayley home."

June huffed at the officer, but then took Hayley's arm. "Fine, I'll take the trouble-maker home."

She steered the teenager out of the station. Erin turned her attention back to the officer, who had disappeared to help another parent who was demanding his son be released.

She scanned the small office for another officer. The handful of officers and civilian staff for a Monday evening were overwhelmed by the crowd in the lobby. At least she hadn't run into her father.

Stupid kids. Who throws a party on a Monday night?

"Erin?"

"What?" She turned and snapped at the voice behind her and found herself looking up into the face of Will Patton. "Oh, God. I'm sorry. I thought you were…someone else."

She shook her head and closed her eyes. When she opened them, he was watching her with a concerned expression.

"Is everything okay?"

He was taller than she had realized, but then again, the two times she'd seen him he'd been lying down—first on the trail, then in a hospital bed. Dressed in a suit that emphasized his broad shoulders, he seemed even more imposing. And even more handsome. His face was composed of hard planes, softened by full lips. His hazel eyes were flecked with green and gold and Erin had to look away quickly to avoid staring.

"My little brother just got picked up by the police," she said.

"Can I do anything?" Will asked.

Erin looked up and tilted her head. "Can you not charge him? He's a good kid. He went to the party to get his sister out of there."

Will smiled. "The police bust these kids all the time. Nothing ever comes of it. Your brother will be fine. What's his name?"

"Colin White."

"I'll keep an eye out for the paperwork. If it looks like he's in trouble, I'll let you know. But if all they have on him is that he was present, they're not going to refer the case to my office," Will said.

Erin took a deep breath. "Okay, thanks."

Her heart rate began to slow and some of the tightness in her shoulders eased, only to be replaced by a fluttering in her stomach when Will gave her a reassuring smile.

Behind the counter, Erin saw a familiar figure step out of his office. She couldn't recall how long it had been since she'd seen her father, and now she saw him twice in one week. In a town the size of Lost Coast Harbor, it was a small miracle that she could avoid him as much as she did.

Chief Jerry Grady stepped forward, made eye contact with Erin and waved her toward him. Her eyes narrowed and she didn't move.

"Erin." Jerry's bark drew more attention than she wanted, so she reluctantly excused herself and moved through the crowd to the counter. Her father held the low swinging gate for her, and then led her through a room filled with desks, back to his office.

"Have a seat," he said, taking the chair behind the mahogany desk.

She didn't want to, but she did.

"Your stepbrother's in a world of trouble," he said, leaning back.

"He's my brother, and he's a good kid."

Jerry Grady had faded from her life as soon as they'd moved out. Other than a few trips to visit her paternal grandparents, she rarely saw him. When she was a freshman in high school, she saw him drive by in his cruiser and realized that he was getting gray. Then she'd done the math and was surprised to discover that she hadn't talked to him in fifteen months. Two birthdays had gone by without his presence, and she hadn't even missed him.

Most of that nonchalance about being abandoned by her father came from the fact that well before then, she had found a new one in Alan White, her mother's new husband. Alan had provided a foundation that Erin had never had in her young life. Bedtimes were set, meals were eaten at a table, and above all, she was no longer required to be the responsible party. If she hadn't had that, Erin was sure she'd have skipped college, probably married right out of high school, and would be working at a local store for minimum wage, barely scraping by. It was a life she saw all around her. Now she was focused on making sure her two younger siblings didn't fall into that trap.

"Your *half*-brother was just caught at a party with enough beer and liquor to get the whole town drunk."

"What do you want?" Erin had little patience for Jerry's games. But she got the hint. He had the power to make her brother's life hell. Or make this go away.

He gave her a long and unreadable stare. "Is having dinner with my daughter once in a while too much to ask?"

"Why?"

"What do you mean, why? You're my daughter. I'd like to know what you're doing. How you're doing."

"I mean, why now? I'm thirty. We've lived in the same town for the last five years and I've never heard from you." Not to mention all the years before she went off to college, when he mostly ignored her. Erin couldn't think of what had changed that suddenly Jerry wanted to be a father.

"And I've never heard from you, either," he said. "I would just like the opportunity to get to know you better. I know I haven't been a great father. Not even a good one. But I'd like another chance."

The words were the right ones, but there was something off in the delivery. She wasn't buying it.

"I'll think about it," she said.

"There are advantages to having a father who's the police chief, you know," Jerry said.

"Not that I've seen."

He gave her a tight smile. "Tell you what. You come by for dinner tomorrow night and we'll talk about it. I'd like to hear more about this clinic you're planning to open."

Erin startled at his mention of the clinic. She hadn't been hiding it and had broadcast the need for donations and support throughout the medical community. But hearing Jerry talk about it, a project so close to her, kicked that uneasy feeling into overdrive.

"Why are you interested in the clinic?"

"It's my community, too, Erin," he said. "Have you heard

if you're going to get the Hastings pledge?"

Her heart dropped. The money felt like it was barely within her grasp now, and slipping away fast. She shook her head. "No, it's still up in the air."

"It's a good cause. You should talk with the prosecutors," Jerry said. He stood and she followed. "I'll release Colin to your custody for now."

"And then what happens? Are you going to charge him?"

Grady paused at the door. "I don't know yet. These decisions can take a few days."

She clenched her jaw at the implied threat. Her choice was to let her little brother face charges that could ruin his chance at a good college or put up with Grady over dinner. One meal together in twenty years. She could bear that for Colin.

"What time is dinner?"

"Come by around six," Grady said with a smile, holding the door for her. She ignored his triumphant expression. He had won this battle of wills and he knew it. So did she.

Erin stormed out of the chief's office and back to the lobby to wait for Colin's release. She threw her purse onto the worn bench by the door and stood, hands on hips, glaring toward the chief's office. How dare he hold Colin hostage? She should just tell him to fuck off. They'd get Colin a lawyer and he'd be cleared. Eventually.

The door behind the front desk area opened and an officer led Colin through. His dark curls were mussed, as usual, and his face stricken and pale. His T-shirt draped loosely from shoulders that were broad, but still thin, the result of a growing spurt last summer that was all height and no weight.

His eyes met Erin's and the tension in his face and frame dissolved.

The officer put the paperwork in front of her and Erin signed it with a slightly shaky hand, and grabbed Colin in a tight hug.

"You little idiot," she said with affection. "What the hell were you doing there?"

A hand on her shoulder reminded her that they weren't in private. She turned and was surprised to see Will behind her. He nodded toward the doors.

"You should talk out there," he said quietly.

Erin nodded. "Of course."

She introduced Colin to Will and her little brother offered his hand with a polite greeting. She kept an arm around him as they walked out, Will right behind them.

The line of minivans had disappeared. Erin unlocked the passenger-side door for Colin and closed it behind him.

Will walked with her to the other side of the car, but stopped her before she opened the door. His hand on her wrist sent a tingle through her arm, a pleasant warmth that she wanted to feel again.

"Are you all right?" he asked.

Erin turned toward him, studying him in the pale illumination from the street lamp. The overhead light brought out his cheekbones and cast his eyes into shadows. The fine mist was settling on his thick dark hair.

Erin nodded, her eyes still on his face. God, he was really good looking. Objectively, she'd recognized this fact from the moment he'd fallen in front of her, and again when he was lounging in the hospital, trying to charm the nurses.

But now, standing in the dark and cold night, alone… she couldn't take her eyes off him.

His lips turned up slightly and her stomach fluttered. She'd been staring too long, too intently. The heat burned up her neck to her cheeks.

"You're not wearing your sling," she said.

"I wore it most of the day, but I'm feeling better," he said. "How about the dinner I promised?"

Erin shook her head. "You don't have to do that."

As soon as the words slipped out, she wanted to take them back. His gaze intensified and the flutters in her stomach grew to tremors. She didn't even like cops, and though he wasn't in uniform, that's basically what he was. He was the end result of law enforcement. He worked with her father, for fuck's sake.

"I want to."

She shivered and tried to tell herself it was the chill from the fog, but knew it wasn't. It had been way too long since a man had looked at her like that.

Oh, what the hell.

"I have to get Colin home," she said.

"Tomorrow then," he said. He still held her hand, his thumb casually stroking the inside of her wrist. The touch was intimate, familiar. Long-dormant parts of her body woke in a wave of longing and heat.

"I can't tomorrow. I, uh, have to—I have plans," she said, with genuine regret that she was turning down dinner with Will for dinner with Jerry.

Will raised an eyebrow and Erin realized she was brushing off the only man who'd taken her breath away with a touch in, well, forever.

"It seems that an awful lot of your vocabulary revolves around what you have to do," he said, his head tilted slightly as he watched her. "How about this? I'm going down to the Crab Shack for dinner in about an hour, because it's the only place open on a Monday night in this town. I'll get a table for two. If you *want* to join me, I'd love the company."

What she wanted was a nearly foreign concept, something Will seemed to have picked up on. She could defend herself, argue that she did what she wanted. That would be a lie, though. And she did want to meet him later.

"And if you don't show up, you'll be making me look like a loser," he said with a smile that made her stomach do a slow somersault. He let go of her hand and she missed the touch.

"I'll be there," she said.

It was a good opportunity to take Jerry's advice and talk to a prosecutor about the donation to the clinic, her rational mind said. It was just dinner.

But with a man whose slightest touch sent her reeling, her body reminded her. So don't be late.

CHAPTER SIX

The restaurant was nearly empty and the waitress was happy to leave them alone in a corner booth. The candle in the heavy glass holder cast eerie red streaks across the table and reflected off a silver ring on Erin's right hand as she twisted the cloth napkin with her fingers.

Will had planned on calling her earlier, seeing if she'd go out with him that evening, but before he knew it, it was after six and he was still comparing evidence in the windowless storage room at Lost Coast Harbor Police Department. Valerie Childs hadn't told him what to look for, hadn't given him any direction. But he understood what she was trying to tell him.

There was something going on with the police department. Something beyond incompetence or laziness that he'd seen in other small town police forces. This was rotten. And it was just what he was looking for.

Will was familiar with corruption. He had detected it a year ago in Meridian, another remote Mendocino County town. Bad arrests, illegal searches, informants who didn't seem to exist. After six months of tossing cases from that police force, reporting the abuses to his boss, to the police chief, and threatening to go public with the records he'd been compiling, he'd finally gotten somewhere. The district attorney's office had to take action, grudgingly, with an investigation into the police department.

And to ensure that Will couldn't be involved with the review of the police force's practices, he had been promoted to the farthest outpost in the county.

He wasn't sure why Valerie had trusted him, but guessed it was because he was an outsider, like she was. Maybe she saw him as an ally. Maybe she, too, suspected that Grady or one of his trusted officers had been working with Hastings, tipping him off when law enforcement got too close, or ignoring obvious criminal activity on the docks.

Now he just had to figure out where to go from here. And maybe the woman across the table could help him figure that out. Who better to tell him about the police chief than his daughter? And it wouldn't be a chore to explore Erin Grady, or what she knew.

"You're holding up well for someone who just had to get your kid brother from lock-up," Will said.

"I get plenty of practice handling crises," Erin said, her smile showing off deep dimples.

They were close enough in the small booth that he could detect a hint of her perfume, something floral and light and a little sweet and he found himself leaning in even more.

"I hope this is okay. There aren't a lot of options on a Monday night here," Will said, glancing around the nearly empty dining room of the Crab Shack restaurant, a dockside family diner that looked like it had served Lost Coast Harbor for several generations.

"Not in the winter," she said. "When the tourists return in the summer, the restaurants stay open, but it's not worth it when it's this slow."

"It was this or that place down the harbor. What's it called, the Vista del Mar?"

"The VD by the Sea? I don't recommend that place unless you're looking to buy drugs or get into a fight," she said, with a smile that made his breath catch in his chest.

The waitress returned with a merlot for Erin and Will's beer. They placed their orders and the waitress returned to the bar, where a small crowd was watching a college basketball game, the cheers and groans occasionally filtering into the dining area.

She looked up from her glass of wine, her eyes troubled. "I know I'm probably not great company tonight. I did try and warn you off."

He smiled. "Not a chance. And your brother's going to be fine, you know."

Erin gave him a worried look, but nodded. "He's so smart, but book-smart. I don't worry about him not doing well in school when he goes off to college. I am concerned that he'll be so busy thinking deep thoughts that he'll walk into traffic."

Will smiled. "Sounds like a good kid. Did you talk to your dad about the charges?"

"No, I haven't called—Oh, you meant Jerry. No."

"You call your father Jerry?"

"We're not close."

She sipped her wine and looked away and he studied her

face. Tense again. It wasn't that she wasn't close with her father, she might actively hate him.

"How long have you been estranged?"

"Since birth, but my parents divorced when I was nine."

"Did you have any relationship with him at all?"

Her eyes flashed as she glanced back at him. "Look, if you're on the prowl for daddy issues, you can keep going down to the Vista del Mar. I'm sure you'll hit the jackpot. But my mom remarried a great guy, who raised me like I was his own. I have healthy self-esteem and no need to seek approval from a male authority figure, okay?"

Will's smile grew into a full laugh. "Got it. I'll stop asking about your—about Jerry."

"Thank you," she said. "If you wouldn't mind, I really don't like talking about him. I'll talk about anything else. Sports. Weather. Or you can tell me something about yourself. How long have you been in Lost Coast Harbor?"

"About four months. I transferred from Ukiah."

"Did you grow up in Mendocino County?" she asked, her fingers absently playing with the stem on the wineglass.

"No, I'm from San Diego. I went to law school in Los Angeles. Mendocino County wasn't where I ever thought I'd end up."

Erin smiled and tilted her head. "Do you like it here?"

He let his gaze linger on her face, her skin caressed by the warm glow of the candle. "It's growing on me."

Her mouth opened slightly and he had a strong urge to kiss it, taste those pink lips, explore beyond them. Her eyes widened and he felt that pull again when he realized she felt the attraction between them, too.

"Tell me about yourself, Erin Grady," he said, lowering his voice. "Why are you here?"

"In Lost Coast Harbor? It's my hometown. I was born and raised here."

"But you must have gone away to college. And nurses can work anywhere. Why come back here?"

She raised her chin and met his gaze. "I went to college in San Francisco, but my family's here. They're important to me. The more interesting question is why you're here."

Her answer wasn't complete, and he suspected she was withholding something. But he wasn't being entirely upfront either, so they were even.

"I got a promotion to supervise the district attorney's office here."

"And this was your reward?" Erin laughed and tilted her head back. "Well, at least you must keep busy here."

"What do you mean?"

"Lost Coast Harbor. It's a corrupt little town," she said with a smirk.

He raised an eyebrow. "Is it?"

"Have you not noticed our major arms trafficker who has tentacles into nearly every part of the town's economy?"

Will nodded slowly, watching her carefully. "I have. It was a little awkward explaining to my boss that I was renting a house from Peter Hastings, the man we'd just helped arrest for gun running."

"Hastings or his family own most of the rental properties in town. What they don't own, the Donnelly family does. Plus, Hastings has nearly all the commercial property around," she said, casting a quick glance around the nearly empty restaurant. From their booth, a half-circle of aged fake leather, they had a view of the bar, where the patrons were captivated by a basketball game on the large-screen TV. Erin's eyes narrowed as her gaze swept the bar, lingering on a man perched on the last barstool—Detective Todd Butler. A slight frown crossed her face, then she looked away and back at Will.

The waitress interrupted them to drop off their dinners, disappearing nearly instantly. The atmosphere of the restaurant could best be described as gloomy, with worn captain's chairs around ancient wooden tables and a dull carpet that was thick with decades of cracker crumbs. But the food was excellent. The town might be a cesspool of corruption and insular to an extreme, but Will hadn't had a bad seafood meal yet.

He knew he should try and keep the conversation light, not scare her off, but his curiosity was too great. He needed someone with a deep knowledge of Lost Coast Harbor, and even if she didn't want to talk about her father, Erin could give him some insight into the town.

"Were there rumors about Peter Hastings before his arrest?"

"No, not at all. He was respected, well liked. Everyone here has either worked for Hastings Enterprises at some point or has a family member who did," she said. She frowned and tilted her head. "Can I ask you something?"

"You can ask me anything."

"What about Hastings' charitable contributions? What will happen to those now?"

Will paused and tilted his head. "If the checks were already cut, I would imagine the charities will keep their money. But if not, they're probably out of luck. Did he help a lot of local causes?"

A brief cloud passed over her face, disappointed in his answer. She blew out a sigh. "Yes, he did."

"Like what?" Will asked.

"Like the mental health clinic I'm trying to get started," Erin said. "He was going to give fifty thousand dollars."

Will frowned. "I'm sorry. I didn't know."

"It's not your fault. I've been waiting to hear if there was any chance I could still get the money. I just thought we were close enough to start looking for a building to lease."

He reached over and put his hand on hers and the heat from her soft skin made his heart beat a little faster.

"I'm not involved in the case. The FBI investigated and the U.S. Attorney in San Francisco is prosecuting. Other than assisting them, if they request more help, I have nothing to do with it," Will said. "You could talk with Spencer Bourne, the federal prosecutor. I'll put you in touch with him."

"That would be nice," she said. "Why aren't the local police investigating Hastings?"

"It's a big case, and the feds have more resources to go after him," Will said.

Erin looked thoughtful as she sipped her red wine, then licked a drop off her lips. At her unconscious gesture, his imagination took over and all he could think of was reaching across the table and licking those wine-scented lips. All the blood in his body rushed to his cock. Fuck, he needed to get control. To focus. This was his chance to get what he needed. And yet, he couldn't stop looking into her eyes and wondering what would happen if he just forgot that she was Chief Grady's daughter.

"Is that the only reason?" Erin asked. "Just hypothetically speaking, Peter Hastings' operation wasn't a criminal enterprise that one could do single-handedly, right?"

That was what Will was counting on. For an operation the size of Peter Hastings' to go undetected for so long, he had to have protection. Will might not be allowed near the federal prosecution, but the police corruption angle was a way into it, if he could figure out who was helping the gun runner.

There were several possibilities. Deputy Chief Stan Hutchins, who was retiring within a few weeks, was the second in command and had a wife who had been fighting cancer for several years. Financial pressure like that had led to many public corruption cases.

And there was Chief Jerry Grady, of course. He'd been with the Lost Coast Harbor police force since he was in his twenties. Now in his early sixties, he had to be close to retirement. He knew everyone in town and had been close friends with Peter Hastings since childhood.

Then there was the man in the bar—Todd Butler. He was a detective, the most senior in the department. Talk around the courthouse was that Butler would replace Hutchins, and eventually would succeed Chief Jerry Grady. With Valerie Childs' suspicions, Butler was now on Will's short list of potential suspects. Other than those three men, no one else on the force had been there long enough or had enough clout to protect such a large operation.

Erin looked up at him through thick lashes and he let out a slow breath and tried to recall her question.

"No, it's unlikely that Hastings was acting alone. And the two henchmen who were arrested with him wouldn't have been the end of it."

Her glance flickered back to the bar, and Will looked in that direction, too. Todd Butler had shifted in his chair so he could watch them and was staring intently. When Will didn't look away, Todd raised his drink and nodded in a chilly greeting. Will gave a small nod in return.

"You know him?" Will asked.

"A little," Erin said. "He comes into the ER sometimes. Harasses my patients—you know, the ones he put in hospital in the first place, and then wants to question while they're being stitched up."

Will knew the type. "That happen a lot?"

Erin's breath hissed out. "Yeah. Lost Coast Harbor residents seem to always be resisting arrest."

"Maybe we should get out of here," Will said, waving the waitress down for the check.

As they walked past the bar toward the exit, Butler's stare burned into Will's back. He held the door for Erin and returned the unfriendly stare for a long moment before leaving. Will had never had any problems with the detective before, but his presence with Erin seemed to be rubbing Butler the wrong way.

He and Erin walked in silence through a half-filled parking lot toward where their cars were parked.

As he helped her into the driver's seat, Will looked back to the restaurant and saw Butler watching from the building, a lit cigarette illuminating his face, then obscuring it behind a cloud of exhaled smoke.

"Where do you live?" he asked.

She looked at him, then past him to the restaurant where Butler stood, staring. "Oh."

"Just humor me."

She smiled. "You want to make sure I get home safe?"

"I'd hate for you to be charged with resisting arrest."

She raised an eyebrow, but shrugged. "I'm on Cormorant Drive, at the west end of the street, the last house on the right."

It was a few blocks from his own house, and he nodded before shutting the door. "I'll be right behind you."

She pulled out of the parking lot, and Will watched Butler drop his cigarette and walk away from the restaurant and toward a row of cars. Will climbed into his SUV, but didn't pull out of the parking lot, watching Butler's city-issued patrol car turn left and follow Erin's car up the hill toward the center of Lost Coast Harbor.

Tailing a car in Lost Coast Harbor was a joke. Especially on a quiet night in the dead of winter. The only three cars on the small town's streets made their way up the hill from the harbor area, past the small business district and the city's center square, and then farther west and north through the darkened residential neighborhood that sat perched on the western edge of the town. Erin's house was on a street that ended just before the cliffs. The taillights of her car disappeared as she turned the corner, several blocks ahead of Will. Butler's brake lights flashed, and he pulled a U-turn, coming back down the hill.

As his car approached Will's, the light bar flashed red and blue briefly, before Butler continued down the street and around a corner. Will tensed at the message. Butler was watching—either Erin or himself, Will didn't know. Perhaps at the chief's direction.

He parked in front of the last house on the street, where Erin's Jeep sat in the driveway. He stepped out of the car and saw her door open. The rest of the street was quiet and dark. He walked up the path to the steps, waited for Erin, then escorted her to the door and waited as she unlocked it.

"Thanks for dinner."

He looked down at her in the dark. "You're welcome. Thanks for your help Saturday."

They were inches apart and on the threshold of something. A fierce desire to grab her, kiss her, pin her against the wall flooded his body.

"Want to come in?"

The question was nearly a whisper, falling from her perfect lips. God yes, he wanted to come in.

Without answering, he reached up and cupped the back of her neck, his fingers sliding through silky strands of hair. When he leaned down, she met him halfway. A jolt of lust, pure and bright, coursed through him at the first touch of her lips. He groaned at the taste of her lips and pulled her closer. Erin returned the kiss with a passion that matched his own.

He reached for the doorknob, fumbled with it and felt Erin's hand on his, helping open the door without breaking the kiss.

"Wait." Erin's whisper brought him out of the haze, his heart racing and his blood pumping.

He looked down at her, but she was looking inside and

not at him. Her hair fluttered as a breeze blew through the open door.

"Something's wrong."

CHAPTER SEVEN

A blast of cold air greeted Erin as she stepped into the foyer and she froze in place, her body sensing the danger a fraction of an instant before her mind did. Then the breeze brushed her face and her brain registered the alarm, snapping her back to her senses. Her lips still tingled where Will had kissed her, and her head spun as she tried to put the pieces together.

"What's wrong?" Will was close behind her, his hand on her shoulder.

"The patio door is open."

He pulled her back, pushed her behind him and stepped into the house.

"Did you leave it open?"

"No."

"Stay here."

Erin hugged her arms around herself, for warmth as well as comfort, as he disappeared around the corner into kitchen. Her mind raced back to the hurried manner in which she'd left the house. She'd been rushed, but she was certain she'd closed the sliding glass door to the patio after feeding the cat.

And out of habit, she had very likely flipped the lock up. She lived alone and her house backed up to a public footpath, so she was careful about security.

She held her breath, straining to hear Will in the house and finally heard heavier steps coming toward her. Erin met him in the living room, where the door to the patio was open wide, letting in cold, damp air.

"They came in through the back bedroom window. It's busted and the screen is missing," he said, covering his hand with his sleeve before he flipped on a light.

Her legs felt shaky as she took in the room. It wasn't disturbed, except for muddy footprints on the carpet, but the thought that someone had been in her home chilled her more than the cold air let in by the open slider door. Erin started toward the door to close it, but Will's hand on her arm stopped her.

"Don't touch anything," he said, pulling his phone from his pocket. "I'll call it in."

Erin nodded, then listened to him relay her address and the state of the house to someone at the police department. *Great.* More interaction with her father.

She walked to the entrance of the hall and looked in both directions—toward her bedroom in the back of the house, then into the guest bedroom in the front of the house, where she could see the light from her laptop computer on the small desk. In the bathroom, the medicine cabinet was open.

Will disconnected the call as she returned. In the living room, her TV was still on its stand and her wireless speakers sat on the bookcase across the room. Whoever broke in wasn't looking for electronics.

"The good news is your cat didn't get out," he said.

"What?"

"He's sleeping on your bed."

Erin laughed, then covered her mouth with a shaky hand. That wasn't the right response to having one's house burglarized, but her nerves were shot. She walked down the hall, Will behind her, and found the black cat curled up on the corner of her bed. When she walked in, he opened his eyes and blinked at her. She stroked his head and his body vibrated with the purr.

"Making yourself at home, are you?"

"What's his name?"

"He's not my cat and I don't know his name."

"There are cat dishes on the patio."

"I feed him, but he's not my cat."

"He sleeps on your bed and depends on you for food. I think you own a cat," Will said, running a hand down the cat's sleek fur and getting an affectionate head bump in return. "An officer will be here in a few minutes to take a report."

The window in the corner of her bedroom was pried open, the frame torn and ragged from someone using a crowbar on it. The weathered wood and single-paned glass hadn't stood a chance against that level of force. Erin had planned to replace the old windows with double-paned glass, something to keep out the cold wind off the Pacific Ocean. Someone moved up her plans for her, she thought, shivering in the cold bedroom.

"Let's wait outside," Will said, taking her arm and leading her back through the house, both of them careful not to touch anything. By the time they walked out the front door, the black and white squad car was parking at the curb.

Officer Sean Hollis climbed out and walked to the door, looking even younger in his uniform than he had behind the counter of the police station earlier that evening.

"We walked in to check on the cat, but didn't touch anything," Will said.

"The evidence tech is on his way from a scene across town, but it may be an hour or so before I can let you back in," Sean said. "Is anything missing?"

Erin shook her head. "I wasn't in there long, but I didn't see anything, except the bathroom medicine cabinet was open. I wouldn't have left it like that."

"Did you have any prescription drugs in there?" Hollis asked, opening a notepad and taking a pen from his pocket.

"Just over-the-counter stuff, aspirin, ibuprofen, that sort of thing."

He asked a few more questions, and then a black SUV pulled up and parked. "That's my tech. When he gets suited up, I'll need you to walk through with him and note anything that is broken or stolen."

Erin followed the two police officers into the house, Will close behind her, and pointed out the open medicine cabinet and the broken window. Then she pointed to the chair by the door leading to the master bath.

"My gym bag is gone," she said.

"What was in it?" Sean asked.

"Gym clothes, shoes, toiletries. The usual."

"Nothing of value?"

She shook her head. "No, not at all."

"Can you describe the bag?"

"Dark blue, with a white logo from a pharmaceutical company. I got it for free at a conference last year," she said. "Do you think whoever broke in was looking for drugs?"

Sean gave a noncommittal tilt of his head. "Maybe. That's not unusual."

He handed her a business card. "If you notice any other items missing, give me a call. And if you'd like to give us an hour or so, we'll get some prints and photos and get out of here."

Erin tucked the card into her pocket and then ran a hand over her hair. Her heart rate was approaching normal again, but her insides still felt shaky. It had been a nice evening, sandwiched between two fairly crappy events. She'd even had a glimmer of hope that things might end with getting to know Will in a more biblical way. That would have been a nice distraction from the family drama.

Will handed a card to the officer. "My cell phone is on the back. Can you give me a call when you're finished?"

Will put an arm around Erin's shoulders and led her down the front stairs into the darkness.

"Where do you buy plywood at this time of night?"

"I have some in the garage," she said. "I'll put it up when they're done."

Again she found herself staring into his face in the harsh light of the streetlamp and what she saw there didn't make her feel any less shaky. Dark hair, falling over his forehead, his hazel eyes intent on hers, and God, those lips. She looked away. Just when things were going well, another drama arose and Will probably figured she was a hot mess. He wouldn't be wrong.

"I'll help," he said, walking away. "Tools in the garage?"

Her instinct was to take care of herself. She'd been doing that for years. But his deep, low voice sent a tremor through her and made her want to let him take care of her. In more ways than just nailing a sheet of plywood over the window.

An hour later, the police were gone and Erin and Will had nailed the plywood over the broken bedroom window, then he helped her sweep up the glass and wipe away the fingerprint dust residue. The chill in the house was on the run, thanks to the crackling fire Will had insisted on starting, but the thought of sleeping just feet from the plywood-covered window made her shiver again.

Will returned after taking out a bag of broken glass to the trashcan. "Where are you staying tonight?"

It was like he read her mind.

Her back straightened and she raised her chin. "I'll stay here. I lock my doors, and a friend gave me some pepper spray, so I'll be fine."

Will said nothing, but walked back to the open kitchen, where he poured two glasses of wine. He had taken off his jacket and was wearing his white dress shirt, fitted across his broad shoulders and with the sleeves rolled up to reveal tanned forearms. His eyes met hers as he handed her one glass and she took a sip, swallowing the wine without tasting it.

It was unnerving how at home he'd made himself, and how comfortable he looked in her kitchen. And how easily he'd taken over in the middle of her crisis. That was usually her role. She was the reliable one, good in an emergency. Fully capable of nailing up her own plywood. And that wasn't even a euphemism, though it could have been.

Erin made the short walk to the living room and sat on the couch, facing the fireplace. When Will sat next to her, her stomach fluttered. When his leg touched hers, the flutters grew into tremors, even with the fabric between them.

Will watched her with a hint of a smile and leaned in before she could say anything. "I don't want to leave you here alone. Is there someone who can come stay with you?"

She could call Bree, and she'd be here in minutes. But that wasn't who she wanted to spend the rest of the night with.

Erin shook her head. "No."

"You could stay with someone…?"

"No. I'm fine."

His eyes narrowed and his brow furrowed just the slightest—an expression of frustration or anger, she couldn't tell which.

"Someone just broke into your house. They may not have gotten what they want, but they've taken an inventory and could return."

"It was probably just someone looking for drugs. They figured out I don't have any and they won't be back."

He looked over at the wide-screen TV and the wireless speakers, then back to her with a shake of his head. "Just because it's a small town doesn't mean it's safe and nothing bad can happen to you here."

Erin set her glass on the coffee table and crossed her arms in front of her. "I'm not being run out of my own home by some moron, or a couple of bored teenagers."

Will moved closer and reached past her, setting his wine next to hers and the nearness took her breath away. She raised her chin to look him in the eye to protest his bullying, but found herself speechless again, her heart pounding and unable to pull her gaze from his eyes, hooded with need.

God, kiss me. Again. And again.

He reached up and slipped a hand behind her neck, his fingers stroking the soft skin on her nape. Each brush fired her nerves, a heat that spread throughout her body.

This was crazy. She wasn't into one-night stands, or hook-ups, or even casual flings. But her last relationship had ended a couple years earlier. She was due, damn it. She was a grown woman and could decide to have casual sex if she wanted to. Just because that wasn't her usual style, didn't mean it was necessarily a *bad* idea. She was just too busy, and worked too many nights. And she knew too much about any potential partner, the hazard of living in a small town for most of one's life.

Will's lips brushed across hers and his hand tightened on her neck and any moral objection she might have had flew out the window. Her heart pounded as the kiss grew deeper, more demanding. She inhaled the faint hint of his scent and the rough friction from the slight scruff on his face over-whelmed her. She ran a hand up his hard chest, flattening her palm to feel as much of him as possible.

"Damn."

His gruff whisper didn't make sense, but the sound made her shiver. Before she could respond, he kissed her again. Her arms were around his neck, pulling him closer. It wasn't enough.

He shifted on the couch, reclining against the arm and wrapping an arm around her so she lay on top of him, their bodies fitting together. Placing a knee on either side of him, Erin straddled him, eliciting a rumbling growl. His hands traveled down her body, cupping her ass and pulling her hard against him. The contact was rough, dominant, and so fucking hot.

His hand at the back of her neck tightened and he kissed her again, deeper, sending swirls of heat throughout her, settling between her thighs.

"God, you taste good," he groaned.

With a rough yank, Will unzipped her sweatshirt and pushed it off her shoulders and then pulled it off her arms and let it fall. That left her with only a thin white T-shirt as the thinnest of barriers between his hot gaze and the lacy bra beneath. He licked his lips and grasped the thin fabric, pulled it up and over her head. His breath escaped in a long shudder as he cupped one breast, encased in pink lace.

Expensive lingerie was Erin's secret vice. Her work wardrobe consisted of shapeless scrubs and there was rarely a reason to get dressed up in Lost Coast Harbor, so she indulged in the priciest and sexiest underthings she could find. And she'd happily pay twice what the bra cost her, just to ensure that reaction from Will.

He pulled himself up close again, his lips caressing her neck as she arched her back.

"Do you taste as good here?" he asked, pinching one nipple and rubbing the lace against her tender skin, sending a thrill through her body.

She moaned and tightened her legs around him as his mouth traveled down, past her collarbone, his breath hot on her skin.

"Oh, God. Please, Will, please," she gasped as his lips grazed the top of the lace cup.

His lips covered the sensitive tip gently, and then more urgently. Bright flashes of light danced behind her closed eyes and Erin gripped his biceps to keep from herself steady.

Will's arm tightened around her and he started to roll their bodies, but jerked his arm back, a wince crossing his face.

"Your shoulder," Erin said, scrambling to climb off his body. "Oh my God, I'm sorry. Are you okay?"

"It's fine, really. Come here." He grabbed her with his good arm, bringing her back to him. She watched his face for any sign of pain, but he just smiled. "It's just a little tender and I forgot."

Will kissed her and shifted so she was under him. "I was distracted," he whispered, running a finger along the cup of her bra, drawing a shiver from her. "This was a nice surprise."

His hands roamed over her skin, leaving trails of heat behind that made her arch into his touch. Will's lips followed his fingers, tracing the pattern on the lacy bra, then down to the waistband to her worn jeans.

Erin reached for him, craving his touch in a way that surprised her and left her dizzy with lust. It had been a while since she'd been in this position, but even then, it hadn't ever been like this, such a deep and primal longing. A passion that overrode all her judgment, and any inhibitions she might have had about sleeping with someone she'd just met. All she wanted was more of Will. More of his touch. More of his skin to touch.

She fumbled with the buttons on his shirt, opening enough

to slip her hand in and feel the hot skin beneath her fingers, the hard muscles bunching under her touch. His breath grew ragged as her hands crept down his torso. Lower still, across tight muscles that flexed at her exploration. He grabbed her hands and pulled them up over her head, pinning them with one hand while the other played with the lace edge, pulling it down incrementally to expose her to his view.

"I want to touch you," she whispered, barely able to get enough breath to form the words. But she didn't struggle against the strong grip on her wrists. There was something daring, forbidden about letting him take control.

"I want you to touch me," he said, his low voice sending a tremor through her. "In time."

He bit the sensitive peak, softly, but enough to send her nerves soaring.

"Oh, God," she moaned.

Every nerve ending in her body was trembling at the new wave of sensation. She gasped, giving herself over to the feeling. This was what she needed. And more. She wrapped her legs around his hips, pressing her aching core against his hard bulge. *Yes.* That was what she needed.

Will growled and pulled away, cool air chilling her where his lips had just been. Fumbling with his pocket, he pulled out his phone and Erin heard the buzzing. He started to throw the phone, but glanced at the screen and paused.

"Is everything okay?"

Will turned back to Erin, his eyes still intent on her, but something had shifted. He leaned in and kissed her, but it lacked the hunger that had just nearly consumed them. Then he adjusted her bra, covering her with a reluctant groan.

"I have to go." His voice was hoarse and his regret sounded sincere.

Erin lay still, suddenly feeling the chill that still lingered, or maybe there was a new cold front moving through the living room.

"Now?" She was sprawled under him, half-dressed and panting.

"I know. I am so very sorry," he said, his gaze roving over her again with regret. "I'll make it up to you."

She flopped back on the cushions and stared at the ceiling as Will stood and adjusted his own clothing. She sighed. Maybe this was a bad idea anyway. One nice dinner and a whole lot of sexual chemistry didn't cancel out the fact that he worked with Jerry and was basically an over-educated cop. So what if he seemed to know just how to kiss her so that her clothes melted off?

"Come here," Will said, finishing with the buttons on his shirt and extending a hand to her. He pulled her to her feet and she looked for the T-shirt that had been stripped off her body just minutes earlier. It wasn't in sight, so she pulled on the sweatshirt and zipped it up, depriving him of the pink lace view.

He put both hands on her shoulders, then moved them to her neck. As disappointed and angry as she was, his touch still sent a shiver up her spine. It made her angry with herself that she was apparently so desperate that she'd let herself be treated like this.

"Can I grovel for forgiveness tomorrow? Dinner at my place?"

"I have plans."

He smiled. "I promise not to behave myself."

Despite herself, she felt the stirrings in her gut again. Damn it, she was going to fall for his charm.

"As tempting as that is, I'm serious about having plans," she said.

He bent down and kissed her, sending her traitorous heart racing again.

"Think about it?" he whispered, his lips brushing her ear.

"Maybe." Her voice wavered and she closed her eyes.

"I'll take that. For now."

After another lingering kiss, he was gone. And she was more confused than ever.

CHAPTER EIGHT

Will sat in his cold SUV, parked at the end of Erin's street and cursed himself. That was the worst timing ever for a text message. What the hell was he thinking? He should have just ignored the phone, but then he saw that the text was from FBI Special Agent Shane Glover, the lead agent on the Hastings case. His attention was split between learning if the agent had news on the Hastings case and discovering what other delights were under Erin's clothes.

He could have refocused on Erin's delicious curves and smooth skin, but then his conscience kicked in. He was trying to get information about her father, not trying to seduce her. But that pale pink lacy bra made him wonder who was seducing whom anyway. Erin Grady was full of surprises.

He shifted in his seat and tried not to think about how Erin tasted and felt writhing under him, how eagerly she returned his kiss.

The buzzing phone in his hand brought him back to reality—the reality that he was investigating Erin's father. Even though they weren't close, a corruption investigation focusing on her father, especially in a small town, could have a drastic impact on her life. And when she found out, she may not ever speak to him again, let alone let him taste her.

"Hey, Shane," Will said. "This better be important."

"It's a Monday night in Lost Coast Harbor. I can't imagine I'm interrupting anything too exciting," Shane said. "But it is important. I need someone who can follow up on an angle up there."

"What sort of angle?"

In the brief pause, Will heard the sound of a keyboard clacking as Shane worked. "You investigated the police corruption in Meridian, right?"

Will didn't answer right away. His role in the probe of Meridian's police department wasn't widely known and he wasn't involved with the official investigation in any way. His boss had made sure of that.

"I spotted some irregularities in Meridian Police Department's reports, but I'm not involved in the investigation," he said.

"Yeah, I know. You refused to bring charges on any of their cases. You discovered the town's police chief was basically living in Florida and had abdicated his responsibilities to lead his department. You also spotted a number of illegal searches, seizures, and arrests that could have led to innocent people being arrested and jailed."

Shane had done his homework.

"What do you need from me?"

Will kept his eye on the house at the end of the block as he spoke. Rain threatened, but he still had a good view of Erin's house. He still wasn't comfortable with her staying there alone. At least he could be nearby if her uninvited guests returned.

"I need someone to look into the LCH Police Department," Shane said. "But as you might guess, I'm not the right guy for the job. I'm not going to blend in. They're not going to trust me."

That was an understatement. Shane had come to Lost Coast Harbor nearly two weeks ago to coordinate the search warrant executions at Hastings' business and his house. He was tall—at least six-four, and broad as a barn. He was also completely bald and sported numerous tattoos. If he were a betting man, Will would put money down that Shane had spent most of his law enforcement career undercover.

"I was specifically told by the assistant U.S. attorney on this case that the feds would be handling this mess and I was to report any leads to you guys and let you take it from there," Will said.

The message had been made clear to him—let the big boys handle Hastings. They hadn't said anything about investigating potential accomplices, so Will had focused on that.

"Nothing's changed as far as I know. But the prosecutor doesn't direct my investigation. I do. And I need your help," Shane said.

"Why me?"

"You're not police, so I can trust you. And you haven't been in LCH long enough to have become corrupted. You seem to have a good sense of right and wrong and you do the right thing, even when it's hard."

An image of Erin sprawled out on the couch flashed through his mind, those perfect breasts teasing him from behind the pink shimmering lace. His jaw tightened. Was he doing the right thing by getting her into bed without being up front about her father? Probably not. At the time, it had felt right, though. It felt very right.

Leaving her abruptly to take a work call? The jury was out on whether that was the right thing to do.

"Why not Valerie Childs? She's new to the department, and she's in a better situation to see if someone in her department is on the take."

"I thought about it, but I need someone outside," Shane said, and Will heard a long exhale. "Look, I know it's not easy to look at the police in cases like these. But you know we have to. You think Hastings ran that operation without a friend in the police department? Not a chance."

"I know."

"You in?"

"What happened that made you call me now? What have you learned?"

In the background, he could hear Shane typing again, in a pattern that echoed the patter of the rain on the roof of the car.

"Some of the documents we seized from Hastings indicate that the man had a network of people he was paying off. I don't know who, yet. Or why. The former office manager has been helpful in unraveling some of the papers. I think if we track some of these payments down, they're going to lead to some interesting places," Shane said. "What do you know about the police chief?"

That he's got a hot daughter who likes sexy lingerie and looks damn good in it.

"He's been chief for about sixteen years, on the force for

well over a decade before that. He's divorced, has one adult child, and seems to be a popular guy in town," Will said.

"And he has a really pricey boat parked down at Hastings' dock."

Will raised an eyebrow. "Lots of people have boats here. We're on the coast."

"Yeah, but this one is far more expensive than most. Can you go check it out?"

Will watched an ancient pick-up truck turn onto the street leading to Erin's house, the headlights concealing the driver from his view. It parked at the end of the block and a woman with a wild mane of platinum hair jumped out, slung a backpack over her shoulder, and slammed the door before walking up to the front door and letting herself in. He breathed easier knowing Erin had called a friend to stay with her and she wouldn't be alone.

"I'll check it out. Anything else?"

"I need more information about the department's staff and sworn officers. I can get the official rosters and some information without raising any eyebrows, but I'll need your help for the details."

"Sure, I can do that," Will said, still distracted by the house at the end of the block.

"And, uh, keep this under wraps for now."

"Got it."

The call disconnected and Will sat still for a few more minutes, staring out the windshield that was blurred with rain. There was some comfort in knowing he wasn't alone in suspecting something dirty going on at the police department.

The light over Erin's front porch blinked out and snapped Will out of his thoughts. With her friend staying, he was cleared to go home. Yet he stayed another minute, just watching the street.

Finally, he started the SUV and flipped on the windshield wipers, then pulled away from the curb and onto the street leading down the hill, back toward his own house.

CHAPTER NINE

Will staggered out of the house after a restless night of little sleep. Dreams flipped between images of Erin, sexy and sprawled out on his bed, and then angry and hurt when she learned he had been using her. But that wasn't exactly true. He wanted Erin from the first moment he'd seen her, well, at least as soon as the pain and shock had subsided. Initially, her family connections had seemed like a nice perk, but those plans faded fast.

Now, the fact that she was Chief Grady's daughter just complicated matters.

He went through his morning court appearance on autopilot, then returned to his office to start reviewing his notes on the evidence boxes that Valerie Childs had given him. That might help him with his task for Shane Glover, too. His secretary handed him his messages, and he saw Valerie Childs was at the top of the list.

He closed the door to his office and put the messages aside, dialing another number instead.

"You're calling to apologize, right?" Erin's voice on the other end of the call made his pulse pick up. Sweet and sexy and not taking any shit from him.

"Yes, I am. Since you answered, does that mean you'll forgive me?"

"Maybe. You did leave me in a rather unfortunate state."

Will exhaled at the memory. That pink bra had been a nice surprise. His heart pounded at the thought of picking up where they'd left off. "Have dinner with me tonight. I'll make it up to you."

He heard the soft intake of her breath, and smiled. He'd gotten to her, too. *Good.*

"Unfortunately, I can't tonight. I'm having dinner with my father."

"Your stepfather?"

"No, with Jerry," she said, her voice reflecting her frustration.

"Why? You said you're not close."

If Erin did have a relationship with her father, even an estranged one, that was going to make telling her about his investigation that much harder.

"We're not. But he's insisting on it."

"I'm sorry to hear that. What time are you getting out of there?"

"As soon as I can."

Will dropped his voice, even though he was alone in the office. "Can I offer you dessert?"

He heard that soft intake of breath again and his heart rate increased.

"Maybe…"

"Come on, Erin. Let me make it up to you for running out last night."

"Yeah, I suppose you do owe me dessert for that."

"I'll bring dessert," he said. "You bring that pink bra and anything else that goes with it."

Erin laughed and at the sound, a deep warmth curled throughout his gut. "What time?"

"How about eight o'clock at my place?"

"Sure, I guess so," she said.

Will hung up the phone with a smile, then immediately dialed the police department and asked for Valerie Childs. Her greeting was far less warm.

"I left a message hours ago," the detective said.

"And I was in court all morning. What's the emergency?"

"We need to talk."

"Yeah, we do."

"Not here. I'll come to your house tonight."

"No." Jesus, that would be great, having another woman show up while he was trying to seduce Erin. "I'll meet you this afternoon. Somewhere we can talk privately."

He heard her sigh with frustration. "Fine."

"Hey, any news on the break-in last night at Erin Grady's?"

"We've submitted the prints to the DOJ. Nothing came back yet. Could take a couple more days," she said. "Where do you want to meet?"

"You're more familiar with this town, so you tell me."

She was quiet for a moment. "You familiar with the Vista del Mar?"

"The VD by the Sea?"

Valerie laughed. "Yeah, that's the one. Meet me there in 30 minutes."

Will glanced at the schedule on his desk and agreed to

the meeting, then hung up. It would take him five minutes to drive to the Vista del Mar, so he took his time packing up his notes before he gave an excuse to his secretary and walked out to the parking lot.

The rain had lasted through the night, but the sky overhead was now clear and blue. The town looked like it had been washed clean, sparkling in the bright sunlight. This was why the tourists made their way along the treacherous coastal highway to spend their vacations on the beach, hiking in the redwoods that lined the cliffs, and shopping the stores that lined the town square. Lost Coast Harbor's glory days were long past with the drop in logging and fishing industries. Those economic mainstays were still the biggest employers in town, but at a far lower rate. Now the town's economy was largely based on its fading charm, luring families to the coast to spend their vacation dollars.

Will pulled his SUV into a parking lot at the docks that was more potholes than pavement. He stared out the windshield at the building across the lot, the Hastings Enterprises headquarters. Peter Hastings' family had built their wealth in fishing and then expanded into transportation. The company still owned most of the property down at the docks, and its shipping operation took up a good portion of the industrial section. The operation was now still run by the Hastings family, but with the federal government watching every move, just looking for an excuse to seize the entire business and shut it down.

Will walked across the uneven pavement to the bar at the foot of a pier. The door to the Vista del Mar was a faded blue with chipped and curling paint, and Will wondered briefly what he'd find on the other side. Everything he knew about the dive bar came from police reports he reviewed on a regular basis. It wasn't a stop on the tourism trail.

The bar was dark and the floor was sticky with the residue of spilled beer. He passed the jukebox and a pool table, and the long, empty bar to the table in the corner, where Valerie Childs sat, her back to the wall and facing the front door. The table was near the emergency exit and a window that overlooked the pier, if one could see past the grime. Will gave the bartender a nod, but didn't order anything.

Valerie had a cup of coffee in front of her.

"Nice place. Come here often?" Will asked, taking the seat across from her, but scooting the chair back so he, too, could keep an eye on the door. They were the only people in the bar, but who knew when the regulars would start arriving. And if the clientele was as rough as the interior design, he didn't want to be hanging out when they showed up.

"You better order something or Frank will kick us out. I recommend the coffee."

Will glanced over at the bar and the bartender glared in return. He motioned to the coffee cup and the stout man behind the bar nodded without expression. He waddled across the bar and set a mug of murky brew on the table, then left without saying a word. Will pushed the cup a few inches away. The coffee looked older than the bar's front door.

"Did you look at the two files?" Valerie asked. She was holding her cup, but not drinking it, like she needed something to do with her hands.

"Yes. Why did you want me to look at the Katri and Acuff files?"

Valerie scowled at him. "You read the reports?"

"Yeah, they were identical. Same wording, same confidential source." It was troubling, but it wasn't conclusive proof that Todd Butler was a dirty cop. He could just be lazy.

"I don't think there's a source," she said.

"Why are you telling me this?"

She shrugged. "You've seen shit like this before."

"Yeah, and it landed me here."

"Just tell me, am I being paranoid or is Butler crossing a line?"

"What happened when you attempted to search Acuff's car, the night you couldn't get backup?"

Valerie set her coffee on the table. "Butler is the head of our drug task force. He coordinates any drug busts and all intel with the sheriff's department, can call the feds, if it's something they're going to take on. So, naturally, I called him when I had Acuff on the side of the road. I asked him to call out the drug dog, but he refused."

"Did he say why?"

"No. He asked my location and I told him where I was, and he said it was in the sheriff's jurisdiction."

"Was it?"

"No, I pulled him over within the city limits. But even if it were, I'd been following the RV through town and could have stopped him. Butler could have called in the sheriff to assist, especially since this was a suspected drug haul."

"Did he say anything else?"

"No. Not then. Later he accused me of trying to horn in on his task force," Valerie said, her brow furrowed. "I'm not. I just made detective and I know Todd has twelve years more experience than me. And I know that he'll never put me on his task force."

Will sat back and studied Valerie. It couldn't be easy being the only woman in the police department. But she seemed tough and smart. She was trying to do the right thing by cleaning her department of bad cops. Will could respect that, though he understood the consequences probably better than she did.

"Why are you coming to me with this?" he asked.

She shrugged. "I wasn't sure who to go to. But you have experience, so I thought I could trust you to do something about it. Was I mistaken?"

"I don't know how you ended up in Lost Coast Harbor, Valerie, but for me, this is punishment. For doing exactly what you're asking me to do."

"Maybe it will be different this time," she said. She pulled a folded piece of paper out of her jacket pocket. Unfolding it, she laid it on the table between them. "I found this."

Will moved in and looked over the long list of payments on the page.

"Where did you get this?"

She shook her head. "That's not important."

"Yeah, it is. This is an internal FBI document."

"I'm in charge of tracking inventory from the search warrants until the feds come move it."

"They didn't take it with them?"

"Not all of it. There's a repository of documents, computers, stuff they haven't picked up yet."

"And they left this behind?"

She shrugged and Will wondered if she had some help

from Shane Glover.

"What does this show?" He looked at the dates, which stretched back about two years.

"Payments from Hastings' company to various parties."

Will looked at the list, then back at Valerie. "Why are some of these highlighted?"

"Those are the payments that can't be explained as business expenses. Either the companies don't exist, or the companies' principles can't be tracked down."

The sums were huge, and several names on the list were paid on a regular basis. None of the names were familiar to Will.

"How is this related to Acuff, Katri, and the police force?"

Valerie ran her finger down the page to the name that showed up in the list a dozen times.

Solstice Enterprises, Inc.

Valerie straightened in her chair and turned toward the one window in the back of the bar. Will followed her gaze to the large white boat docked along the pier. Through the speckled glass, he could make out the name of the boat across the back.

Winter Solstice.

It was a sport fishing yacht, at least forty-two feet in length. Growing up in San Diego, Will had worked several summers cleaning boats at the public harbor. He was familiar with the brand. It was a quality craft, with a powerful engine that could handle anything the rough California coastline kicked up. The cabin would be well-appointed, comfortable enough to live onboard. And it was expensive. If he had to guess, the price tag on such a boat, even used, would be well past a half-million dollars.

"Who owns that?" he asked.

"Chief Grady."

CHAPTER TEN

It had been years since she'd been in the house by the park, more than a decade. But the walls were still painted a rich cream in the living room, with dark wood wainscoting that gave the room a stately feel. Her mother had chosen the color and Erin had a vague memory of sitting on the floor and watching Leanne brush on the paint that covered a darker shade.

The furniture in her father's house was new—a sleek leather couch and matching chairs, coffee and end tables, and pewter lamps, all of which looked like they were ordered directly from a high-end catalogue. Classy, expensive, and soulless. The room had no character, no warmth. There was a single framed photo on the bookshelf and it was of a fish.

"Caught that in Cabo," Jerry said from behind her.

Erin turned and took the glass of wine he offered. She'd brought the wine, certain that dinner with her father was going to drive her to drink. He was carrying a glass of scotch, three large ice cubes clinking together in the cut crystal tumbler. It was his second since she'd arrived a half hour earlier.

Sure hope I never need a kidney, she thought, taking a sip of the cabernet.

"Have you been there?" Jerry asked, seemingly undeterred by his daughter's boycott of the conversation.

"Cabo? No, I haven't," Erin said.

"You should go. I have a vacation rental down there, outside of Cabo San Lucas. Nice little town. Good fishing. Let me know if you want to use it," he said.

Erin took a sip of the wine and gave a noncommittal nod.

"How's your mother?"

She tensed at the question. "She's fine."

She had yet to talk to her mother, but was getting twice daily updates from Alan who assured her that Leanne was going to be fine once they adjusted her medication.

Jerry studied her in a way that made Erin feel like one of the criminals he went after. "I heard Leanne was back in the hospital."

Erin's eyes narrowed and she returned his steely stare. "Yes, but she'll be fine."

She had no idea how he would know, but it was a small town and gossip traveled fast. Still, the thought of him keeping tabs on her made her stomach sour. If he'd cared, there had been years when he could have expressed it. She'd prefer to think they were equally estranged from each other. She had no idea if he had a girlfriend, if he had friends, if he was going to retire from the police department, or if Jerry was happy with his life. Frankly, she just didn't care. She'd always assumed he felt the same.

Jerry's expression didn't change, but he gave her a slow nod. "I'm glad to hear that."

Damn it, had he just stolen the high moral ground from

her? That thought pissed her off. How dare he care about Leanne's health now. Why not twenty years ago when she'd been diagnosed and was struggling to maintain her sanity while raising a small child on her own?

"I better go check on the steaks," he said, walking toward the kitchen. "Why don't you set the table?"

The plates and silverware in the dining room were in the same place they were when Erin was nine—in the built-in cabinet lining one side of the dining room. She put out plates and silverware, found the cloth napkins in the drawer, and then poured herself another glass of wine. *Just get through one meal.* The sooner it was over, the sooner she could go see Will. That thought brought a hesitant smile to her lips.

When he'd bolted from her house last night, she'd been furious, hurt, and disappointed. She'd been ready to write him off. But then Bree had come over to stay with her, and when she told her friend what happened, Bree had taken Will's side. His job was in public safety and there might be a valid reason for him to have to leave suddenly. And incredibly good-looking men, with a job and an education, didn't exactly grow on trees in Lost Coast Harbor. Erin had agreed to give him a second chance, if she ever heard from him again. When he called and apologized, she found that it was harder to stay mad at him than she thought.

Another hour or so and she could go see Will in person, maybe pick up where they'd left off. A bit of the anger and tension she'd been carrying all night melted away at the thought.

The dinner far surpassed her expectations. Jerry clearly had plenty of experience grilling a steak, and the simple salad and fresh bread rounded out the meal. They kept the dinner conversation light, staying away from talk about family history.

"Stan Hutchins is retiring next month," Jerry said.

"I don't think I know him," Erin said.

"Sure you do. He's the deputy chief, been my second-in-command for years."

Erin had no idea who Jerry was talking about, but she took another bite of the steak so she couldn't argue with him over it.

"Todd Butler will get the promotion to deputy chief," Jerry continued, as if they were having a conversation and not a stilted monologue. He looked up from his plate and gave Erin a small shake of his head. "Guess that's a lot of insider politics that you don't care about."

"I'm really not that familiar with your department," Erin said. Nor did she care to learn, and thankfully, Jerry seemed to pick up on that and dropped the subject.

He finished his dinner and pushed his plate back, then took another sip of his drink.

"I'm afraid I didn't plan for dessert. Not much of a sweet-tooth," he said with an unpracticed smile.

Erin returned the smile, trying to make the uncomfortable situation a little more bearable. It was nearly over. "It's okay. I have plans for later and can't stay too long. Thank you for dinner. It was very good."

"Thank you for coming over," Jerry said.

It felt like a truce, one that Erin hadn't planned or wanted, but a truce nonetheless.

"I really should have invited you sooner," he said. "I didn't think you'd come."

She wouldn't have, if Jerry didn't have some leverage over her. He hadn't yet mentioned what was going to happen to Colin. The fact that he had to blackmail her to come to dinner sat between them, unremarked upon, but still there for both of them to see.

"Your half-brother seems like a nice kid."

She nodded, watching him warily. "Colin is amazing. He's smart and talented and he has a bright future ahead of him. He wants to develop new energy sources that don't rely on fossil fuels."

She left it at that. If Jerry really wanted her to believe that he had somehow changed into a caring and decent person, he'd do the right thing and leave her brother alone.

Jerry nodded thoughtfully. "I looked at the police reports again and I don't see any reason to pursue charges against him and his friends. But tell him that if I catch him at another party, I won't be as lenient."

Erin smiled, and this time it was genuine. "I'll tell him."

"Good," he said, tilting his glass so the amber liquid swirled and coated the ice cubes. "Tell me about your clinic. How's that going?"

She paused for a moment, tamping down her irritation at his question, still not convinced he cared about a project so close to her heart.

"It's a little slow. Peter Hastings pledged fifty thousand dollars toward it, and now with him in jail, I can't count on that," Erin said. "It took me a year to raise that much from other sources. It's a setback."

"What do you need?"

She raised an eyebrow at the question. "Besides money? A building, for starters. Something I can remodel into a clinic. I'd prefer something near the hospital, but at this point, I'd take any commercial building that was affordable."

"And you'd work there?"

Erin nodded. "Yes, along with other support staff and nurses."

Jerry was quiet for another minute, then stood and retrieved a folder from a drawer in the hutch. "I'd like to offer you this. If it will help you."

He slid the manila envelope across the table and Erin opened it. "What is this?"

"The deed to a parcel of land. It's zoned commercial, a few blocks from the hospital. I've owned it for a few years and I'm not going to develop it. My accountant says the write-off is more valuable."

Erin blinked at the page, her thoughts racing. "You want to give me a piece of property?"

"Yeah. Is that so hard to believe? I understand the mental health issues in this community. Probably as well or better than you do. Hell, most of them end up arrested and that doesn't help anyone."

The slight edge to his voice surprised her and she looked up from the documents and caught a flash of unreadable emotion in his eyes. Her brow furrowed. "Is there a catch?"

He gave a short, caustic laugh and shook his head. "No strings attached. If you're interested, we'll have my lawyer draw up the paperwork to transfer it to you, or to your clinic or whatever we need to do. Will it help you?"

Having some land would give her instant equity that she

could use as collateral for a construction loan. She could then pour her cash resources into start-up costs, like building permits and an architect, and for operating expenses until the insurance money started flowing. Her heart skipped a beat at the possibility.

"Yes, it will help me," she said, her voice barely above a whisper. Her throat was constricted, tight with a wave of emotion.

Jerry gave a firm nod. "Then let's get it done."

"I don't know what to say," Erin said, her heart pounding. "Thank you."

He pushed his chair back from the table and picked up his plate. "It's a good thing for the town."

He started to clear the table and Erin jumped up to help, carrying her dishes into the kitchen. That room had been remodeled and now had state-of-the-art appliances, including a commercial range with a gas grill where Jerry had cooked the steaks.

"Let me help you clean up," Erin said, placing her plate in the sink.

"No need. I've got a girl who comes in and cleans and she'll be in tomorrow. I'm not that messy, so she doesn't usually have much to do," he said with a short laugh.

As foreign as the idea seemed, maybe Jerry wasn't a bad father or lousy husband, or even a bully who would use a teenager's fate as leverage to coerce his daughter to have dinner with him. Now he just seemed like a lonely man, nearing an age when most people looked forward to spending time with their families, but without anyone to turn to. His parents were dead and he had alienated his only child. It could be that was his motive in making the gift to the clinic.

"What are you doing later?" he asked.

"What?" Erin asked, shaken out of her thoughts and conflicting emotions.

"You mentioned that you have plans later. What are you doing?"

"Oh, right. I'm meeting Will Patton."

He nodded with an approving expression. "I didn't realize you two were seeing each other."

She hoped her face wasn't turning pink, but from the heat, doubted that she was hiding her feelings very well. "We just met, so we'll see what happens."

"He seems like a good man," Jerry said, rinsing off the platter and stacking it in the sink.

"Yeah, he does." Erin hurried back to the dining room to gather the rest of the dishes and to avoid further questions about Will. The donation and his mercy toward Colin had thawed her feelings slightly, but she wasn't comfortable sharing details of her life with Jerry. Maybe they'd come to a place where they were civil, but he was still the same man who left his nine-year-old child with a bipolar mother and no support. The man who had cut her out of his life for years.

Though he was also the man who had paid for her college tuition when scholarships hadn't covered the whole amount.

When she returned to the kitchen, she was more conflicted than ever. Jerry was loading the dishwasher and gave her a sheepish smile. "I can't help it. I'm too much of a neat freak to let the dishes sit overnight."

"Why have a housekeeper, then?"

He shrugged. "She does the deep cleaning that I don't

have time to get to. She only comes once a week. I hate clutter, so I manage the daily chores. I think it's why your mother and I were so ill-suited."

Erin smiled at the thought of her mother's haphazard art studio, which spilled out into the rest of the house. If it weren't for Alan, the entire house would have been taken over by canvases, paint and supplies, mingled with laundry and dishes that Leanne was too busy to wash.

"She'll never be described as a neat freak," Erin conceded.

Jerry wiped his hands on a towel and leaned back against the counter. "You should get going. I don't want to keep you from your date with Mr. Patton."

"Okay. Thanks again for dinner. Thanks for everything." She was still at a loss for words about the donation, trying to absorb what it meant.

"And uh, I hope you're taking precautions at your house now. The window got fixed?"

She hadn't mentioned the break-in, but of course he'd know about it. His police force, responding to a call at his daughter's house—he had probably known as soon as it had been called in.

"Yes, it was replaced today."

He frowned. "You have an alarm?"

"No. But I lock my doors. I'll be fine."

"I've asked my patrol to keep an eye on the house," Jerry said.

"You don't have to do that."

He gave her that stern expression she knew best from Jerry. The look of a police chief who was used to getting his way. "I'll decide if it's necessary."

At least it was just a patrol car driving by her street once in a while, not an officer at her side. "Fine."

"Good. Now go on and enjoy your date," he said.

Erin paused for a moment, unsure what to do. Hug him? He was her father, but she hadn't hugged him since she was a child. Shake hands? That seemed too formal. In the end, she gave him an awkward smile and thanked him again, then left without doing either of those options, but with the paperwork grasped firmly in her hands.

As she drove down the sloping road toward Will's house, her emotions and her logic warred over the out-of-the-blue offer. She supposed it could be guilt. Or he could be altruistic and want to help the town by supporting the clinic. She frowned. He'd never come across as very civic-minded to her.

She shook her head and forced the thoughts from her mind. With his gift, she could provide a much needed service to her hometown. With a clinic in Lost Coast Harbor, lives could be changed, or even saved. People like Rob Katri could get the help they needed, and maybe Leanne could have more hands-on medical care that would prevent the periodic hospital stays.

Erin parked on the street in front of Will's modest ranch-style house and sat for a moment, still stunned at her father's actions. She didn't know why he did it, but in the end, it didn't matter. All that mattered was that he made the offer. She could take it from there.

CHAPTER ELEVEN

William poured two glasses of wine and brought them to the couch in front of the fireplace. Erin sat on the edge of the sofa, the soft light from the fireplace illuminating her creamy skin. When she smiled at him, he caught a glimpse of her dimples.

"My third glass tonight," she said. "I should be careful."

"You don't have to work tomorrow, I hope," Will said, leaning back into the cushions.

She shook her head. "No. This is my transition week, after more than three months on weekend overnight shifts. I agreed to cover a Saturday shift, but otherwise, I have some time off before I go back to daylight shifts."

"Three months? You must have really pissed someone off."

Erin nodded, her eyes sparkling in the low light. She looked almost proud of herself. "I did."

"What did you do?"

"I punched a pharmaceutical salesman who pinched my ass."

Will shook his head. "Sounds like he deserved it. Did he have to do penance, too?"

She rolled her eyes. "No, not that I know of. He's a friend of one of the senior doctors on staff. They have all the power. They can get away with anything. I was given a stern talking-to and advised that next time I was sexually harassed, I should go through proper channels."

"That's unfair."

She shrugged and smiled. "I don't regret it. I don't actually mind the overnight shifts too much. And that rep stays the hell away from me now."

He knew that feeling, being pushed to the limit and then snapping. Just trying to do the right thing, and meeting that wall of resistance. "Sounds like we have something in common."

"Oh, yeah?"

He hadn't meant to go there, but what the hell. "I caught a police department falsifying evidence, refused to prosecute their bogus cases, and instigated an investigation."

Erin's eyes widened. "What happened after that?"

"I got transferred here."

Heat rushed through him as he shared his history with Erin. Only a few close friends knew the details of his banishment. It had been four months, and he was still raw with anger about how he'd been treated, as if he'd been in the wrong.

"They sent you here in retaliation?"

"Technically, it was a promotion."

"I'm so sorry," she said with a laugh.

He found himself smiling, and the anger faded as he looked at her. "I'm not."

At that, her cheeks flushed pink. She ran her tongue along

her bottom lip and his mouth went dry. Christ, she was beautiful. He swallowed and took a deep breath. She'd been in his house for less than ten minutes. It would be bad manners to grab her and kiss her deeply and yank that soft black sweater over her head and see what lace and silk was underneath.

"How was your dinner with your father?" he asked, trying to distract himself.

She tilted her head and looked into the fireplace with a thoughtful expression. "It was fine. Not what I expected."

"Why is that?"

"Because it wasn't horrible," she said, relaxing into the couch with a smile. "And he did something that I wasn't expecting."

Will imagined a scowling Chief Grady. "He smiled?"

He'd learned a lot about the man since meeting with Valerie Childs at the Vista del Mar. He was divorced for twenty years and didn't seem to have a girlfriend, but Valerie told him that he used to date a bank manager. They broke up last year when she took a job out of the area. He was respected, but not beloved, according to Valerie. What was more interesting was his finances—at least the small bit that Will was able to find out in a few hours. Chief Grady owned his house outright, had a second house in Mexico, and was able to buy the most expensive non-commercial boat sitting in the public harbor—all on a civil servant's salary.

Maybe the man was really good at managing his money.

Or maybe he was supplementing his income.

Erin laughed again and brought him out of his thoughts.

"Well, yes, he did smile. But he also gave me a plot of land."

The wine soured in his mouth. "He gave you land?"

"Well, not to me, to the clinic. Jerry just donated a parcel close to the hospital." Erin's voice grew more animated as she told him the story.

"How long have you been working on this?"

"About two years. A friend of mine in San Francisco is going to move up here to run it. She's a psychiatrist. And I've already spoken with some of my coworkers who are willing to come to work for me in administration and on the nursing staff. My friend Maddie helped me write up a business plan. Getting the land means I can take out a construction loan and I can use the other funds I've raised for the start-up costs."

As she spoke, she turned sideways, pulling one leg up so she was facing him on the couch. Her wine went untouched as she hurried through her tale of good fortune.

"This is really important to you," Will said.

She nodded. "It is."

"Why?"

She looked down and was quiet for a moment. "We need a psychiatrist in Lost Coast Harbor. Our last one moved away and we just haven't been able to lure a replacement to such a remote location."

She finally took a sip of the wine, but Will sensed she wasn't done explaining what made her so passionate about her project.

"It's also personal," she said, and then paused and looked up at him. Her expression grew more guarded, and when she spoke, her voice was lower. "My mother has bipolar disorder. This is important to me because it will help her, and people like her, who need to be able to manage their mental health better."

She searched his eyes, as if to see if he understood, and the pain lurking there was impossible to hide.

"How long has she been living with this?" he asked.

Erin shrugged. "All of my life. She was diagnosed finally when I was about seven years old. And that helped, having a diagnosis. But it's an unpredictable disease and she still has bad spells."

He looked down and realized that at some point, he'd taken her hand. He stroked the smooth skin with his thumb and let her talk.

"She's having one right now," Erin said. "My stepfather took her to Santa Rosa and admitted her at the hospital there. She's getting good care, but it's difficult to be so far from her. If we had a clinic and a doctor with admitting privileges, she might be able to stay home or at least be in a local facility, getting better."

Words escaped him. His own family life was stable, so stable it could safely be described as boring. His father was an attorney specializing in corporate litigation. His mother taught science at a community college. He and his sister grew up with just enough privilege that all of life's hard knocks were somewhat cushioned. He couldn't imagine what Erin's childhood was like—with a mother who suffered from mental illness and a father like Chief Grady.

"Did you live with your father growing up? When your mother was ill, I mean."

She shook her head. "No, my mom and I moved out and I always lived with her. She had one episode when I was about thirteen, when she had to be hospitalized for about a month. But by then, she had married Alan. Colin, my brother, was a baby, so we stayed with my Aunt June. And there have been other spells, where she had to go get treatment, but they're rare. She's usually able to manage everything."

"I cannot imagine what that must have been like," he said, still holding her hand in his, her skin warm beneath his touch.

"I know it wasn't a conventional childhood, but it was a happy one. My mother is wonderful. She's a brilliant artist, she's adventurous, and just a great mom," Erin said.

He drank the last of his wine and set the glass on the end table, not letting go of Erin's hand. He liked the feel of her small hand in his, the way he could feel her pulse.

"Why is Chief Grady offering you the land? You said you weren't close."

"We're not. He basically abandoned me and my mom, and right when she was at a terrible time, too. She had just been diagnosed and was trying to figure out the medications, what worked, what didn't, what made her sleep all day," Erin said. "And he just wasn't around much when I was growing up. I'd go months without seeing him."

Her anger was deep, pushed down over decades, and Will wondered if she was even aware of it. On the surface, she kept everything light and playful, but it was a thin veneer. His heart ached at the thought of a young Erin struggling with her parents' issues, and the grown up woman in front of him still trying to keep everyone else patched together.

She sipped at her wine and looked back at the fire, which was now banked red coals glowing from the stone fireplace.

"But I have to say, he's come through when I needed help. He helped me with tuition and rent when I was in school in San Francisco," she said. "Maybe I should give him more credit than I have been."

While Erin spoke, Will was keeping a running tab on Jerry Grady's expenses. It wasn't cheap to put a kid through college, especially not in San Francisco. What was that—four or five years of tuition and books, plus a monthly rental tab that was higher than most people's mortgage? That added up fast, even for the top cop in Lost Coast Harbor.

Erin finished her wine and then shook her head. "I'm sorry, I'm going on and on. I'm a little excited about it."

"I can see why," he said. "This property that the chief is giving you, how long has he owned it?"

"A few years, I guess. He said the tax write off is more valuable to him now," she said.

Erin reached over and fumbled in her large purse, pulling out a manila envelope. She withdrew the paperwork and handed it to Will.

"I'll give this all to the attorney who is helping me, but this is everything I know about it so far."

Will looked over the copy of the deed and a parcel map. The property was two blocks from the hospital where Erin worked, in a cluster of buildings that housed other medical practices and related businesses. It was a perfect location for what she had in mind. But the timing, coming so soon after Hastings' arrest, made Will suspicious. Erin had been working on the clinic for two years. The chief could have donated the property earlier.

Erin shifted on the couch, her knee bumping his leg, and

brought Will out of his thoughts.

"Is everything okay?" she asked, tilting her head as he set the papers down.

"Everything's fine," he said, taking her hand again. He had to tell her about his suspicions and clear the air between them before they went any further.

"So where's that dessert you promised me?" she asked, flashing those dimples at him.

She looked so happy that he couldn't do it. Not tonight. He'd tell her, if he had something concrete that would affect her father. Until then, he wasn't going to be the one to wipe that smile off her face.

He reached forward and smoothed her hair away from her face, letting his fingers slide through the silky strands until he was cupping her neck, then he pulled her toward him and kissed her—long, hard and deep. Her lips tasted of the wine and when a sweet sigh escaped her, every muscle in his body tensed.

Without breaking the kiss, she moved until she was straddling him, her lean thighs on either side of his. They were nearly back where they'd left off before they got interrupted the night before. Her hair fell forward like a veil as she leaned over him. He tilted his head back and let his hands travel down her back, over the soft sweater, then lower, pulling her closer.

He'd only meant to kiss her, but once he started, he didn't want it to end.

"I knew it."

Her whispered words in his ear made his gut tighten. "You knew what?"

"You lured me here with the promise of dessert, but really you only wanted one thing."

He laughed as she continued exploring his skin with her soft lips. "Oh, I want one thing."

His hands found the bottom of her sweater and he slipped his hands underneath, stroking soft, hot skin. She shivered at the touch and pressed herself against him, grinding against the obvious bulge in his pants.

"You guys are all the same," she said, gasping as he flattened a hand against the small of her back and kept her pinned to him.

"I beg to differ," Will said, moving quickly and flipping them so he was on top of her.

He kissed her again, deeply, until she was gasping and clawing at his back through his T-shirt.

Then he stood up.

Her eyes were clouded with passion as he stood over her. "Where are you going?"

He gave her a long stare, taking it all in—the mussed hair, the flushed cheeks, the way her sweater clung to her curves. He wanted her, so much. But he could be patient. "To get dessert."

She shook her head, her eyes sparkling with laughter. "Get back here."

He shook his head and held out a hand, which she took, a puzzled look crossing her face.

"Come here." He pulled her to her feet and then tugged her to the kitchen.

"No, no, I was kidding," Erin said with a laugh.

Will turned and lifted her to the counter, kissing her

again.

"I know. But I wasn't." He lingered over her lips, then smiled. "Stay right here."

He pulled a small dish from the refrigerator, uncovered it and grabbed a spoon from a drawer. Erin watched him, a smile hovering over her slightly swollen lips. He was the reason for the just-kissed pout and that thought gave him great satisfaction.

"What is it?" she asked.

"Chocolate mousse."

Her eyes widened. "You made this?"

He nodded, then dipped the spoon into the bowl and held it up close to her lips. Erin licked her bottom lip, her eyes still on his. Then she opened her mouth and he slipped the dessert between her lips. Her eyes closed.

"Mmm, so good," she said.

He smiled as she opened her eyes. She ran her tongue along her lips again and he moved closer.

"More?"

She nodded. "You really made this?"

"I did."

"How did you learn to do this?"

Will dipped the spoon back into the creamy dessert. "It's not that difficult."

"I can't believe that," she said with a laugh. "But I'm not much of a cook."

He slipped another bite into her mouth.

"My dad is a corporate lawyer and has a huge firm, so he was always having clients over for dinner. But my mother hates to cook. She taught herself a very small number of recipes that she could whip up to impress guests," he said. "After watching her make the same three dishes over and over, I had the steps memorized."

And the rich chocolate mousse was a simple and predictable way to win over a date, too. It hadn't failed yet, and from the look on Erin's face, that streak was continuing.

"It's delicious," Erin said, and ran her tongue over her bottom lip.

"I know."

She smiled and he fed her another spoonful, feeling himself grow harder as her eyes closed again. *Fuck.* That expression. That rapturous peace, mingled with the anticipation of more pleasure to come.

"It's amazing," Erin said with a sigh. "Aren't you having any?"

He looked down the length of her body. Her soft curves covered by the snug tight sweater, the long and lean thighs. He'd been thinking of her, and of how he'd left her last night. Only a complete idiot would leave a passionate and playful Erin Grady to advance his career. He'd make it up to her.

"I'll get my dessert. Later."

Erin's eyes widened and she drew a quick breath, then pulled him closer. He was standing between her legs, which she wrapped around his thighs. She raised her face to look him in the eye and his own need reflected back.

"More," she whispered.

"Chocolate?"

"No."

He abandoned the dessert and leaned in, holding her face in his hands, kissing her in a slow caress. His tongue explored her mouth. Deeper. Slowly, he slid one hand down her neck, skimming down the soft fabric of her sweater. His palm flattened against the small of her back and he pulled her closer, to the edge of the counter. Pressing her against him, letting her feel how much he wanted her.

Nothing had prepared him for this physical reaction. It was more intense than anything he'd felt before, and the more he learned about her, the more he wanted her. The more he touched her, the more of that he needed. It was an ache that he couldn't relieve.

His hand traveled down and grasped her thigh and kept her tight against him until she groaned and gasped for breath.

"God, Will," she moaned, her body straining against his. Her breath brushed his ear, hot and eager and set his nerves on fire.

He picked her up, keeping her legs wrapped around him. He ignored the slight stab of pain in his shoulder as her arms tightened around his neck as he carried her out of the kitchen and down the hall. Some things were worth a little suffering.

ERIN TIGHTENED HER GRIP AROUND HIS NECK AS WILL carried her down the hall. Her lips tingled from his kiss.

They tumbled onto the king-sized bed together, grasping at each other in a frantic attempt to shed the clothing that kept them from each other. Erin ran a hand down Will's back, to the hem of the shirt, and eased it up and over his head. His back was solid under her hands, hot and smooth skin over taut muscles that bunched at her touch. She exhaled and closed her eyes, letting herself sink into the sensations beneath her fingers. Will's hands tangled in her hair, tugged her head back, and his lips scorched a path down her neck. The contact sent a jolt of electricity through her, leaving a tingling trail in its wake.

Will moved down her body, exploring over the top of the cashmere sweater to her waist, then beneath the fabric, his hands hot on her skin.

"I've got to know what's under here," he said, his voice rough as he pulled the sweater up, baring her stomach by inches.

He lowered his head, kissing her skin as it became visible. She moved to help him remove her top and throw it aside, and then heard his groan at the sight of the red lace-trimmed silk bra.

"Jesus, Erin. You're killing me."

The pink lace bra she'd been wearing yesterday wasn't planned, but she'd enjoyed his reaction to the lingerie. Tonight's red silk set was no accident. It was designed to impress and seduce. Will ran a finger across the lace trim along the top of the cup and into the cleft between her breasts. He raised his eyes to her and in the dim light from the hall, she saw the heat there. Pure unadulterated lust.

He turned his attention back to the lingerie and his breath brushed across her skin. She arched, wanting more than the heat of his breath, and Will gave a low laugh.

"What do you want, Erin?" he asked, then ran his lips across the nearly sheer fabric. "This?"

"Yes-s-s-s." Erin's voice wavered at the contact, the heat that penetrated the fabric.

Then the hot breath was gone and his attention moved south, his lips grazing her stomach, stopping at the button of her jeans. His fingers fumbled only briefly with the fastener and then he was tugging the jeans from her hips. She moved to help him, lifting herself off the mattress so he could slide them down her legs. A low rumble escaped his chest as he saw the matching lace there, too.

Erin reached for him, but he moved away, exploring the newly bared area. His fingers traced where the lace met her skin, from her hip to the tiny red bow, centered several inches below her belly button. His lips followed and she gasped at the intimate contact, but wanted so much more. His breath penetrated the lace barrier and she squirmed. Will positioned himself between her legs, brushing his lips against the soft skin on her inner thigh, and Erin's legs trembled at the touch.

"Did you wear these for me?" he asked in a low whisper, then kissed her through the thin lace. "Because you can do that, anytime you'd like."

He pulled the fabric to one side and stroked her with a finger, easing it inside of her, driving her crazy and making her writhe under his attentions. Her muscles clenched around him and her breath caught in her chest. She clutched at him, her fingers sinking into his hair as the tension built.

"Oh, my God," she gasped, arching her body. It was too much. She felt the crest of the orgasm building.

Will withdrew, then thrust into her again, this time with two fingers, while his tongue lapped at her clit, circling and teasing until she was vibrating with need.

"Yes, Will, please." She could hardly form thoughts, let alone words. Her world had shrunk to this bed, her needs reduced to one thing—him. His body, his touch. Everything else melted away.

She arched again, and with a long cry, came undone.

Will crawled his way up her body, kissing her skin, removing the damp panties, the silky bra, and then continuing his way to claim her mouth.

"These are pretty," he said in a gruff whisper, putting the lingerie aside. "But not as pretty as what's underneath."

His mouth captured a breast, his teeth raking lightly across her nipple, making her cry out again. Erin gripped his arms, desperate for an anchor as her body crashed in the wake of the mind-shattering orgasm. He kissed his way up her body, his lips brushing her collarbone, her neck, sending tingles through her. Erin ran her hands up his bare chest, the muscles tightening at her touch, and then explored lower.

When her fingers found the button of his jeans, he hissed out a breath. Emboldened, she unbuttoned the fly and slid her hand along the large, firm bulge. She tugged his pants lower, wanting to see him all, impatient to have him all. Then she was holding him in her hands, stroking his length, reveling in the soft skin and the way he hardened with her touch.

"I need you," he gasped, as she stroked him. "Can't wait."

Will groaned and moved away to push the last of his clothes away, and returned to her gripping a condom in one hand. She took it from him and with a teasing smile, set it aside and pushed him onto his back.

"I have needs, too, Will," she said, kissing his way down his chest. Using her lips and her hands, she explored his body, the ridges on his abdomen. His breathing grew rapid and his body tensed as she caressed the length of his cock, then leaned in, running her tongue along the rim, then taking him into her mouth.

"Erin, oh, fuck," he groaned.

The words fueled her and she gripped his shaft, taking him deeper, gently sucking and stroking, swirling her tongue over his head.

"Come here, baby," he gasped, pulling her up to kiss her. "That's too much, too good. I need to be inside you, Erin."

She found the condom, opened it, then rolled it on him, enjoying the power she had over him when she held him in her hands.

His hands roamed over her body, more frantic now than his leisurely exploration earlier. He pulled her so she was on top of him, her legs straddling him. His cock rubbed against her swollen clit, sending a sharp jolt through her body.

Erin reached down and guided him to her entrance, easing herself down onto him. She closed her eyes at the sensation, her body trembling and tightening around him. She found a rhythm that made him growl with pleasure. His hands roved from her hips to her breasts, cupping them, teasing, playing with the sensitive peaks until she cried out, another orgasm building within her.

"That's it, Erin. Come for me. Let me see you come," he gasped, his body tensing beneath her. His fingers tightened on her skin, holding her close.

Will grabbed her hips and thrust deeply, sending her over the brink and into another wave of sensation.

She leaned forward, her forehead against his. Their mouths met in a deep kiss, and he thrust again. He wrapped an arm around her and rolled them over, keeping himself inside her, his body heavy on top of her.

Will drove into her again and with each thrust, she raised her hips to meet him, her legs locked around his hips. She felt him tense, and gripped his back. The tremor that rocked his body sent her into another wave of pleasure and she whimpered with the unexpected aftermath.

He stroked her back as the waves subsided, then he rolled to the side and stood up to discard the condom. When he returned, he pulled her close and nuzzled her hair. Erin ran a hand over his chest, feeling his heart pounding, echoing her own.

They lay still, catching their breath, for a long period until Erin wondered if Will had fallen asleep.

While her body was exhausted and sated, her mind was going a thousand miles an hour. This was supposed to be a fling. Nothing serious, just a good opportunity for some fun, sexy encounters. But holy crap, she was so totally unprepared for the chemistry between them.

CHAPTER TWELVE

Will made the drive from Lost Coast Harbor to Ukiah in less than two hours—a good pace considering the thick layer of fog that obscured the coast road for the first part of his trip. Once inland, the fog lifted to a gloomy overhead bank of gray that the sun could barely penetrate. He had given his few court appearances to his two coworkers to handle, making the excuse that he had to be at the main office for a mid-day meeting, then headed east.

He would have rather slept in, wrapped around Erin's soft and warm curves, surrounded by her scent. But she had left early, well before daylight, before the sight of her car in front of his house set off a flood of gossip. The memory of the previous night warmed him in the cool interior of the SUV and made his heart rate pick up a little. She had a few days off before she had to work, and he hoped to spend more time with her. His mind ran through all the things he wanted to do with her—and to her—on his return to Lost Coast Harbor that evening.

Jesus, how did he get so attached to her, so quickly? He blew out a breath and tried to focus on the familiar city streets, looking for the restaurant where he was meeting Shane Glover. The FBI agent's early morning text indicated it was urgent they meet. Urgent enough that Shane was driving two hours north from his office in Oakland to meet him.

He found Shane in a corner booth at a diner that served breakfast twenty-four hours a day. It was on the outskirts of a truck stop and in the two years he'd lived in Mendocino County, Will had never been tempted to eat there.

"The coffee's not bad," Shane said, greeting Will with a grin. "Or I've become used to the swill at my office."

Will slid into the booth and waved at the waitress for a cup of coffee. "It must be important for you to come all the way up here."

Shane nodded and ran a hand over his smooth head. The waitress poured a mug full of fragrant coffee and left menus on the table before leaving them alone in the quiet corner of the diner.

"Yeah, I needed to be in Santa Rosa this afternoon for some interviews anyway," he said, eyeing the sparse crowd. His constant watching and scanning of the other diners made Will uncomfortable, but he knew it was just the agent's training kicking in.

"So what's up?"

"Someone's poking around in your background," Shane said.

Will frowned. "My background?"

"Someone in the LCH police ran a full criminal history report, the works."

At this, a chill ran up his spine. "That's illegal."

Shane shot him a skeptical look. "Yeah, I know. But these

guys up there, they're so remote, they're used to doing what they please. No one reins them in."

Will thought about the reports by Todd Butler. The detective's refusal to backup a fellow officer in the field. The expensive sport-fishing boat owned by Erin's father. Yeah, they were operating under their own rules up there.

The waitress returned and took their order, and they were silent until she walked away.

"Got anything for me on the police department?"

"The chief seems to be flush, even with his expensive toys."

"Why do you say that?"

"He just gave his daughter a parcel of land in the city limits."

Shane paused, his coffee cup halfway between the sticky tabletop and his mouth. "He's giving away land?"

"It's for a clinic she's going to start."

Shane's eyes narrowed. "That's a pretty nice gift."

"He'll get a tax write-off."

"Why now?"

Will didn't respond right away. That had been his question, too. He reached into his jacket pocket and pulled out a few pages he'd picked up from the assessor's office on his way through Ukiah.

"It's undeveloped, zoned commercial. I just picked up the public records," Will said, looking over the paperwork. Shane leaned in and studied the deed.

Will frowned and flipped through the pages, then started at the beginning. "This is odd."

"What's odd?" Shane asked.

"The dates," Will said. The waitress returned with their

plates and he pushed the papers aside.

Shane covered his eggs with a generous portion of hot sauce and started eating, but Will's appetite had faded.

"What about the dates?"

Will put the paperwork in front of the agent. "This says that Chief Grady purchased the property two weeks ago. But Erin says her dad has owned this parcel for several years."

"Erin? You're on a first-name basis with the chief's daughter?"

"Yeah. The previous owner was 1221 Properties, Ltd., a real estate trust. I can't tell from this how long the trust owned the parcel."

Shane shoveled in a forkful of egg. "I can look into 1221 Properties. What about his daughter? What's her story?"

Will didn't want to talk about Erin with Shane Glover. "They're not close. She's a nurse at the Lost Coast Harbor Medical Center."

Shane finished off his breakfast and sat back in the booth, sipping his coffee. "She's not close with her dad, but he gives her a piece of property?"

"He's not giving it to her," Will said. "It's for the mental health clinic."

"When did Ms. Grady and her dad fall out? What sparked it?"

"Her parents split when she was young and they haven't been close since," Will said. Which didn't explain why Grady had paid for Erin's college tuition or subsidized her rent in San Francisco for five years. That was definitely information the federal investigators would want to know. He should be the one to tell them about it. A small measure of guilt wormed into his gut, but he pushed it aside and stayed silent.

"And then he waltzes back into her life with a present like this?" Shane gave a suspicious snort. "Yeah, I'm not buying that. I'll take a deeper look at Erin Grady. I have a hard time believing she wouldn't know if her father is on the take."

"*We* don't know if her father's on the take," Will said.

"All the signs are there," the agent said with a shrug.

Will needed to change the subject and fast. He didn't like where Glover was going. "There's someone else at the police department we need to look at. Todd Butler, a detective."

"Yeah, I met him," he said. "Butler was a little too gung-ho when he assisted on our raid. That's why I requested Detective Childs be the liaison to my office on this case. What do you think of him?"

Will didn't think much of Butler. Something about the way he was staring at Erin and Will in the restaurant the other night, then followed her back to her house. And those reports Valerie had shared. Either the man was lazy or he was sketchy. Will didn't have enough information yet to decide which.

"He's the senior detective on the drug task force. I have a drug case pending that's a little weird. The defendant says he got pulled over in an RV filled with pot, and Butler called off the drug team the officer wanted to bring in."

That got Shane's attention. "When?"

"A few months ago. I'm not sure how relevant this is to Hastings, though. It could be sloppy work."

Shane tilted his head. "What's your gut say?"

Will paused, then met Shane's gaze. "I think it's all connected. I just can't prove it."

"Well, get me some proof."

"Why am I working for the feds on this?" Will asked. "I can bring this case myself if I make it."

"You trust your boss to go after another corrupt police department?"

The rage inside him simmered as he recalled the weeks he tried to get someone to take the Meridian case seriously. Will stabbed at his eggs. "What have you heard on that?"

"The investigation into Meridian is being quietly closed up with no findings of wrongdoing," Shane said. "You didn't hear?"

Will shook his head. "No. I'm not in the loop."

Shane snorted. "Yeah, I bet. They couldn't have gotten you out of the way better than by shipping you off to Lost Coast Harbor. If they'd fired you, you'd be able to say it was in retaliation for doing your job. But by giving you a promotion and transfer, you can't complain."

Will nodded, his jaw tense. Shane had more inside information on the Meridian case than he did, and read the situation well.

"You want out of Lost Coast Harbor? This is the way to do it. You work with us, and we don't forget that." He took another sip of the coffee, then set down the mug. "You've got a former supervisor in the San Francisco U.S. Attorney's office."

Shane Glover knew a lot about him, Will thought. He nodded. "Yeah, I do."

"She says good things about you," Shane said. "And you know Spencer Bourne, the federal prosecutor on Hastings, right?"

Will nodded. "Met him a couple of weeks ago on the Hastings case."

"He sends his regards."

"What's that supposed to mean?"

"There's always a need for good prosecutors in their office," Shane said, slapping down enough cash to pay for both of their breakfasts. "That's a direct quote from him."

"If I play ball with the feds," Will said. That was the promise he'd been looking for. Do his job, find out who was aiding Peter Hastings, and get the hell out of Lost Coast Harbor.

Shane grinned. "You got it. Don't get too comfortable in Lost Coast Harbor. You probably won't be there long."

He slipped out of the booth and stood.

"I'll be in touch. You've got my number if something comes up," he said. "And be careful around the police up there. They're investigating you, as much as you're looking at them."

Will watched the agent cross the diner and leave, then walk across the parking lot and get into a tan sedan that nearly faded into the background. He stayed in the booth for a long moment, watching the car turn south toward Highway 101.

If he wanted to move up in his career, this was the best opportunity he'd ever have. Just help the federal prosecutors build a case against the Lost Coast Harbor police force and he could move up several rungs on the career ladder. Get out of Lost Coast Harbor, stop prosecuting misdemeanor DUIs and petty theft and vandalism cases. Start going after big cases, making a difference, and putting real bad guys away for real time.

If that was what he wanted.

He folded the property records and put them back in his jacket pocket, then slid out of the booth. He walked out of the restaurant and into the light rain that was his near-constant companion.

He climbed into his car and sat there without starting the engine. For several minutes, he stared sightlessly past the windshield that was dotted with drops of water.

His mind flashed back to an image of Erin, smiling at him. Her eyes laughing as she flashed those dimples at him. Then a memory of last night, her on top of him, of running his hands up her lean body, cupping her breasts, and her eager reaction to his touch. *Christ.* He gripped the steering with both hands, leaned his head back, and stared at the ceiling.

It was no use. His mind insisted on replaying key moments from last night, and not just the naked moments. Her passion for the mental health clinic, how she'd opened up to him about her mother. The way he felt gut-punched every time he saw her. And all he could think of was that he had to get back to her, needed her again.

But first, he'd have to tell her what he was doing in Lost Coast Harbor. She deserved to know.

The buzzing of his cell phone distracted him from his increasingly guilty thoughts and he glanced at the screen as he started the car.

"Hey, Valerie, what's up?"

"Thought you'd want to know we got the prints back on Erin Grady's break-in."

He hadn't been expecting that so soon. "That's great. Who

was it?"

"Rob Katri," Valerie said.

"The case file you made me review?"

"Yeah," she said, then paused. "Butler is going to go pick him up."

Alarm bells went off in Will's mind. "Why Butler?"

Valerie's voice, already quiet, dropped even lower as she answered his question. "He says the chief wants his daughter's case handled by the senior detective."

Fuck. Butler had a reputation, according to Erin, of roughing up suspects. He could really mess this up.

"Can you go with him? Make sure he doesn't beat the shit out of the guy?"

Valerie blew out a frustrated sigh. "No. They're on their way."

"Anything else I should know?"

"No, just thought you should be aware of what's going on."

"Okay. I'm on my way back from Ukiah. Call me if something comes up. And thanks, I appreciate you letting me know what's going on."

"No problem. I heard you and Erin are together now. Thought you'd want to know."

"Wait. How did you hear that?" It had literally been a matter of hours.

"I'm a trained investigator. And this is a *very* small town. Get used to the gossip, Will," she said, then disconnected the phone.

"Damn it," he muttered, turning north onto 101. He didn't trust Butler to not blow the case against the burglar with a stupid excessive force issue. And there was no way he'd get back there in time to do anything about it.

CHAPTER THIRTEEN

"Nice," Bree declared. "Sophisticated, yet slutty."

Erin grinned at Bree's declaration as she held up the black lace bra and panties set for her friends' approval. She, Maddie, and Bree were just going to meet up for lunch, but then Erin had seen the salesclerk at her favorite boutique hanging up new arrivals in the window and dragged her friends inside for an impromptu shopping trip.

"I thought it was more classy than slutty," Erin said, eyeing the price tag. A little expensive, but what else did she have to spend her money on? And she was quickly becoming addicted to seeing Will's face as he uncovered the lingerie under her nondescript clothes. The demi-cup brassiere and hipster briefs, each with scalloped-edge lace edging, would definitely do the trick.

"Sure, more of a high-class escort." Bree's eyes narrowed. "Care to tell me why we're shopping for black lace before noon?"

"Oh, no reason." Erin bit her lip to keep the smile off her face, but it useless.

"Yeah, that would be easier to believe if you didn't have

that just-fucked grin on your face. Spill it," Bree said. Then she held up a hand. "Unless it's my brother."

"It's not Adam," Erin said with a laugh. She and Adam Rogers had been together for just over a year, a few years earlier, and were still friends. "I tried to get Adam to agree to a friends-with-benefits type relationship, but he takes sex way too seriously. Which is a shame because he is really good at it."

Bree balled up a pair of overpriced panties and threw them at Erin. "I'm sending you my therapy bills."

"That's fair," Erin said.

"So who likes the lace?" Bree asked. "Is it the lawyer who ran out the other night?"

Erin glanced away and hesitated. She told Maddie and Bree everything. They were her best friends. And yet, she liked the idea of keeping Will to herself. She looked back at her two friends, waiting impatiently, and sighed.

"Yes."

No use in lying anyway, since Bree came to stay with her after the break-in and was smart enough to figure out that Erin's bad mood wasn't just related to the burglary. She'd been more than a little frustrated at the interruption and had vented that—loudly—to her friend.

Maddie raised an eyebrow. "Isn't he the new district attorney?"

Erin nodded and glanced around the shop, but they were the only ones in the lingerie section at the back of the store.

"Is he working on the Hastings case?" Maddie asked in a low voice.

Erin shook her head. "I don't think so. It's a federal case, and it doesn't seem like he has anything to do with it."

He had a lot of questions about Hastings and the town, but Will had said his job was to head up the misdemeanor and petty crimes prosecutions—and that certainly didn't describe the Hastings case.

"When can we meet him?" Maddie asked.

"I don't know. I mean, we had dinner the other night, and then last night… well," Erin said, the just-fucked grin making its way back to her face.

Maddie smiled, but her eyes were concerned. "Good, but be careful."

"I'm a nurse, Mads. I know how condoms work," Erin said.

"That's not what I meant," she said, with a laugh.

Erin hugged her friend. "I know. Don't worry."

After handing over her credit card and receiving the small pink bag in return, Erin nodded toward The Sweet Spot, the bakery across the park where they were going to get sandwiches or some of Annabel's aromatic homemade soup for lunch. "Do you guys mind making a stop to see the property for the clinic after lunch? I'll drive. It's not too far."

"So you're going to take the property?" Bree asked.

Erin glanced away, not wanting to see the look on her friend's face. Taking the parcel was selling out—letting her father buy his way out of thirty years of crap parenting with some paperwork. But on the other hand, shouldn't she be allowed to leverage the emotional baggage he'd bestowed on her for something she actually wanted? She could do so much with this unexpected gift.

A memory of Jerry trying to smile during their dinner

leapt into her mind. He was trying to connect with her, in his own awkward way. As much as she wanted to still believe he was just a jerk, the evidence was mounting that he wasn't. At least, not as big of a jerk as she thought he was.

"Of course she's going to take it," Maddie said. "That property's worth at least twice the amount of the Hastings' pledge."

Erin simply shrugged. "It's not final yet. But I can't really think of a reason to turn it down."

"I hate that your father ends up looking like a hero by doing this," Bree grumbled.

Erin had the same thought, but standing on principle wouldn't get the clinic built. Jerry had put her in a no-win situation. Damn him.

Maddie begged off lunch to return to the nursery that she had just purchased, so Erin and Bree crossed the town square and entered The Sweet Spot, the warm, cookie-scented air enveloping them like a hug. They stood over Annabel's display of cookies, cinnamon rolls, and assorted pastries, which Erin knew from experience were as tasty as they looked.

"I feel a sugar coma coming on," Bree said, leaning in close with her hands on the glass.

"What can I get you girls?" Annabel asked, wiping her hands on her apron. She had only been in Lost Coast Harbor about three years, so she'd still be considered a newcomer for several more years. Her arrival had caused quite a stir, at least among the men—single and otherwise. She had the baking skills of Julia Child and the curves of Marilyn Monroe. Top that off with a cloud of blonde curls, her round, green eyes, and her penchant for retro red lipstick, and her bakery was suddenly a very popular place for the retired geezers to gather for coffee and gossip.

Erin had always liked her. Annabel kept to herself, worked hard at the bakery, and always had a smile on her face. She made a mental note to drag Annabel along the next time she met Maddie and Bree for drinks at Donnelly's.

"What's the soup today?" Erin asked.

"Minestrone. And I have rolls that are just about to come out of the oven," Annabel said.

"Make it two of those," Bree said. "And a large piece of cheesecake."

Annabel moved back toward the kitchen and Bree and Erin took a table by the window that overlooked the town's plaza. A few people milled around on the sidewalks, huddled under the awnings to avoid the light drizzle. Erin turned her attention back to Bree, who was giving her a suspicious look.

"What?"

"What does your mother say about Chief Grady's bribe?" Bree asked.

"I don't like that it comes from him, but it's a perfect location and it's free. I can't turn that down. I'll find out tomorrow what my mom thinks. I'm going over to see her then."

"How is she?"

Erin shrugged. "I don't know if Alan is telling me everything. I think if she were doing better, he'd come home. But he says she's improving."

Annabel appeared with two bowls of soup and a basket of hot, fragrant rolls.

"I've been meaning to give you a donation to the clinic, Erin. I'd still like to, if you're accepting them," Annabel said, pulling spoons out of her apron pocket.

"Of course. Thank you! That's very generous."

"Well, we'll see how generous I can be when I look at my bank account."

"Every little bit helps."

Annabel flashed a smile that lit up her face and returned to the kitchen.

Bree grinned and scooped up a spoonful of the soup. "So, back to the subject of you sleeping with the district attorney…"

"Jesus, Bree. Keep it down. There are still at least a dozen people in this town who don't know all my secrets."

"Well?"

"Well, what? You want details? Positions? Orgasm counts?"

Bree nodded enthusiastically. "Yes."

Erin laughed. "Too bad."

"At least tell me if this was this a one-night deal or if you're going to see him again."

Erin shrugged again and felt her face warm as she recalled the previous night. It was good. No. It was far better than good. But she couldn't get too attached. Not that she was looking for that. She'd been single long enough to know that she didn't mind it. If all she got out of Will was some recreational sex, that was fine. Or so she told herself.

"You're blushing, so I take that as a yes, you want to see him again. Preferably naked," Bree said.

There was really no point in trying to keep her private life private in this town.

"Sure, I'd like that. But he's not staying in Lost Coast. You should see his house. It looks like he moved here yesterday,"

Erin said. "He's fun. Despite the fact that he works in law enforcement."

"Well, nobody's perfect," Bree said. "It's about time you found a decent booty call. You were getting as bad as Maddie there for a while."

"Maddie's getting it on the regular now."

"That means you're in danger of becoming our new spinster friend," Bree said, tilting her head with sympathy.

Erin hadn't exactly been celibate. Since she and Adam parted, she'd dated a few men. But no one kept her interest for more than a couple of months. Maybe Bree was right about her spinsterhood.

"This is good for you," Bree said. "You work too hard. You need to relax more. Or at least get laid more often."

"Great advice, thanks," Erin said. "And I'm not lonely."

Even to her own ears, she didn't sound convinced of that. But blessedly, Bree dropped the subject while they finished their lunch.

As they stepped out of the bakery, Erin's gaze strayed to the historic courthouse on the other side of the square, scanning the street for familiar faces. The lunch crowd was starting to trickle out of the courthouse and Erin caught herself looking for one tall, broad-shouldered figure among them.

It wasn't that she expected him to call her, since he was at work. But she did feel a little awkward about sneaking out of his bed so early that morning. At the time, she'd figured it'd be less awkward than running into someone she knew on her walk of shame.

"Erin?"

Bree's voice brought her out of her thoughts. "I'm sorry,

what did you say?"

"He must have been damn good to have you so distracted," Bree said, a wide smile on her face.

Erin shook her head and saw a familiar figure standing next to her car—but not the one she had hoped to see. Detective Todd Butler pushed himself off the front end of the Jeep where he'd been leaning, watching Erin and Bree approach.

"Miss Grady," Butler said.

"Officer Butler," Erin said, trying to keep her tone neutral. It was tough. She'd had just enough dealings with the detective to know that she didn't like him, and certainly didn't trust him. And then there was the way he'd studied her and Will in the restaurant the other night. It was flat-out creepy.

"It's detective," he said, then smirked and looked Bree over from behind his mirrored sunglasses. The man couldn't be more of a cliché. From the glasses to the close-cut military-style haircut to the suit jacket, pulled back just enough to show off the holstered sidearm at his waist.

"How can I help you?" Erin asked. As the man was blocking her path to the car, she didn't think it was an accident she was running into him.

"Tried to find you at the hospital, but they said it was your day off."

Erin's eyes narrowed at the thought of Butler going to her workplace. "Yet you found me."

His smirk grew.

"Wanted to let you know that we got fingerprints back and know who broke into your house," he said.

She stared at him, but ended up just watching her reflection in the surface of his glasses.

"What we don't know is why he broke into your house and and didn't steal anything of value."

"I wouldn't know. Maybe we interrupted him." Erin started toward the car, but Butler remained standing in her way.

"Right. You and the new DA. How long have you guys been an item?"

"Is that part of your investigation, *detective*?" Bree asked.

The detective gave Bree a brief glance, then turned back to Erin. "It is, if Ms. Grady is trying to ensure that she'll get off the hook for doing something illegal."

"I haven't done anything illegal," Erin said, glaring at Butler.

"Well, it's not like you haven't called in those types of favor in the recent past, right? I mean, your little brother walks away from his legal troubles because of your connections," Butler said.

Erin crossed her arms in front of her. "That's not what happened."

"Did Rob Katri break into your house because he knew you had drugs there?"

Erin's eyes grew wide and she gasped. "Rob broke into my house?"

"Why would he think he could get narcotics there, do you think?" Butler asked.

"He wouldn't think that. Rob hasn't ever been to my home," Erin said, moving around him. "I'm done talking with you."

Butler moved to the side to let her pass and unlock the passenger side door for Bree.

"I think you and I will be talking again real soon, Ms.

Grady," he said.

Erin stepped back toward him to walk around the back of the Jeep.

"Nope. We're done," she said.

She climbed into the driver's seat and started the Jeep. She gave only the briefest glance in the sideview mirror before pulling away and leaving him behind her, but it was enough to see him standing there, watching her drive off.

She had a horrible feeling that he was right—that she wasn't done dealing with Butler.

Chapter Fourteen

Erin raised her hand and knocked on the front door of Jerry Grady's house, knowing that there would be no response. The house had an empty feel to it. The neighbors' houses were lit up with warm porch lights spilling out into the early dusk. Jerry's house sat back from the curb looking dark and cold, and as grumpy as a house could look.

Not that she was projecting, Erin thought, knocking again and looking for a place to leave the envelope in her hand. The paperwork included a letter from the nonprofit that thanked Jerry for the generous gift. Erin signed it, but her attorney wrote it. It also included a sheaf of papers involving the property transfer and tax documents that she didn't want to leave on the doorstep. Unfortunately, the envelope was just thick enough that it wasn't going to slip into the mail slot in the door.

She could deliver it to the police station, but it wasn't related to his job and she really didn't want to run into Detective Butler, who gave her the creeps.

"Erin Grady? Is that you?"

Erin turned at the sound of the woman's voice. A familiar figure stood on the lawn between Jerry's house and the bungalow next door. Beulah Foster looked exactly as Erin remembered her from when she'd lived here 20 years prior— her white hair curled around a cherubic face, and her velour tracksuit that married comfort and her daily power-walking habit. If she gave the older woman a hug, she'd probably still smell like Shalimar and cookies.

"Hi, Mrs. Foster. How are you?"

"If you're looking for your dad, he's probably either at work or down on his boat," Mrs. Foster said.

Erin walked down the steps from the porch toward Jerry's longtime neighbor.

"Thanks, I guess I'll try back later," she said.

"No need, just head down to the dock. You can't miss him. His berth is on the first pier. Big ol' fancy boat, on the north side," Mrs. Foster said, then smiled. "Nice to see you around again, sweetie. You and your father patching things up?"

"Nice to see you, too," Erin said. "How are your children doing? I heard your daughter was living in Seattle."

It didn't take much to divert Mrs. Foster's attention to her own family and away from Erin's, but it meant that Erin was stuck standing in the cold, hearing about Mrs. Foster's daughter and her four gifted grandchildren. That wouldn't have been too bad, but she'd worn a dress for the first time in ages. As soon as she delivered the papers to Jerry, she had to attend Hayley's school musical. Though she'd worn boots, thick tights, and had a wool coat over her dress, by the time she got into the Jeep, the cold had seeped through all her layers and her fingers were stiff and frozen.

They were barely thawed after the short drive through Lost Coast Harbor to the public docks. Erin parked as close to the entrance as possible, which was unfortunately close to the town's biggest dive bar. She locked the Jeep and hoped that it would still be in one piece in the short time she intended to visit Jerry.

She rarely had occasion to come down to the harbor except to eat at the Crab Shack, which was more on the tourist trail than the bar, not-so-affectionately known as the VD by the Sea. The wind came in off the ocean with a bitter chill. Erin pulled the collar of her coat up to her chin and stepped onto the dock, which swayed and creaked.

Ahead of her was a huge white boat, one of the few that were lit from within, and she figured it was the fancy old boat where Mrs. Foster said she'd find Jerry. The boats around it were silent and dark, so she walked up to the bow and wondered how one knocked on the door of a boat.

Behind her she heard footsteps and turned, meeting Jerry's surprised gaze. He was carrying a brown grocery sack on one arm and a six-pack in the other hand.

"What are you doing here?" he asked.

She held up the envelope.

"I wanted to bring this by. You weren't at the house, and Mrs. Foster said you were probably here."

He nodded toward the short ladder. "Come on up."

Erin followed him onto the boat, and then down the short and steep flight of steps into the main cabin. On the left was a neatly appointed galley and eating area and on the right an L-shaped upholstered bench and narrow dining room table.

"It's bigger down here than it looks from outside," Erin

remarked, looking around.

"Yeah, it's my retirement home," he said, setting the grocery bag on the counter.

Erin raised an eyebrow. "Are you retiring?"

He shrugged and looked around the cabin. "Not right away, but eventually. In the meantime, I spend as much time down here as I do at the house. I sleep better down here."

Jerry's fishing rods were hung on the wall on hooks, along with more photographs in the same theme as in his house—fish, Jerry fishing, Jerry holding up a fish with a wide smile on his face. His coat hung on a peg by the steps, and a pair of rubber boots sat below them, everything tidy, just like his house.

But unlike the house, this felt warm and lived in. A thriller novel lay on the bench, near a reading lamp. On the shelf opposite the eating area, Erin saw something familiar—her own face at age seven. Her front teeth were missing and her face was framed by choppy bangs, the result of her own hair-styling attempt. If he had tried, Jerry couldn't have found a worse school photo of her.

Jerry unloaded the groceries and offered her a beer, which Erin declined. He opened a bottle and took a drink.

"Have a seat," he said. "What did you bring over?"

"Paperwork from Mr. Minton," Erin said, handing him the envelope and then taking a seat on the bench. "If everything in there looks okay, call him and he'll have you come in to sign the papers."

Jerry nodded, thumbing through the pages. He slid the papers back into the manila envelope and stood, walking a few steps to the largest framed photo. He pulled the frame from the wall, revealing a small safe behind it. He tapped in some digits, and then slid the envelope in.

When he turned back to her, he was smiling and looked more relaxed than she'd seen. The lines around his mouth, usually harsh, were nearly faded. He sat on a stool that he pulled out from under the table and faced her.

"I'm glad that you decided to take the property," he said.

"Well, it's perfect, really. It's a great location," she said. "Thank you. It was a very generous gift."

Jerry shrugged and shifted on the stool.

"Well, it's a good cause. God knows, most of the nutcases end up in my custody—"

Erin's frustrated sigh cut Jerry off before he could finish his sentence. Just when she thought she'd misjudged him, her father reminded her who he really was. Inflexible, judgmental, and lacking any empathy.

"Oh, for fuck's sake. They're mentally ill. They need treatment, not your moral judgment," she snapped.

"Hey, watch your language," Jerry said.

"If you wanted a say in my upbringing, you should have stuck around," Erin said, standing.

"Ah, Jesus, Erin. Don't go," he said. He stood and reached out, then raised his hands as if surrendering. "I'm sorry. I shouldn't have said that. Okay?"

Gray eyes, as familiar as her own, stared back at her and she backed down. He was giving her a gift that would let her do something she'd dreamed of doing. The paperwork wasn't even final yet, so she better behave. At least a little. And she knew that she was sensitive to mental health issues, and probably overly defensive.

She took a deep breath and let it out slowly, a meditation technique that her mother had taught her to tame her quick temper. It sometimes worked.

"Okay," she said, but remained standing.

"Good. Well, we were almost having a civil conversation there for a minute." Jerry shook his head with a small smile. "We're probably out of practice. Maybe we could have dinner again."

Erin pursed her lips at the thought. Another hour of stilted conversation, trying to avoid all the emotional landmines they'd each planted over the years. It didn't sound inviting. Yet, his reaching out to her seemed sincere and she couldn't see what he'd gain by it.

"Sure, I guess so."

Jerry looked at her, seeming to notice her dress and boots for the first time. If he looked close, he'd also notice the lipstick and mascara, but she doubted that he saw her often enough to know she rarely bothered with cosmetics.

"You look nice. Got plans tonight?"

She nodded. "Hayley's in a play at the high school."

"Are you taking Patton?"

"No."

"But you're seeing him?"

Erin eyed her father. "Why?"

He gave a frustrated exhale. "Because, like it or not, I am your father and I am curious about your life."

Erin sighed, and hated how much she sounded like Jerry. "I just met Will. We've seen each other a couple of times."

"But you like him?"

Erin narrowed her eyes at him. "Yeah, I like him."

Jerry had no idea the thin ice he was treading on. She didn't like talking about Will with her best friends. Trying to have a conversation about him with Jerry was just about killing her.

"Sure I can't get you something to drink?"

Erin shook her head. "No, I really should go. I just wanted to make sure you had everything from my lawyer."

She started toward the steps, then paused. "Hey, if I can ask a favor."

Jerry's eyebrows raised in a surprised expression. "Of course."

"Rob Katri's not a criminal. I mean, he is. He has a criminal record. What I mean is, he's not a threat. He has a terrible addiction and he needs mental health treatment. Please just consider that, okay?"

It wasn't a favor for herself, so it wasn't like she was using her connections to Jerry's authority, she rationalized. This wasn't at all like what Butler had accused her of doing.

Jerry shook his head and seemed genuinely puzzled. "Why are we talking about Rob Katri?"

"Because your detective told me he's the one who broke into my house. Said he was probably looking for drugs," Erin said.

An artery in Jerry's throat bulged and his eyes turned cold. "Detective? Which detective?"

"Todd Butler."

His face flushed a ruddy red. "Tell me what he said. When did you talk to him?"

Erin was taken aback by the reaction. "This afternoon. He said he thought Rob was at my house to find drugs."

Jerry nodded. "Did he say if Katri was in custody?"

"No," Erin said. Her father's tension was contagious and her shoulders tensed. "What's going on?"

His lips tightened. "Nothing. Just, uh, stay clear of Butler, okay?"

Erin nodded, though his command made no sense. Butler worked for him. Jerry should have known about Rob's prints.

"Is everything all right?"

"It's fine," he said, the words clipped. Then he forced a smile. "Thanks for tracking me down. I'll get the documents back to Barney this week."

He went ahead of her and opened the hatch.

The air hit her in the face, a bracing cold wind off the ocean, as soon as she hit the top step. But even with the bitter cold, she could see the attraction of sleeping down on the dock. It was quiet, and the boat's gentle sway was relaxing.

Jerry made sure she made it down the short ladder to the dock, then stood above her.

"Take care, Erin," he said. "Keep in touch."

She looked up at him, bathed in the orange light of the overhead security lamp on the dock. The harsh light cast his face into shadow, but she saw the regret there.

"I will," she said. "And I mean it. Thank you."

He raised a hand in a short wave and she turned to walk back toward the parking lot, her gaze falling on the boat's name as she did. Her step faltered at the script that arced across the stern—Winter Solstice.

Her heart skipped at the sight and she looked up to where Jerry had been standing, but he was gone. She stared at the cursive black letters for several long moments, absorbing the words.

She had grown up hearing her mother tell the story about her birth. It was the afternoon of December 20 and her mother's labor was progressing fast. But Leanne wanted her daughter to be born on the winter solstice and through sheer will, she managed to hold off giving birth until the calendar said December 21. Then she wanted to name Erin after the event, but Jerry had drawn the line there.

Maybe he wasn't a bad guy after all. He had saved her from being named Solstice Grady. That alone should buy him some goodwill.

Erin hugged her coat around her as she crossed the parking lot, keeping an eye on the rough crowd loitering near the front door to the Vista del Mar. Again a tall, broad-shouldered figure waited for her, leaning against the front of her Jeep. This time, though, her insides quivered as she recognized Will in the low light and thickening fog.

"What are you doing here?" she asked, standing in front of him.

He shifted, his hands stuffed into the pockets of his heavy coat. "What, a guy can't stalk the woman who snuck out of his bed at four o'clock in the morning?"

Heat flushed her face and she hoped the darkness hid the tell-tale blush. "I said good-bye."

His eyes dropped and his lips parted and her whole body flushed hot at the memory from that morning. His hands pulling her back into the warm cocoon of blankets, his lips and his fingers convincing her to stay just a little longer.

"I remember," he said with a smile. "What are you doing down here?"

"I had to drop some paperwork off for Jerry," she said.

Voices were getting louder across the parking lot as some of the VD's patrons spilled out of the bar.

"Can I buy you a drink, get you out of the cold?" Will asked. He grinned and her stomach did that slow flip again.

Fuck me. That man was way too pretty. Too bad she had to turn him down.

"I'd love to get a drink, but my sister is in a play and I have to go to that."

Will gave her a serious look, and even though he was dressed casually, she could picture him in the courtroom, cross-examining a witness on the stand. "You have to do a lot of things."

She shrugged. "Well, yes. This is a family obligation."

"Can I join you?"

The suggestion surprised her. "Really?"

"Yes. If that would be okay."

She paused, a warm flood of happiness filled her. "It's a musical."

He smiled. "Is that a warning?"

"Yes. I wouldn't be going but Hayley is probably my best bet for a kidney if I ever need one, so I should stay on her good side."

Will laughed and the sound warmed her. "I don't scare off that easily."

He was going to regret this, but the thought of spending another evening with him, even listening to Hayley's slightly off-key rendition of Broadway classics, was too tempting.

"You've been warned," she said and let him lead her to his SUV.

HE SAT NEXT TO ERIN IN THE DARK THEATER, TRYING TO block out the amateur musical production and focus on the warm, soft hand enclosed in his own. Will stroked the soft skin on the inside of her wrist, brushing his thumb across and feeling her pulse beat beneath his finger. It might appear chaste, two people holding hands in a theater. But it was anything but innocent. With every stroke, his thoughts returned to the prior night's passion and what he intended to do to her later.

Erin shifted and looked up at him through thick lashes, her lips slightly parted and turned up. Her playful and sexy smile made his entire body hum with pleasure. She crossed her legs and he glanced down and took in the long expanse of her thigh. It was the first time he'd seen her in something other than scrubs or jeans. The simple dress was modest with a high neckline and long sleeves, but when she'd taken off her coat, he'd seen that the hemline hit her mid-thigh. The tall dark boots and tights showed off her legs—long and lean—and his brain fixed on the memory of those legs locked around his hips.

He squeezed her hand and she licked her lips—a signal his cock picked up on. He moved in his chair to get more comfortable, and was grateful the lights were low and they were in the back of the theater.

Erin's hand slipped from his grip and ran up his thigh. Will grabbed it before she could move any higher. She was staring straight forward at the stage, but he saw her smile widen. He gripped her hand with his other hand, then put his arm around her, pulling her close.

"Stop that," he whispered.

"No one can see us back here," she said, her voice hardly above a breath.

He drew even closer, and her hair brushed against his face. "Just wait until later."

She turned her head and her lips were right there, inches from his, and there was nothing he wanted more than to close that distance. Instead, he tried to look unaffected as she licked her bottom lip. He suppressed a groan, but barely.

"Later, huh?" she whispered.

Against his better judgment, he prayed that the high school production lasted long enough for him to stand up in public without a massive bulge in his pants. He managed to calm himself enough to stand and applaud with rest of the auditorium when the lights finally came up, and then he followed Erin to the backstage entrance so she could congratulate her sister.

"Oh my God, Erin! Did you see that I totally forgot the lines in the third stanza of the finale? I can't believe I did that!"

Hayley White was a younger version of Erin—same light-brown hair, same wide smile framed by dimples. But where Erin was all obligations and responsibilities, Hayley had a fearlessness about her, an enthusiasm and energy that only a sixteen-year-old could maintain.

Erin hugged her sister and introduced Will, and within a minute, the teenager bolted off to be with her friends, promising to get a ride home from Colin, who was waiting off to the side of the chaos.

Erin shook her head as she led Will through the backstage area to an exit that let them out in the parking lot behind the high school theater. "That's Hayley. She's never still for long."

"You seem to know your way around back here," he said, taking her hand again as they walked through the mist. "Were you one of the theater kids in high school?"

Erin laughed. "Yeah, a few minor parts. Mostly I know my way around the back because that's where I'd sneak off with my boyfriend to make out."

Will had an instant image of her, young and enthusiastic as her sister, and envied that young man. "Damn, did I miss my chance to make out with you behind the stage?"

"Play your cards right and I'll show you the other favorite place for romance for bored teenagers in Lost Coast Harbor," she said with a giggle.

As they reached his SUV, he pulled her close and smoothed her hair away from her face. "What do I have to do to convince you to take me there?"

She bit her bottom lip and he leaned in, flicking his tongue across that pout. She gasped, opening her mouth, and he took advantage and kissed her, finally claiming the lips that had been tempting him for the past two hours.

Erin pulled away, took his keys from his hand and unlocked the door for him. "Get in. Let's go for a ride."

Her smile tugged at something inside him as he climbed into the passenger seat.

She drove east of the town, then turned north and took an unmarked road that wound through the trees. They were climbing in elevation, but in the dark, Will had no idea where they were.

After about ten minutes, she pulled onto a dirt road and slowed down to a crawl, navigating ruts in the road like a pro. The SUV swayed and bounced another fifty yards and then the road widened into a turnaround. She pulled the vehicle up to the very edge and parked, turned off the engine and cut the lights.

Below them was the town of Lost Coast Harbor, a crescent of lights that looked like sparkling jewels against a blanket of black velvet where the Pacific Ocean disappeared into inky nothingness. A few stars peeked through the clouds.

"What a view," he said, unfastening his seatbelt and turning toward Erin. She was looking down on the town, her face illuminated by the moonlight.

He reached over and hit the button to release her seat belt. Erin smiled and let him pull her closer. "So, this is where you and your boyfriend would come to make out?"

"Generations of teenagers have spent time up here," she said. "The awkward groping these trees have seen…"

He laughed, moving closer, inhaling her scent.

"You didn't have a place like this in San Diego?" she asked, running a hand up his arm.

"Sure, but Balboa Park was more heavily patrolled and we always got kicked out too soon," he said.

"Ah, cock blocked by the cops?"

He grinned. "Something like that."

"Do you miss living in San Diego?"

He shook his head. "No, not really. It's nice to go back, but I haven't lived there in years. I went back for a year after law school, but that job didn't last. I wasn't sorry to see San Diego in my rear view mirror."

Erin turned in the driver's seat, shifting so she was facing him. "Were you a prosecutor there?"

He shook his head. "No. My dad does civil litigation and through his connections, I got hired at a firm there. It was a good job, but I really hated the work. It was boring and required a lot of long hours, and I just didn't see myself staying there long. When the recession hit, they laid off all the first and second year associates, and I didn't really mind."

"Then what did you do?"

"I couldn't find another job at a big law firm because they were all in same situation, so I took what I thought was a temporary job at the Riverside County's district attorney's office," he said. "It was the best thing I could have done. It was a great job and I finally felt like I hadn't wasted my parents' money on law school."

"What did you like about it?" she asked, her gaze curious.

"Everything. It was important work. When I won, the bad guy went to prison. Even when I lost, the system worked like it should," he said. "My first jury trial was a drunk-driving case, which I treated like it was the second coming of OJ Simpson, of course."

Erin laughed. "Did you win?"

"I did win. And then got reprimanded by my boss for calling a half-dozen officers to testify, when one would have sufficed," Will said, smiling at the memory of that time, that rush of learning that this was what he wanted to do. "But she kept me around, and kept throwing me into the courtroom to learn the ropes. I worked my way up to felony trials pretty quickly."

"Like what kind of cases?"

"All kinds—whatever they'd give me," he said. "It didn't feel like work. It's rewarding to feel like your effort is making a difference. And criminal law is interesting—there's always an intellectual challenge, new techniques to learn. I only wished I'd figured out earlier that this was the kind of law I wanted to practice."

Her lips turned up. "You sound like you miss it. Don't you still get to do that?"

He shrugged. "It's not the same here. I'm in a branch that doesn't handle any big trials. We have to turn the felony cases over to the main office for prosecution. So it's a lot of misdemeanors, arraignments, minor things."

"How did you end up in Mendocino County?"

"Unfortunately, the recession caught up to the county offices and budget cuts meant my position was eliminated," he said. "My former supervisor had just moved to San Francisco, to the U.S. Attorney's Office there, and she said as soon as she has an opening on her team, I'm in. But her work is specialized and those openings don't come up too often. So I applied for several positions around the state and the only district attorney's office hiring at the time was Mendocino County."

"And then you got sent out here, to Lost Coast Harbor," she said.

He nodded. "Yes. You know the rest of that story," he said. "Why are you back here, Erin?"

She shrugged. "It's home."

He shook his head slowly. "No, that's not the answer. Tell me why you came back here."

She frowned. "My mom got sick. I'd been out of school for a year or so and was working at SF General. It was great. Exciting. I liked the people I worked with. But she had to be hospitalized for several weeks and my brother and sister were young. It was so hard on Alan, my stepdad. I figured it was time to come home."

"This isn't where you thought you'd be after college?"

She shook her head. "No, when I went off to school, I swore I wouldn't be back here. But you know, things change. You make the best of it."

"How is she doing?" he asked.

"Better. She should be home in a few days," Erin said.

"But overall, when she's not hospitalized, how is she?"

Erin paused, watching him in the dark car with a thoughtful expression. "She's usually just fine. It's a chronic condition that can be managed."

"So why have you stayed?"

She ran a tongue across her bottom lip. "I stayed because I'm needed here. I grew up with a mother who had bipolar disorder. It's not easy. I just want to make sure Colin and Hayley don't go through that."

He wasn't surprised. Erin's entire life was centered on others. Her siblings, her mother, her patients.

"I can't imagine what that was like. It was just the two of you?"

Her eyes clouded and he thought he'd pushed too far, but then she raised her chin and met his gaze.

"It wasn't all bad. I mean, now I look back and wonder why someone didn't step in, but at the time, I didn't know. I guess I thought all ten year olds knew how to buy a week's worth of groceries while there was still money in the checking account, or how to cover for my mom's absence at a parent-teacher conference."

For a long moment, Will just stared at her. Childhood shaped everyone and this explained so much about Erin. Why she came back to Lost Coast Harbor, why she stayed, and what she did.

"You take care of everyone in your life," he said, smoothing a lock of hair from her face. "Who takes care of you?"

Her lips turned down. "I take care of myself. I don't need someone to take care of me."

Will ran a thumb across her pouty bottom lip. He didn't doubt that she believed it. That stubborn tilt to her jaw said she was independent and self-reliant. She was tough, and strong, and he wouldn't want her any other way. But God, he just wanted to hold her and care for her for a change.

"Not tonight."

Her eyes widened at the contact of his fingers along her cheek. "No?"

Her voice dropped to a husky whisper that made his cock harden.

"I'm going to kiss you," he whispered.

Her eyes widened and her lips parted in a small smile. "You are?"

He ran his fingers through her hair until his hand was at the back of her neck.

"And then, I'm going to push that indecent dress up just a little higher, and see what you wore for me tonight," he said, feeling her heart beat under his fingers.

She started to reach for him, but he stilled her hand, covering it with his. He shifted so he could pull her closer.

"I know it's something sexy," he breathed into her neck, then pressed his lips against the soft skin below her ear.

"Lace? Silk?"

Her breath escaped in a rush as he ran his hand down her body, over the curves that had been tempting him all night. His fingers played with the hem of the short dress and Erin shifted as his hand moved under the fabric, over the thick tights.

"Let's get these off you," he whispered.

She kicked her boots off and wiggled out of the tights and he ran his hands over her soft, warm skin. His hands roamed higher, up the back of her legs, along the curve there and moving higher still.

His mouth went dry as he realized the lace and silk he was reaching for wasn't there. Instead, his fingers brushed her soft, hot core, making her squirm against his hand.

"Jesus, Erin," he breathed.

He pulled away and she followed after him, but he gently pushed her back. He reached down between the seat and the passenger door, pulling up the lever that let him ease the seat back as far as it would go.

"Come here." He pulled her with him until she was on top of him and his hands again worked their way up the back of her bare legs.

Her hair fell forward and he reached up and brushed it away, gripping a fistful of it and then guiding her to his mouth, kissing her deeply. Their tongues met and every muscle in his body tensed.

He moved her so she had one knee on either side of him, then reached down and stroked her, his fingers sinking into the heat.

"So hot. God, so wet for me."

She whimpered as his fingers delved deeper, penetrating her and stroking her until she trembled.

"I need you inside me," she moaned.

He slid another finger into her and kissed her, thrusting his tongue in a matching rhythm to his hand. Her legs shook and she tightened around his fingers. He moved, shifting her for a better angle, cursing that he'd been too impatient to get her to a bedroom. Hell, even the backseat would have been more comfortable. A twinge of pain in his shoulder reminded him that the bike crash hadn't been that long ago, but he quickly pushed that away and focused on the woman writhing on top of him.

She gasped and moaned, her body tensing as he brushed a finger against the bundle of nerves.

"Come for me, Erin," he groaned. He crooked the fingers inside her to find that spot that drove her crazy. He eased his fingers in deeper, until she threw her head back and cried out his name, her body shaking with the force of her orgasm.

She collapsed on his chest, breathing heavily and trembling. He pressed his lips to her head, breathing in her scent while her tremors faded. With a deep sigh, she pushed herself up, her hands on his chest, straddling him. Her hair was mussed, her lips swollen, dress hiked up to her waist and she was so beautiful it took his breath away.

Erin's hands fumbled with his belt.

"I'm not going to be the only one half naked here," she said, unfastening his pants and freeing him.

His balls ached at the first touch of her hands on him, stroking and caressing until the need built. Erin shifted and then moaned in frustration. "This car, I can't—There's not enough room."

Will gripped her hips and pulled her closer to him, her wet core hot against his cock, a sensation that nearly did him in. "You want to wait until—"

He didn't get the question out before Erin leaned in and kissed him, her hips rocking against him, one hand stroking him, and he forgot to breathe for a moment.

"No, I do not want to wait." Her voice was husky and impatient. "But I want to taste you."

Any blood remaining in his head shot south and left him light-headed, watching her run a finger across the tip of his cock, through the bead of moisture there. Then she raised her finger, looked him in the eye, and sucked the tip of her finger—and his body jerked. She gave a low laugh and continued stroking him until he groaned.

"Damn it, Erin," he gasped, as his balls contracted. "Fuck, that feels good."

He reached for her hips, cupping her ass with both hands. He needed her, needed to bury himself in her.

"Get that damn condom before I come. I want to be inside you."

Erin found his wallet, withdrew the condom and rolled it on quickly. Raising herself on her knees, she rubbed against him and positioned him at her entrance, then eased herself onto him with a shudder.

"Oh, God, Will, yes," she murmured, her head tilting back and her eyes half-closed.

His breath caught in his chest at the sensation of being surrounded by her, a part of her. So hot. So sweet. He nearly came at the shock of it.

He held her close and thrust into her, relishing every soft cry from her lips. She leaned in, brushing his lips with hers. He reached one hand up and grabbed her head, deepening the kiss, demanding more. Demanding everything.

His fingers flexed, gripping her hip. His balls tightened, the release threatening to give way. Erin cried out and ground against him, and her body clenched around him. The release tore a shout from his throat and the pulsing continued as Erin moved against him.

Spent, he gathered her against him, both of them panting. He stroked her hair and breathed in the scent of her perfume and their sex. He closed his eyes and tried to remember every detail of her—how she felt in his arms, the playful way she teased him in the auditorium, the sound of her laugh.

He knew had to tell her about her father, and the expanding investigation, but holding her in his arms, he didn't know how.

CHAPTER FIFTEEN

When she was young, Erin thought her mother was the most beautiful woman in the world. Long hair that varied in color from blonde to gold to a deeper shade of honey. She wore flowing skirts, dangling earrings, and bangles around her wrists. Leanne Grady was a free spirit who would proudly wear a garland of daisies in her hair if her daughter brought it to her. She was an artist, and she taught art at the local schools, where she was popular among students and other teachers. But she was also deeply troubled and when Erin was six years old, the first signs of mental illness appeared.

As she parked in the visitor section of the private hospital, Erin remembered the first time she came here to visit her mother. She was nine years old and didn't understand the nature of Leanne's illness, or why her mother couldn't come home. Over the years, there had been several more stays at the hospital's psychiatric ward. The most severe was when Erin was twenty-four and still living in San Francisco. It was six weeks before Leanne was released, and by the end of that difficult time, Erin knew she had to move home. She got a job at the LCH Med Center and left her friends and her job at San Francisco General behind for her hometown. That way, if Leanne had another breakdown, Erin would be close by to care for her siblings, help her stepdad, and manage Leanne's care.

It had been the right decision. She had a good life in Lost Coast Harbor. A bit boring, sure. But she was able to spend time with Colin and Hayley, and with her mom and stepdad. She'd reconnected with Bree and met Maddie—her two best friends. She had a job that she loved and coworkers she mostly liked. And if she could get the mental health clinic open, she'd be able to give something back to her hometown.

The doors slid open with a faint hiss and Erin walked into the familiar lobby, and then checked in at the reception desk. A few moments later, a nurse arrived to take her upstairs to her mother's room.

"Your father has been here every day since she arrived. He's so nice," the nurse said.

Erin smiled to cover the stab of guilt that she hadn't come to visit yet. Alan had been staying with friends in Santa Rosa so he could be at the hospital every day for visiting hours. During the day, he worked from their living room as best he could, advising his staff at Lost Coast Harbor High School, conducting conference calls, and writing reports. Then he'd spend two hours with his wife, unsure whether he'd be greeted with a sobbing, hysterical woman convinced that angels were surrounding the hospital, or a woman too medicated to speak. On a good day, Leanne might be lucid, but sad that she was putting her family through hell.

"How is my mom doing?"

The nurse gave a quick nod and a smile that disappeared too quickly, an expression that Erin understood to mean that there wasn't much good news to share. It was a look she'd worn herself many times before.

"Well, we're working on getting her medication adjusted, but as you know, that can take some time."

"How is she today?" Erin clarified. She knew far too well how tricky bipolar disorder could be.

"You're catching her on a good day."

Alan was already in the room, sitting with Leanne on a couch under the window that overlooked a courtyard. He stood when Erin walked in and gave her a hug. "It's great to see you."

He motioned for Erin to take his seat on the couch. "I'm going to go and get us something for dinner. I'll be back in a little bit, okay?"

Leanne nodded and her lips turned up, but it was a shadow of her usual smile which would light up her face. Erin took her mom's hand. "We'll be here. Bring back something good."

The door closed behind them and Leanne held open her arms. Erin sank into the embrace and nearly sobbed with relief. She'd been trying so hard to hold everything together in the last few days, and it wasn't until she felt her mother's arms around her that she realized what a toll it was taking on her.

Leanne's hands stroked her hair and Erin lingered for a few more minutes, composing herself.

"How are you doing?" she finally asked.

Leanne gave a wan laugh. "Well, I'm back in the looney

bin, but other than that, I guess I'm okay."

Erin pulled away and studied her mother—the same pretty face, surprisingly few wrinkles for a woman in her mid-50s, and long flowing hair. Her eyes were a bit clouded by the medication, and she looked tired, but she'd clearly retained her sense of humor.

"Are they taking good care of you?"

Leanne squeezed her hand. "They're good to me."

Maybe this hospital visit wouldn't last too long, Erin dared to hope. "What are they prescribing for you?"

Leanne rattled off the names of some anti-psych meds, but then shook her head. "I want to visit with my daughter, not a nurse."

She brushed Erin's hair away from her face. "How are you?"

Erin gave her mother the sanitized version of Hayley and Colin's recent misadventure, leaving out the part where Jerry blackmailed her into having dinner with him. Then she updated her mother on the rest of the gossip she was missing out on.

"So, there is something else," Erin said, unsure how to approach the subject of Jerry's donation, or even if she should bring him up. But maybe Leanne could use some good news. "Your ex-husband did something I wasn't expecting."

Leanne tilted her head, doubt crossing her face. "What did Jerry do?"

"He wants to donate a parcel of land to build the clinic on. It's near the hospital. And it would be perfect," Erin said. "I think everything is finally coming together."

Leanne frowned and closed her eyes for a long moment.

"Oh, dear."

"What?"

Leanne took Erin's hands and gripped them tight.

"Mom, what's wrong?"

"Don't take it, Erin." Leanne's attention now was sharper, her voice stronger, like she was fighting through the medication fog.

"But, why?"

The unease that always rode with Erin on these trips grew inside her gut.

Leanne shook her head. "You don't want to owe him."

"What are you saying, Mom?"

"He's not a good person, Erin. I've tried not to say anything bad about Jerry because he's your father, and you might want to have a relationship with him one day. But sweetie, please. Just tell him no. Tell him you don't need the land."

A knot of tension grew within her and a dull ache throbbed at her temple.

"I do need it."

Her mother's grip on her hands tightened. "There's got to be another way to raise the money. You'll find a way, a different way."

"Why is this so important?"

Leanne's brow furrowed. "Erin, he's not a good man."

Erin shook her head. "That's not enough. You need to tell me why."

Her mother took a deep breath. "He's crooked. I've always thought that, since just before we divorced. I never said anything because, well, who'd believe the crazy ex-wife? I've never even said anything to Alan. But please trust me on this.

Don't do this."

Erin's head spun with her mother's confession.

"Why did you think he was crooked? Did something happen?"

Leanne tilted her head and gave Erin a sad smile. "Maybe I should have done something sooner, but I didn't want to rock the boat, you know? I just wanted to get away from him, get you away from him."

"Is this why you left him?"

Leanne shook her head. "We were never going to last. Our marriage was impulsive and a terrible idea. But I got you out of it, so I'll never regret it."

She'd been so confused when her parents divorced—the sudden move from the only house where she'd ever lived to the small, drafty duplex. Her father had worked long hours, and when he was home was gruff and distant, so she hadn't missed him that much. But he had provided a measure of security that disappeared. It was a chaotic time. Their fortunes veered between extremes. One week they would be eating ramen noodles and cutting coupons, and the next week Leanne would sell a painting and they'd take an extravagant trip.

"Mom, whatever Jerry was up to, that was a long time ago."

Leanne's mouth tightened. "I don't think he's changed."

Erin's eyes narrowed as she tried to fit this information into what she knew about Jerry. Sure, he was cold and distant, even with his only family. But being a jerk wasn't illegal. If what Leanne suspected was true, then Jerry wasn't just a bad father. He was a dirty cop.

They didn't have a relationship, but he'd come through for her when she needed something. Something big, like tuition. Or a place to build a mental health clinic.

"When I went to college…" She started the question, but couldn't finish.

Leanne sighed. "I went to him and told him that I needed him to pay your tuition and to help you out while you were in school."

Erin looked away, toward the window, but she wasn't seeing the landscape below. "Did you threaten him?"

"No. Not really. But I knew he had the means to help you get an education. He owed you that," she said.

"Maybe he just felt guilty, for not being a good father."

"Jerry Grady doesn't feel guilt. He can justify his worst behavior. I knew that if he thought I'd expose him for what he really was, that he would support you. Finally."

"So I already owe him." Erin said softly.

"No, you don't." Leanne's words were firm, her eyes focused on Erin's.

"Did he pay for my tuition with money he got, like, from bribes?"

Leanne hesitated, then nodded. "I think so."

Few in Lost Coast Harbor who believed Peter Hastings was guilty thought that the criminal activity ended with him. It was too vast a scheme. Maddie and Gabe suspected the same, and Erin had to admit that her father, Hastings' childhood friend and the top cop in town, was the most likely person to have been paid off. Those were rumors, though. It wasn't proof that Jerry was involved.

"Did he take money from Peter Hastings?"

Leanne shrugged. "They've been friends since they were kids. They bought some properties together early on, flipping houses and stuff. I don't know, but I would guess that if Peter were in trouble, Jerry would try to help him."

The vent above her head kicked on, blowing cold air down Erin's neck, making her shiver. "Would he take money from Hastings to make the trouble go away?"

That was what Butler had accused her of, using her connection to her father for protection. "And why now? Why is he giving me this property?"

"I don't know, sweetie," Leanne said, pulling Erin into a tight embrace again. "I just don't want you to be dragged into his world. I don't think it's pretty there."

The door opened and the scent of posole from the Mexican restaurant across the street wafted in with Alan's arrival. Erin pulled away and tried to act normal, like she hadn't just uncovered her family's darkest secrets. Alan was someone she could go to when she needed advice. His moral compass was true, and he was the person she'd normally turn to when confronted with this news. But he had so much on his plate already, she didn't want to add more.

Erin took a bowl of the steamy and fragrant soup, though her stomach roiled at the thought of food. She pushed thoughts of Jerry and his possible corruption to the back of her mind. She'd have a long drive home later tonight during which she could rehash the conversation with her mother. As if she could stop from doing that.

Erin hugged her mother goodbye soon after they'd eaten. It hadn't been a long visit, but it had worn on Leanne. Her eyes were closing for long moments, and she rested her head on the back of the couch while Erin and Alan caught up. She had smiled and kissed Erin goodbye, and didn't bring up Jerry or the gift to the clinic.

Alan walked Erin to her Jeep with one arm around her shoulders. "It did your mom good to see you."

"I hope I didn't upset her," Erin said.

"Why would you have upset her?"

She studied Alan's concerned expression in the waning evening light. It was an expression she knew well—he could always tell when something bothering her.

"Jerry offered to donate a piece of property for the clinic," she said. Her stepfather's face registered surprise, then concern. "Mom doesn't want me to take it. She says Jerry's crooked and can't be trusted."

Alan squeezed her shoulders. "What do you think?"

"I don't know. I don't like that he gets to be some sort of local hero by giving me a piece of land he's never bothered to develop in all the years he's owned it. But I could really use it. If Jerry was involved with Hastings, I can't take that. I've already been burnt once on a pledge from a criminal."

Alan ran a hand over his hair. "I love your mother, and I generally trust her instincts about people. But you have to keep in mind that right now, she's not well," he said. "I don't know what she said about Jerry, but just a few days ago, she was convinced that dark angels were following our car on the way here."

Erin hugged him and felt the sting of tears in her eyes. Sometimes she wondered what her life would have been like, had Leanne not met and married Alan. He'd been a rock in their lives. But she didn't share Alan's doubts about Leanne's state of mind. She'd looked in her mother's eyes and had seen a woman as lucid as she was on her best day.

"Thanks," she whispered over the lump in her throat. "Are you coming home soon?"

"I think so. Maybe a couple of days," he said, then kissed the top of her head. "I love you, kid. You have a safe drive back home. Stop if you get tired, okay?"

She promised to be careful and climbed into the Jeep quickly, trying to keep the tears at bay until she was alone in her car.

Erin wanted to trust Leanne. Her mother wasn't losing her mind—at least not about Jerry. She couldn't be.

But her trained mind led her back to what she knew about her mother's condition. The individual was still there, her mind was good, but in Leanne's case, there was also more input than usual—voices, hallucinations. That didn't mean she was wrong about Jerry, but still, doubt crept in.

The word of a protective, bipolar mother wasn't evidence of corruption, though. And she needed to know.

There was someone in Lost Coast Harbor who would know, or could help her find out. But if she went to Will, he'd be obligated to follow up on it. He was good at his job, and he had rooted out corruption in other police departments. Opening up this part of her life, her family secrets, would be like drawing a big fat target on her own father.

Chapter Sixteen

"What do you mean you can't find him?" Will kept his voice low, so the question sounded like a snarl. "Lost Coast Harbor is a very small town and Rob Katri is a drug addict. He can't have gone far."

Valerie Childs stood facing him in the supply closet at the district attorney's office, inches from his face. Her hands fisted on her hips.

"If you haven't noticed, we're in a very remote area, with lots of places to hide," Valerie said. "Plus this is not my case. And frankly, it's probably better for Katri to disappear than to let Butler find him."

Will ran a hand through his hair. He had found Valerie waiting for him on his return, demanding to talk to him about Butler. But he couldn't very well have an open discussion about his clandestine investigation into police corruption in front of the rest of the rest of the district attorney's staff. They managed to find a private place to talk—among shelves of paper, crates of file folders, and extra ink for the temperamental photocopier. If anyone saw them slip into the room by themselves, they'd probably assume they were having an affair.

Which would suck if that rumor made it back to Erin's ears, but he'd just have to take that chance.

"Why are you worried about Katri?" he asked.

"Because he's accused of breaking into the chief's daughter's house."

"You think Butler is going to rough him up?" Erin's warning about Butler echoed in his head. Butler was a bully. Will knew the type.

Valerie shook her head. "I know he'll rough him up. But I'm more worried about Erin."

Just hearing her name made his stomach flip. "Why?"

Valerie bit her lip. "Butler has a theory. He thinks that Rob Katri broke into Erin's house because he thought he could get drugs there. He's an addict. He'd just been turned down at the hospital when he'd tried to score there."

"But nothing was taken."

"Nothing was reported stolen."

Will's jaw tensed and his eyes narrowed at Valerie's careful distinction. "You think Erin's a drug dealer?"

Valerie shook her head, her eyes widening. "No, not me. I don't think that. But Butler does. And if he gets to Katri before someone else does, before he lawyers up? He'll pressure him to talk. To blame Erin. To say things to implicate her."

An icy chill flowed through him at that thought. Butler would have no problem manipulating an addict to point the finger at someone else, especially if Katri was detoxing, hurting for another pill or hit.

"Why would he do that?"

"Butler? I don't know. But he's working that angle hard," she said. "Rumor is that he's going to take Stan Hutchins' place as deputy chief, which sets him up to be chief when Grady retires in a year or so."

Footsteps sounded outside the door and then passed as he and Valerie held their breath.

"You've got to get to him first," Will said.

Valerie's chin jutted out. "How am I supposed to do that? If I go out there and start beating the bushes for Katri, that's going to get back to Butler."

Will ground his teeth. He closed his eyes for a moment and tried to focus on the best way to keep Erin safe. "Would the chief protect her?"

Valerie's dark eyes widened. "I don't know about that. From everything I've heard, they're estranged. I've been in LCH for two years and I've never even heard him mention her name."

"She's his daughter. If one of his detectives is framing her, he wouldn't let that happen."

Valerie shrugged. "I'm not sure of that."

"I could talk to him." Even as he said it, he knew he couldn't go to the target of his investigation for assistance. But Grady wouldn't be setting up his own daughter to get arrested on false charges. Right? Surely, he'd rein Butler in and end any speculation about her role in the break-in, or in a drug investigation.

"You're not exactly impartial yourself," Valerie said.

"Have you seen any evidence that Erin is stealing drugs and selling them to addicts on the street?"

Valerie shook her head. "Of course not."

"We need to cut off this line of questioning now. If word of Butler's investigation gets out, Erin's reputation will be shot."

He reached into his pocket and pulled out his cell phone. It was early evening and he wasn't sure where the hell Erin was, but she hadn't returned his message from the morning yet.

"Who's Erin's friend? The woman with the blonde hair? Drives a beat-up old pickup truck." He'd only seen her briefly, when she'd arrived to spend the night with Erin after the break-in, but she'd had a distinct look about her.

"That's Bree Rogers."

"Where does she live?"

Valerie shook her head. "I don't know."

"You can find out."

She sighed. "Yes."

"Text me the address." Will grabbed the doorknob, then paused. "Not a lot of cops would be willing to help me out with this."

She gave him a half-smile. "Yeah, I know. But nobody hates a bad cop more than a good cop. And Butler is a bad cop. A dirty one. He has to be stopped."

"Can you do one more thing for me?"

"What?"

"Find out who ran my name through CLETS."

She exhaled a long breath. They both knew what it meant—someone was willing to, at best, lose their job by tapping into the California Law Enforcement Telecommunication System, the state and federal database, to run an unauthorized background check. At worst, they were risking criminal prosecution. It happened far too often—a cop used the database to run a check on an ex-spouse's new lover, or a neighbor who was giving them grief. It usually backfired, with the cops in far more trouble than their targets.

"I'll see what I can find."

Will poked his head out and saw the hallway was empty, so he ushered Valerie out of the closet and they walked off in separate directions—Valerie to the parking lot and Will to his office. He tried Erin again, but his call went straight to voicemail and he hung up without leaving a message.

In the empty, quiet office, Will tried to focus on the stack of folders left on his desk by his two colleagues. He reviewed the files for the next day's court appearances, made some notes about following up with the officers, and left instructions for his secretary for the next day. It had been a quiet day in the office while he was gone, and it wasn't long before he was finished.

That meant he had no excuses left. It was time to tell Erin what was going on. He couldn't keep hiding it from her. But first, he was going to have to find her.

His phone buzzed with a text and he saw that it was Valerie sending him an address. He was disappointed it wasn't Erin returning his text, but Bree Rogers' address would be good enough. He studied the address, then pulled up a map on his computer to try and find it. He printed out the map, locked the office, and started toward the only person who might be able to help him find Erin before Butler did.

Bree Rogers lived a twenty-minute drive outside of Lost Coast Harbor, in a cabin in the woods that didn't have an address so much as a vague set of directions. Finding it in the dark, especially for someone not familiar with the area, would be challenging. A thick layer of fog obscuring the road in front of him didn't help, either. He nearly missed the turn off a two-lane road and onto a narrow, barely paved drive. The one-lane road twisted between tall trees until Will was certain he'd made a wrong turn. Maybe he'd turned too early and was on an old logging road cut into the forest. Christ, he'd probably end up spending the night out here until he could find his way back.

The road took a hard left and ended abruptly in a clearing. Will stared at the cabin lit by his headlights. It was small, with a cozy porch. Warm yellow light spilled out of the windows. A beat-up truck was parked at an angle in front. As he turned off the engine, the door opened and a woman's silhouette appeared against the brightly lit interior.

"Bree Rogers?" he called out, stepping out of the vehicle and onto the soft dirt.

"Maybe," the woman in the doorway replied. An outdoor lamp snapped on and he stepped into the pool of light so she could see him.

"Will Patton. I need to talk to you about Erin Grady."

He could see her now, leaning against the door frame. Her blonde hair was tied up in a messy knot, and she wore a black T-shirt and faded jeans that hugged her body.

"You're a long way from home, Will Patton," Bree said.

"Yeah, no shit." His foot slipped on wet leaves as he walked toward the porch. "Can I come in?"

Bree looked him up and down, but held open the door.

"What brings you out to the woods?"

"I need to find Erin."

He stepped inside the cabin. Will expected a dark, cozy interior. Instead, he found a cheerful living room decorated with bright wall art and colorful furniture, and a dining room that looked like mission control.

"Did I interrupt your hack-a-thon?" Will asked, nodding toward the three computer monitors perched on a fire-engine-red dining table.

Bree gave him a wide smile. "It can wait. The Pentagon's not going anywhere." She motioned at her large teal sofa and he took a seat. She sat in a chair between him and the dining area. "What can I do for the district attorney's office?"

"I need to find Erin."

"Why? To arrest her?"

Her frank question surprised him. "No. Why would you say that?"

Bree appraised him with a cool look, studying him as if he were a specimen under glass. Or code scrolling by a computer screen, if her dining room was any indication of her interests.

"That detective seems hell bent on blaming Erin's break-in on her."

Will's blood went cold. "What detective?"

"Tall, buzz-cut guy. Butler, I think?"

"Yeah," Will said. "What did he say and when did you see him?"

"Yesterday, early afternoon. Erin and I were downtown and he stopped us to tell Erin that they think Rob Katri broke into her house. And then he hinted that Erin was Rob's supplier."

"Where is Erin now?"

Bree paused before answering, like she wasn't sure he deserved to know. "Probably on her way back from Santa Rosa. She went to visit her mom today. I doubt she'll be home until late."

His shoulders and neck tensed at the thought of her on the road, alone, unprotected.

"Why are you looking for her?" She continued to watch him, her gaze unwavering.

"I'm not helping Butler, if that's what you're thinking."

"So you just want to get…better acquainted?"

He could understand her desire to protect Erin, but Bree's sights were on the wrong target.

"I promise my intentions toward Erin are honorable," he said, flashing her a smile that had won over many jurors.

Bree tilted her head. "Not buying it."

He leaned forward, resting his forearms on his knees and met Bree's direct gaze.

"I like Erin. A lot. I am not trying to throw her in jail. If you don't help me, Detective Butler is going to build a case against her for selling drugs to Rob Katri."

Bree's expression was nearly unreadable, but after a moment she gave him a short nod. "Okay, I like you better than Butler, though that's not saying much. What can I do?"

"What do you know about Rob Katri?"

Bree shrugged. "He and Erin were in the same class in school. I was a couple of years behind them. Rob and I weren't friends, but we knew each other, you know? It's a small town."

"Got an address? A phone number?"

Bree shook her head, but then stood and walked to her

computer. "Give me a minute."

She typed a few commands, and then jotted some notes on the back of an envelope.

"What are you doing here?" Will asked, hoping it wasn't illegal. But he wasn't going to swear out a warrant for her if she was.

She gave him a sweet smile. "Nothing."

"Uh huh."

He took the paper from her and folded it in half, sliding it into his pocket. "What else can you do here?"

Bree sat back in the chair and raised an eyebrow. "Lots. What do you have in mind?"

His eyes scanned the three screens, took in the various drives and other peripheral devices that sat among the tangle of cords. He was fairly computer-savvy and knew enough to know he was well out of his depth with Bree's set-up.

"If I wanted to see something inside the police department, can you access that?"

Bree laughed. "Why, that would be illegal, Mr. Patton."

"Yes."

Her laughter faded and she met his gaze. "Is it important?"

"Yes."

She reached for the keyboard. "Why don't you make yourself useful and make some tea?" she said with a nod toward the kitchen.

The small kitchen was cluttered, with a few days of unwashed dishes in the sink. Will found the kettle and filled it, setting it on the gas range. He located the tea while listening to the occasional tapping at the keyboard coming from the dining room. When the tapping continued, he rolled up his sleeves and washed Bree's dishes, rather than going into the dining room to stand over her shoulder. He didn't want to know what she was doing. And he really didn't want to know how insecure the police department computer system was.

"What is it you need in here?" Bree called to him.

"You're in?"

It had taken her less than five minutes, he estimated.

"I'm good."

"I need to know who ran my name through the criminal database. It's called—"

"CLETS. I know. And it's a more secure system," she interrupted. "Give me a little more time."

He poured the boiling water over the tea bags in two mugs, let them steep, and tried not to think about what he'd just asked Bree to do. If they were caught, he'd be fired—and hopefully, that would be the end of it. But hacking cases were sexy—in legal parlance—and prosecutors tended to go after the perpetrators with blazing guns to make an example of them.

"I can't get to CLETS, at least not quickly, but I can see the logs of who used it here last," Bree said, as Will set a cup of tea next to her.

"That's all I need."

"Here are all of today's requests."

"I need the last few days," he said, putting his tea down to get a better look at the entries on the screen. Out of the lines of text, he could discern the relevant information—dates, Social Security numbers, case numbers. And then as Bree scrolled up to the earlier entries, his own information came into view.

"Stop, right there," he said, putting his finger on the screen.

"The authorization code is here," Bree said, showing him another string of numbers. "This is the name."

"Oh, fuck." The word burst from his chest in a burst of exhaled air.

"What is it?"

Will couldn't answer her. His eyes were focused on the entry and his mind tried to piece the name into what he knew. His heart thumped in his chest and he struggled to focus through the red haze clouding his vision.

V. Childs.

He'd trusted the wrong person.

CHAPTER SEVENTEEN

It was nearing eleven o'clock when Erin turned north onto the coast road that would take her back to Lost Coast Harbor. She'd become accustomed to the overnight shift, so she didn't mind the late hour. Though she was disappointed that it was probably too late to call Will. She could use a physical distraction from the emotional turmoil.

At least with Will, there were no emotions involved, which was perfect because there was far too much emotion going on in the rest of her life. That was what she was telling herself, at least. The fact that the thought of seeing him again gave her butterflies meant nothing. They were just highly sexually compatible. Two healthy and attractive people, finding someone to pass the time with. No need to read too much into this.

Yeah, right.

A beep from her phone indicated that she'd finally driven into the range of a cellular tower after the long quiet drive through the remote hills east of the coast, where all communication devices went dead. She glanced at the screen and saw that Will had called several times, leaving at least one message, and Bree had sent a text.

Glancing back up at the winding road in front of her, she set the phone back down. Whatever Bree needed to talk about could wait. She was more of a night owl than Erin was and would be awake when Erin finally made it home in another twenty minutes.

Then the phone rang and she gave up the fight against the distraction.

"Bree?" she asked, pinning the phone between her shoulder and ear.

The static indicated she was still on the edge of that no-service zone, but there was enough connection to hear her friend's voice.

"Hey, you'll never guess who came over tonight—"

Bree's words were broken up and Erin looked for a place to pull over so she could focus on the call, but the stretch she was driving was a sheer cliff down to the ocean on one side, and a wall of rock on the other.

"Bree, I can't hear you. I'll call you later."

"Wait!"

Erin rounded the last curve before the road widened and headed away from the coast's edge. From here she could see the shimmer of lights along the cliffs in the distance, where the houses on the south end of LCH stood defiant against the offshore winds and driving rain that came in from the Pacific Ocean. Beyond that, a glow from the harbor lights reflected off the low clouds.

She pulled onto a patch of gravel and yanked the emergency brake up.

"Bree? Are you there?"

"I told him to just let himself—"

The call disconnected completely and Bree was gone. With a roll of her eyes, Erin tossed the phone onto the passenger seat. Cell service along this stretch of the coast was spotty at best. Erin pulled back onto the empty road and turned up the music. Bree and her latest boyfriend problems were going to have to wait until both of them were back in civilization.

Minutes later, she passed the faded wooden sign welcoming her to Lost Coast Harbor. And then immediately saw headlights coming up fast in her rear-view mirror, followed by red flashing lights.

"Ah, fuck it." With a groan, she glanced at her speedometer and saw that yes, she was going about ten miles over the speed limit.

Great.

She signaled and pulled over to a wide shoulder where she could get well off the road, then dug in her glove box for her registration and insurance papers. She rolled down the window as the officer approached.

"I know. I was speeding." She held up her paperwork and driver's license and started to hand it through the open window.

"Erin Grady?"

She looked up and nodded, an uneasy feeling sinking into her stomach.

"I'm going to need you to come with me."

Erin studied the electronic display in the front of the cop car. It wasn't one of the usual black-and-white cruisers that patrolled Lost Coast Harbor. This was a black sedan without markings, but with all the bells and whistles on the inside. The officer driving it wasn't in uniform.

"Where are you taking me?" Erin asked, proud that her voice didn't betray her growing panic.

"You can't go home right now," the young woman said. Other than her brief introduction as Erin got into the police car, Detective Valerie Childs was a woman of few words. Erin had seen her at the hospital a time or two, but didn't know her other than those few encounters.

"So…where am I going?"

Valerie kept her eyes on the road. "Some place where you'll be safe."

The car cruised through Lost Coast Harbor on dark and mostly empty streets. The radio squawked and Valerie reached over and turned the sound off. The road to the police station came into view, and slipped past as Valerie continued through the downtown area and into the neighborhood not far from Erin's house.

"That was the turn for the police department," Erin said, watching it slip away into darkness.

"That isn't a safe place for you right now," Valerie said.

Erin gripped her purse close to her body and kept her right hand loose at her side. If an opportunity came, she could open the door and jump out. At least she wasn't in the backseat.

Valerie turned onto the road that led to the city park and slowed, then made two more turns and rolled to a stop at the curb. Erin started to reach for the door handle, but Valerie reached out and put a hand on her arm.

"Don't get out," she said.

Erin leaned back, but every muscle in her body was tensed and poised to leap to freedom at the first opportunity. The detective watched her with no expression, and then raised a cell phone to her ear.

"I have Erin."

"What the fuck! Where are you? What are you doing?" Will's deep and angry voice exploded out of the cell phone in Valerie's hand and the sound made Erin weak with relief. And confused about what was going on.

"I'm not taking her home. It's not safe for her," Valerie said. "I'm taking her to your house. Is it clear outside?"

"What?"

Valerie Childs let out an exasperated sigh and gave Erin a pitying look. "I said, I can't take Erin to her house. Butler says he's got a warrant for her arrest."

Erin felt the breath leave her body. "What?"

A warrant meant, what? That she was going to be charged with a crime? Erin's thoughts went immediately to her family—how they'd react to that news. Her mother, her sister and brother. Her throat threatened to close up as she tried to voice her concerns.

The phone in Valerie's hand went silent. And when Will replied, it was in a normal voice and not a shout, so Erin couldn't hear his answer.

"Yeah, so let us in your house."

Erin studied the detective's impassive expression as she listened intently to the cell phone, trying to discern any clue as to what Will was saying. But all she could hear was her heart beating rapidly and the blood rushing through her veins. This spike in blood pressure would be dangerous over a sustained period, her rational nurses' training whispered in her ear. Based on her symptoms, she'd guess she was at 160/90.

"We'll wait for you. I'm parked on a street about a block west of your place. Make sure you aren't followed."

Valerie disconnected the call and looked over at Erin, who was still trying to breathe normally.

"What did you mean, there's a warrant for me? What does that mean? Are you arresting me?"

Valerie frowned. "I haven't seen the warrant. Butler says he has a warrant for your arrest, trafficking in prescription meds. It's bogus. It won't stand up. But in the meantime, it's going to cause a lot of trouble for you."

Erin felt her eyes sting with frustrated tears. Why was this happening? Why now?

"Butler notified the hospital of the warrant and I think you're going to be put on an administrative leave," Valerie said.

Erin gasped. "Oh my God."

"Do you have a lawyer?"

"A lawyer? No! I mean, I know a lawyer, but he does contracts and sets up businesses and writes wills."

"You'll need someone else. Probably want to call in someone with plenty of experience. Maybe look out of the county. I can give you some names if you want."

Erin's breath was coming too fast. The adrenaline had fully kicked in and she was having a hard time processing anything but her basest instincts, which screamed at her to get away. But her car was on the edge of town, far from where she was sitting.

She was supposed to meet with Mr. Minton on Monday

to finalize the paperwork on the property and establish a timeline for their next steps to get the clinic moving forward. Now she was going to be—what, meeting with a criminal defense attorney? Sitting in jail?

She drew in a ragged gasp and Valerie reached over and put a hand on her arm.

"Hey, it's going to be okay. You didn't do anything illegal."

This was little comfort. "Then why is there a warrant for my arrest? And people go to prison for things they didn't do. It happens. I know."

She thought of Maddie's Gabe, locked in a cage for six years for a crime he didn't commit, and her stomach churned violently.

Valerie nodded, her brow furrowed. "I know. But it won't happen to you."

"Why aren't you arresting me?"

The detective looked away. "Because I wasn't here. I never saw you tonight. And you never saw me."

A familiar dark SUV sped by on the street and after a moment, Valerie pulled the car forward on the empty street, still without lights on. A block later, she turned toward Will's house, where his SUV was in the drive, waiting for the garage door to open. Valerie drove past the house, made a U-turn, and then parked in front of the house and turned off the car.

She watched the street with a steady gaze until Will was inside the garage and the door was closing. A moment later the porch light snapped on.

"Let's go," Valerie said, and Erin climbed out of the car and followed her up to the front door.

Will held the door open for them. Erin passed him, inhaling his scent. He was wearing a dark green Henley and well-worn jeans, and she wanted nothing more than to throw herself at him. But his expression held her back. His eyes were hooded, his lips tight and his movements were stiff, as if his entire body was coiled and ready to spring.

She followed Valerie into the foyer and heard the door slam behind them, and then Will stepped in front of her, partially blocking her view of the detective.

"What the fuck are you doing, Valerie? I trusted you. God, I can't believe this."

He raked a hand through his hair and his jaw tensed. In the low light, Erin could see the tight cords in his neck, the stiffness of his shoulders. He moved, placing himself between her and the detective. Erin tried to see around him, but he kept one arm outstretched, as if to block her access.

"I couldn't take her in. You know that," Valerie said, she tilted her head and gave him a puzzled look. "We talked about this."

"You ran my name through CLETS."

Erin tried to step forward, still unsure what the cop and Will were arguing over, but Will held her back, keeping her next to him, slightly behind his body. Like a shield protecting her from the petite detective facing him. Erin's gaze fell to Valerie's waist and the holstered weapon there and she tensed, but the detective made no move toward her gun.

"No. I didn't do it." She held her hands up, her eyes wide.

"Your log-in credentials were used yesterday to run my name. I've seen the log."

"I was in court all day. That preliminary hearing for the McIntosh case. You can ask your coworker. I wasn't near a computer terminal."

Will's body relaxed slightly, but only enough to risk a brief look away from Valerie to Erin. His gaze swept over her, as if looking for injuries.

This was a different Will from the one she'd seen so far—a very angry, very protective Will. He pulled her into his arms roughly, kissing the top of her head. She closed her eyes and let herself feel safe, let the tension roll away. She sank into the warmth and protection he offered, struggling to keep herself from sobbing with the release and the relief.

"Can we sit down and talk?" Valerie asked. This time, Erin heard the nerves in the detective's voice, as if Valerie had only just realized the danger she'd just been in.

Will nodded toward the living room, then flipped on the light switch, illuminating the cold living room. He kept Erin's hand tight in his and she followed him as he stepped into the hall to adjust the thermostat.

"Have a seat, Valerie," he said. He pulled Erin into the hall and then toward his bedroom. He shut the door behind them and stepped forward, putting his hands on either side of her face, studying her.

At the first touch, the ground shifted and she knew. Something had changed.

Everything had changed.

"Are you all right?" His voice was hoarse and his face was harsh, intense, in the low light coming from the small bedside lamp.

Erin could still only nod, not trusting her voice. If she said anything, she'd just start screaming or crying or otherwise embarrass herself.

His face relaxed by a small measure and he leaned down, pressing his lips to her forehead. She swallowed hard and felt the tears gather in her eyes at the tender gesture.

"What's going on?" She was unable to keep the tremor from her voice this time.

"I don't know. But I won't let you get hurt."

He locked his arms around her, enveloping her against his chest in a protective cocoon. She closed her eyes and listened to the steady thump of his heart.

Too soon, he pulled away and stared at her, his jaw tense with worry. "I have to talk with Valerie."

Erin straightened her clothes and smoothed her hair and hoped she didn't look too obviously distraught when they returned to the living room. Valerie was seated on the couch, the only piece of furniture in Will's living room.

"How did he get a warrant? What's the charge?" Will took a seat on the arm of the couch, pulling Erin down next to him and keeping a hand on her shoulder.

"He used a C.I.," Valerie said, then glanced at Erin. "A confidential informant. Someone he doesn't have to name in the warrant, who swears that you sold Oxycontin to him."

A cold shiver ran through her. "That's not true."

Valerie nodded. "I know. There's no informant."

"Who signed off on it?" Will asked.

"Someone in the main office," Valerie said. "Butler could go around you and your office because of your relationship with Erin."

Erin glanced up at Will's face and studied his profile, the faint growth of beard on his jaw, still tense, and his soft, almost lush lips. Probably once you'd spent time with someone naked, you might call that a relationship. He couldn't claim to be unbiased, at least.

"Who has your CLETS log-in?"

Valerie shook her head. "Nobody does. Maybe the chief could get access to the master list of passwords."

"What's CLETS?" Erin asked.

"A highly restricted database of criminal records," Will said. "Someone ran my name through it, to check me out. Whoever it was also ran my credit."

"Do you think your father would do that because, well, you know…" Valerie's cheeks turned a pale pink as her question trailed off. "I mean, that's something I could see my dad doing, if he had access to that information."

Erin shook her head. "No, not a chance. I don't think he cares that much. What happens if you look up stuff you're not supposed to?"

"It's probably like accessing patient records without a medical reason, like when celebrities check into hospitals and the medical staff in other departments look up their records just out of curiosity," Valerie said.

"You can get fired for that," Erin said. Every hospital employee knew that health records were confidential, even without those boring annual training sessions.

"Yeah, same with this database. And it's a crime," Will said. "Cops have been criminally prosecuted for accessing the database and passing it on to third parties."

"If it were my father who did it, which I doubt, wouldn't he just use his own log-in?"

She saw Valerie shift on the sofa and sit a little straighter. The detective and Will exchanged a glance.

"She's right," Will said. "Maybe the point wasn't to check me out. Maybe it was to set you up. I've undergone a background check and a credit check to get hired by the district attorney's office. There are not going to be any skeletons in my closet on this report."

Valerie frowned, then nodded. "He must know that I've been helping you."

Erin looked between them. "Who knows? And helping you do what?"

Will met her gaze, then looked away, and she saw something new in his hazel eyes.

In a blink, it was gone, replaced by a steely resolve.

"She's been helping me investigate your father."

CHAPTER EIGHTEEN

"How long have you been investigating my father?"

Erin's voice trembled with anger, but beneath that, Will could hear the betrayal. Erin's shoulders were stiff, her jaw clenched. They were alone, just her and Will facing each other after Valerie made a hasty retreat rather than face Erin's wrath. His confession that he'd been investigating her father since they'd met had prompted a flood of profanity from Erin. It was as if her considerable stockpile of curses had been waiting years for an opportunity to drop its payload.

And Will was the target. Deservedly.

"I was transferred here because I found corruption in another small town's police force. No one wanted to see it, so to get me out of the picture, they moved me here. Gave me a raise, a promotion, and a transfer," he said. "But after Hastings was arrested, the FBI asked me about the Lost Coast Harbor police. I've been looking into some irregularities. But it had to be done quietly. I couldn't tell anyone."

Another torrent of curses greeted this news. She ran a hand through her hair as she paced the empty dining area.

"Are you done?" he asked. If he could get a word in, maybe he could defend himself. Maybe.

She shook her head slowly. "Not even close."

He reached out to take her hand and she jerked backward, taking a step that left her against the wall.

"You don't get to do that. You lied to me."

Will shook his head. "I did not lie to you."

"You withheld important information. Like how you were using me to get to my father."

"That's not what happened."

"Tell me again how it was just a coincidence that you met me, that you *slept* with me, while you were trying to throw my father in prison."

He took a step closer, and there was no place left for her to go. She raised her face to look at him. Her cheeks were a delicate shade of pink and her eyes flashed fire at him.

"Erin, I would have wanted you no matter what," he said, reaching up and caressing her cheek, running his finger along her jaw, then down, cupping the back of her neck. "Does this feel wrong? Does this feel like I'm lying to you?"

She wrenched away from him. "Yes, damn it. You can't do that. You can't just touch me and make me forget."

"What do you want me to do, Erin?" he asked, letting her walk away a few feet. "I wanted to tell you about the investigation. I couldn't. It has nothing to do with you."

She threw her hands up in an exasperated gesture. "It's my father we're talking about."

"You don't even like him!"

"You used me to get information about him anyway," she yelled.

"No."

His quiet response seemed to throw her off balance and she stopped pacing and stilled. Her mouth opened, and her eyes still raged, but she didn't respond.

"He probably took money from Peter Hastings. Probably did for years. I can't prove it. Not yet. And I have bigger problems than one corrupt cop. Now, they're your problems, too."

She shook her head, but then stilled. Her anger faltered and the doubt crept into her eyes. She blinked and the rage was gone, replaced with confusion and sadness. His heart constricted. Not that, never that. He'd rather have her be angry with him than be defeated.

He put both hands on her shoulder and leaned in, resting his forehead against hers.

"I am sorry. I truly am," he whispered. "What can I do?"

She shook her head, keeping her gaze down.

"I think I should go."

Instinctively, his arms tightened around her. If she left, Butler could get to her.

If she left, she might not come back.

"Don't go, Erin," he whispered. He buried his face in her sweet, soft hair and felt an unfamiliar emotion—regret. He should have been upfront with her, let her know what he was doing at work. But she might have chosen not to be with him.

There was regret. But more than that was fear. It gnawed at his guts, made him break out in a cold sweat. And he wasn't sure what he was more afraid of—the thought of her being railroaded by Butler, or walking out of his life forever.

Damn it. He had well and truly fucked this up.

"I can't stay here," she said, her voice a soft whisper. She kept her arms at her side. It was the calmness that scared him. She had a quick temper, but it was also quick to fade— and this quiet tension unnerved him.

"You can't leave," he said.

He kept his hands at her shoulder and neck, afraid that if he stopped touching her, she'd walk out of the house.

She squeezed her eyes shut for a long moment. When she opened her eyes, his heart ached at the sight. She was still angry, but there was something else there, too. Hurt.

He'd done that to her.

"Look, I understand how you feel," Will said, but then caught the flash of anger in her eyes. "Okay, maybe not. But it's not safe for you to go home. Valerie is right. Butler's going to be looking for you. He's going to be parked out in front of your house."

She crossed her arms and looked lost. The guilt was killing him.

"Just stay the night. I'll take the couch." Erin's uncertain expression spurred him on. "Please."

Her eyes met his and after a long moment, she nodded. The relief was overwhelming. He'd keep her safe, at least for another night.

"Come on," he said, leading her to the master bedroom. He pulled towels from the linen closet, while she set her large leather purse on the bed and then stood in the middle of the room, her arms crossed tightly across her body. "Can I get anything else for you?"

She shook her head, her hair falling in her face. He could reach up and brush it away. Feel the silky strands and her soft skin. But he didn't.

"Good night."

He shut the door behind him. If it killed him, he was going to give her the space she needed. And it might just kill him. He wanted nothing more than to kiss her, touch her, tell her that how he felt was not in any way connected to his job and what he was doing in Lost Coast Harbor.

He started a small fire and settled in on the couch with his laptop to review the documents that Glover had emailed him a few hours ago. When he heard the water turn on in the shower, he decided to print the documents to cover the sound. Maybe it would keep him from picturing Erin in the shower, steamy and slick, the hot water streaming over her smooth skin, her lean legs, her sweet curves.

Nope. Not working. It took everything he had not to strip down and join her in the shower, damn his good intentions. He could convince her that he hadn't been using her—by, what? By pushing her up against the cool tile wall and taking her until they both couldn't walk? Will closed his eyes and blew out a long breath at the thought of Erin in his shower, or in his bed. He quickly pushed those images away. Not tonight. Not when he'd just dropped this bomb on her.

He tried to focus on the documents in his hand. It wasn't much, but at least the FBI had been able to track down properties owned by Grady. For good measure, Glover had also looked into the trust that owned the parcel before Grady bought it. He flipped between the two lists—Grady's holdings were his house near the park, the boat that was moored in the harbor, and the property he was donating to the clinic. According to the financial disclosures he was required to file as part of his job, he also owned a vacation rental property in Mexico.

The trust, on the other hand, was an investment vehicle that owned two pieces of undeveloped land in Mendocino County, a house in San Francisco, and a commercial property in Ukiah. If it was an investment vehicle, it had just sold the parcel to Grady at a price that must be far below its value. He looked for any information about the trust itself, but Glover hadn't forwarded anything that identified the trustee or the trust's beneficiary.

There was no information on Solstice, Inc. but given that the man's boat was named *Winter Solstice*, Will figured there was a fair chance that Jerry Grady was connected to that, too. Solstice, Inc., a corporate entity out of Delaware, owned some undeveloped property along the coast, south of Lost Coast Harbor. The transfers were fairly recent, all in the last three years. None of the property purchases linked Solstice to the 1221 Real Estate Trust.

Will set the papers down on the end table and picked up the wine. He rubbed his forehead to ease the headache growing behind his eyes. If he could just figure out whether Erin's father was involved, maybe he could convince her to forgive his deceit. Maybe he could fix his monumental fuck up.

He closed his eyes and let his head fall back against the couch cushion. He had to fix it, because he couldn't bear the thought of leaving things with Erin like this.

THE HOT WATER RAN OUT BEFORE ERIN'S TEARS DID, AND she stepped out of the shower feeling no better. This was why she hated crying. It never helped anything. You just ended up with swollen eyes and blotchy skin and a runny nose. And all those things that made you cry were still out there, waiting for you to put yourself back together and get to work fixing them.

Fuck. There was no part of her life that hadn't fallen to shit in the last week. Her mother was hospitalized, her job was in jeopardy, she was facing criminal charges. And Will, well, that had barely gotten off the ground before crashing and burning.

She'd just have to forget him, put him aside and move on.

Though that was impossible at the moment, since he was in the next room. Also, she smelled like him—his shampoo, his soap. She was even wearing one of his dress shirts that she'd helped herself to from his closet. Borrowing his brush, she combed her hair out and sat on the edge of the bed, still hollow inside.

At least she had Maddie and Bree. Her friends would stand by her when news of her imminent arrest hit the gossip mill. She groaned and dug her phone out of her purse. She had to warn June before she heard it via the grapevine, or worse, before Colin or Hayley heard the gossip. Then she saw it was nearing one o'clock in the morning and set the phone aside. She couldn't wake June with this sort of news. She'd call first thing in the morning.

Erin flopped back on the bed and stared at the ceiling. Her whole life, she'd been able to fix whatever problems were thrown at her and those she loved. Maybe she wasn't able to fix her mother's bipolar disorder, but she could make sure that everything at home was as normal as possible. She didn't know a lot of twelve-year-olds who knew how to negotiate with a utility company to keep the electricity on for a few more days.

She was nothing if not resourceful. So why couldn't she figure a way out of this?

There are some advantages to having a father's who's the police chief.

Jerry's words haunted her now. She could go to him and ask him to take care of this for her, like she did with Colin. She wasn't sure if he would even help her, and damn, she hated to ask for help. From anyone, but God, not Jerry. And if he were corrupt, then she would be, too. She'd be asking him to break the law for her.

She rubbed her temples in a vain attempt to ease the pounding there as she tried to think of other options.

As much as she loved Bree and Maddie, there wasn't anything they could do to help her. That left Will.

She sat up, her legs still hanging over the edge of the bed, and touched her face where he'd stroked her cheek. It hadn't felt like a lie. It had felt natural and right. Which made the thought that he'd pursued her because of her last name that much more painful.

Clearly, her hormones couldn't be trusted, because she wanted nothing more than to go to him. Her body ached for him, and her soul longed for the comfort she'd felt in his arms when he had pulled her into the bedroom earlier and hugged her. She'd felt something then, something in his touch that went beyond the crazy chemistry they'd had.

He'd been afraid. For her.

When he'd thought Valerie had betrayed him, he'd put himself between her and the armed police officer.

No one did that. Not for her. She was capable. Reliable. People trusted that she could take care of herself, because she always had. And she would continue to take care of herself.

But it was nice, that feeling of having someone who wanted to help, wanted to take care of her for a change.

The light under the door had gone out and was reduced to a warm flickering glow from the fireplace. Erin stood, her legs unsteady, and walked to the door. She paused with her hand on the doorknob. Then she drew a shaky breath and stopped.

If she went out there, she'd forgive him. Probably the moment she laid eyes on him. She knew herself well enough to know that her temper was fierce, but short-lived. And once she forgave Will, she'd want him. Hell, even now, she wanted him.

She drew her hand back and wrapped her arms around herself, her stomach hollow and her heart pounding. He'd used her to get information about Jerry. She had to remember that, remember that what he'd said was at odds with what he'd done.

He said he'd want her no matter who her father was and there may be some truth to that. She was cute enough, not unattractive. But the reason he'd pursued her was because she was Jerry's daughter.

She couldn't forget that.

She turned back to the bed and climbed between the sheets, which also reminded her of him. There was nothing she could do now, but move forward and figure out how to deal with it in the morning. Then she'd come up with a way to get out of this mess, and get over the man who had betrayed her.

CHAPTER NINETEEN

She kept her voice low and spoke fast, hoping the hospital operator wouldn't recognize her. Fortunately, the harried switchboard operator put her on hold without asking who was calling and Erin spent the next five minutes listening to instrumental versions of her least favorite songs.

She'd waited until Will left for work before she crawled out of the warm, soft bed, showered and grabbed another of Will's dress shirts so she didn't feel quite so exposed walking around in his empty house. Her first task was to call Aunt June and let her know what was going on, and they agreed that it would be a good day for June to take Hayley and Colin out of town to visit their mom. Now, as she waited on hold, she stuck her clothes in Will's washing machine and turned it on. Other than the new black lace bra and panties that she'd accidentally left in her purse, the jeans and sweater were the only clothes she had. She tore off the tags and slipped the new underwear on while waiting for the call to be picked up.

"Dr. Ashette."

She exhaled. "It's Erin."

They often argued over procedures, and yes, she sometimes called him Dr. Asshat, but Erin had developed a grudging respect for the young physician. She hoped her trust wasn't misplaced in calling him.

"Oh, thank God," he said in a rush. "Are you okay? What's going on?"

"I was hoping you could tell me," Erin said.

The ambient noise on Dr. Ashette's end of the call grew softer and it sounded as if he'd closed a door. She could picture him in the small office off the main nurse's station, where he did his paperwork and sometimes napped when the ER was quiet.

"All I know is the police were here asking about thefts from the pharmacy, and they requested your employment records. The hospital put two and two together and then you were put on administrative leave until this gets cleared up," he said. "There is not a single discrepancy in the pharmacy records, but the hospital is going to start a thorough audit this morning, at the request of the police."

"And if so much as a pill shows up missing, I'm going to be blamed."

"Yeah, you got it." He sighed and she could picture him running his hand over his short blond hair.

"I can't believe this," Erin said, more to herself than to her coworker.

"No one can. I mean it, Erin. We're all standing behind you. Everyone. Even Brenda. This is bullshit."

Erin squeezed her eyes shut to stop the sting of tears. She didn't want him to hear her voice choked. After a moment, she managed to swallow the softball-sized lump in her throat.

"Thank you."

"What are you going to do?"

"I don't know."

It was true, she had no idea what to do next. She needed to find a lawyer—and not Barney Minton, who was a nice guy and had volunteered his time to help her with the clinic paperwork, but he wasn't going to know the first thing about defending her against criminal charges.

"Let me know if there's anything I can do, okay?"

"Sure, thanks, doc."

"How's your mother doing?"

"She's all right. They're taking good care of her. She may be home next week. And thank you for asking."

"Of course. Call me if you need anything, got it?"

"Yeah, I got it. Thanks."

She hung up the phone and looked around Will's sparsely decorated kitchen. He had a coffee pot and some pans in the cupboard. A few cans of soup in the pantry. Most of the drawers were empty except for the silverware and a couple of basic cooking tools. The refrigerator held a six-pack of beer with two bottles missing, orange juice, and a head of lettuce that was well past its prime.

The rest of his home was just as bare and cold. The house had an open floor plan and the kitchen opened into a great room that had a dining area across from the fireplace. But other than the couch facing the fireplace, and a small end table, there wasn't any furniture. There was a kayak on the floor against one wall, and Will's wrecked bike lay next to it. Without area rugs, the room echoed and the hardwood floor chilled her bare feet. A short stack of boxes, still packed, were lined up along the other wall. It sure didn't look like someone who moved in four months ago. Or at least, not someone who planned on staying long.

Of course he'd want to move on. He was here for an assignment and once that was done, he'd be off to the Bay Area, for bigger and better opportunities.

And her life would go back to being like it was before—a little boring, a lot of work. Keeping busy to distract from the fact that there was something missing in her life. Except now with more chaos and uncertainty. If she could convince the police that she wasn't selling drugs, and then also persuade the hospital not to fire her, then maybe life would go back to normal.

But there was no way she'd get the property that Jerry offered—not if he really was corrupt. And even a rumor of her involvement with a criminal charge would damage all the goodwill she'd built up in the community, so the donations and pledges for the clinic would dry up, too.

The chill from the empty house penetrated the thin shirt and Erin hugged her arms around her. The walls were closing in around her, but there was nothing she could do about that. Normally, she'd go for a run along the park trail. That's what she did when her mother's illness raised its ugly head and she had to pitch in with Colin and Hayley, when work had her grinding her teeth, or when she was on the verge of giving up the clinic because she was still too short of funds to move forward.

But Will had woken her this morning and made her promise not to walk outside, fearing that Butler was lying in wait out there with a warrant for her. This was foreign to her. She was used to doing things—not waiting for things to happen. She paced the length of the living room in her bare feet to burn off the anxious energy.

As she passed the couch, she saw the paperwork stacked on the cushion and stopped. She paused only briefly before picking up the paperwork and scanning it. If it were confidential, she reasoned, Will wouldn't leave it sitting out.

The washing machine squawked and she carried the papers with her into the laundry room so she could put her clothes in the dryer.

And that's where Will found her a half-hour later—sitting on the laundry room counter, wearing his shirt, reading the documents the FBI had tracked down on her father.

"I brought breakfast," he said. He held up the box from The Sweet Spot. "Is everything okay? No one came looking for you, right?"

She shook her head. "No, I kept the curtains closed and haven't heard anyone outside."

He looked good enough to eat in a dark suit and light blue shirt. Before, she had liked seeing him dressed for court, looking powerful and professional. Today, it reminded her of what he did for a living, and how he did it.

On closer inspection, Will's face was drawn, as if he hadn't slept well—which gave her a small sense of satisfaction. And his expression was contrite, cautious as he set the bakery box on the counter next to her.

"No calls?"

"No. But I called the hospital and spoke with Dr. Ashette. They're doing an audit of the pharmacy."

The sweet cinnamon scent of Annabel's morning buns

drifted up from the box. It was a scent that never failed to make her stomach growl, but not today when her stomach couldn't be trusted to keep anything down.

"The warrant is sealed, so it's not public knowledge. If you were to get pulled over, it's possible that you'd get arrested. When Butler gets the warrant unsealed, it will be made public and you could be arrested if a police officer recognized you."

Erin's stomach jumped at the thought of being arrested. She'd done her best to avoid the police, for many reasons, growing up. She couldn't afford to screw up—too much was riding on her future. Her mother's care, her siblings' futures. And then her job, and her own reputation. And she just wasn't inclined to break the law.

Erin ran a hand through her hair. "I just wish I knew what to do now. I'd feel less anxious if I could figure out how to fix this, you know?"

"I'm making some calls, talking with someone who may be able to help us. Just stay here, okay. Can you trust me?"

Erin shrugged, not ready to do that and not at all ready to talk about it. She held up the papers she'd been reading, the ones that left her with a sinking feeling in her stomach as she read them. "Can you tell me about this? Is it related to Jerry?"

Will frowned. "Those are confidential FBI files."

"Well, you don't have a TV and you left them laying around. What was I supposed to do? Are these related to my father?"

"I don't know. There isn't anything tying him to either of them."

She bit her lip. There was plenty that linked him to the trust and the corporation—both 1221 Real Estate Trust and Solstice, Inc. And Will was smart, he'd figure it out. She should just tell him that the three-unit Victorian in San Francisco was the one she lived in while in college. And that her birthday was December 21, which was also the winter solstice. But that evidence of guilt was also the only evidence she'd seen in thirty years that her father had any affection for her.

No daddy issues, huh? Who the hell was she kidding?

"Do you want me to make coffee?" She jumped down off the countertop and tried to slip past him, but he stopped her with a hand on her arm. She met his eyes, warm and concerned, and quickly turning to hot. She followed his gaze down to the shirt she was wearing and realized that the black lace underthings were showing through the white cotton fabric.

He reached up and touched the collar, tugging at it gently. "I don't think I'll ever look at one of my shirts the same again."

A rush of heat surged through her, settling at the juncture of her thighs. God, just being close to him was enough to make her want more. But when he looked at her like that, like she was something more delicious than whatever was in the bakery box he'd brought, her body ached and throbbed.

She was mad at him, she told herself. He'd used her to investigate Jerry—but at least his instincts were sound. Jerry was up to no good.

"I need to go home," she said. "I have to feed the cat."

"You can't go home. And I fed John Doe this morning."

"You named my cat?"

"Someone had to."

"You were in my house?"

He reached into his pants pocket and withdrew the key. "Bree gave it to me."

"Oh," she said. "Bree knows what's going on?"

He ran a hand through his hair, and her fingers flexed with the desire to feel the short strands under her touch. Instead, she balled her hands into fists at her side.

"Erin, if there's anything I could do—"

His eyes pleaded with her to believe him.

"I know. You were just doing your job," she said, skirting by him to leave the laundry room.

"No." He reached for her and she stopped. Heat from his hand burned through the thin fabric and the tingle started at her elbow, where he touched her, and then flooded through her.

"That's how it started. I had plans," he said, shaking his head, his eyes closed for a long moment. "I thought I could use you. And I thought it would be easy. I was so attracted to you and that was just a great perk."

Hearing him confirm her suspicions didn't help. She turned away.

"That all changed. That changed as soon as I got to know you," he said. "As soon as..."

Her pulse fluttered in her throat and she stared at him, wanting too badly to believe him. What had happened to her self-respect? She was certain that she'd had some once. But now when she looked at him, so contrite and somber, she wanted to tell him that she understood and forgave him.

He brushed a strand of hair from her face. The touch strayed to her cheek, then down her neck. Erin shivered under his hand.

"I'll fix this, Erin," he said, his voice low and deep. A gravelly promise that made her insides jittery. "Do you trust me?"

She met his gaze and nearly lost her resolve in the depths of his hazel eyes.

"Yes," she said. "I trust you."

She trusted him to do what he could to make the criminal charges go away. But nothing beyond that. She couldn't afford to trust him past that.

Erin Grady was a terrible liar. She didn't trust him. Maybe with her body, but not her thoughts. She'd seen something in those papers. Will was sure of it. Given time, she may eventually open up and tell him what she knew. But he didn't have time to regain her trust. Neither did she.

Butler had seen to that.

As soon as he left his house that morning, Will had called Glover, but the agent's phone rolled to voicemail. Valerie was keeping an eye on Butler and would let him know if it looked like the detective was closing in on Erin, or on Rob Katri, who was still at large.

The arrest warrant was sealed, so it wasn't public yet. But somehow the news was already starting to percolate through the town. Valerie was trying to get a copy of it without raising any red flags, and had tracked Erin's Jeep to the impound yard. Without confronting Butler himself, or Grady, there wasn't much Will could do yet. But if Butler arrested Erin, Will would lose some measure of control over the situation.

With his morning court appearances over, it had been an easy decision to come check on his reluctant houseguest. He only had a few minutes, and then he had to get back to the district attorney's office and pretend that nothing was wrong, that he wasn't harboring Erin in his house.

It was hard to leave her, and not just because she was parading around his house half-naked except for his shirt and a pair of black lace underwear. Though that was tempting as hell.

It was too tempting.

He smoothed her hair away from her face, cupped his hand on the back of her head and kissed her deeply. His heart skipped as soon as their lips met. A spark ran through his body. She was so sweet, even in the midst of a crisis.

This was wrong. He should walk away. Leave her alone to figure out how she felt. That would be the right thing to do. But he couldn't untangle his hands from her hair, separate his body from hers, break the kiss and walk away.

With great effort, he pulled away.

"I should go," he said, nearly choking on the words. "Stay inside, okay?"

Erin bit her lip, looked down and nodded. "Sure."

She couldn't be more guarded if she'd built a moat around herself. That was bad enough, but worse was the knowledge that she was protecting herself from him.

"You have my cell phone and you have Valerie's number. Call if anyone comes to the house. Don't answer the door."

"I know," she said, her eyes finally meeting his. "I'll be fine."

She gave him a small, brave smile.

It was never supposed to be like this—wild and sweet and hot. This was supposed to be a distraction, a nice diversion while he plotted his exit from Lost Coast Harbor.

He was so fucked.

Chapter Twenty

A bracing wind hit Will in the face as he walked out of his office and started the short walk to Deputy Chief Stan Hutchins' retirement party. He had been tempted to blow off the invitation, but then his boss had strongly hinted that it would be good politics for him to stop by and represent the District Attorney's office. The thought of socializing with the Lost Coast Harbor police force was even less appealing now that he knew it was rotten at its core.

Donnelly's was on the town square. The main room was warm and spacious, filled with solid wood tables and cozy booths, and there was a pool room in the back where Will had watched a few basketball games since he'd arrived in Lost Coast Harbor. It was a popular local hangout, and he knew that cops loved the place. The beer was cold, the staff efficient, and in the last four months, Will hadn't seen one police report mention the pub.

The door to Donnelly's opened as he approached, and a group staggered out. The noise inside spilled out and Will gritted his teeth and walked in. Though he'd wish the deputy chief well in retirement, that was not who he was here to see.

He nodded at a few familiar faces and shook hands with several spouses who were dragged along to the party. The entire time, he kept scanning the crowd, looking for Butler and focusing on the fact that soon he'd be able to get home to Erin.

He liked the sound of that, coming home to her. Waking up next to her, warm and soft. She was trapped in his house now, until the arrest warrant was recalled—if he could manage that. He tried to think past the current threat, to when she'd be able to return home, go back to her regular life. She was busy—work, the clinic, her family, friends. But there wasn't anyone taking care of her. Not like he could.

Shaking hands and smiling, Will made his way toward the end of the bar where Hutchins and Grady were chatting with a small crowd. A heavy hand on his shoulder stopped him and he didn't need to turn to know it was Todd Butler.

"Mr. Patton, how are you tonight? How about I buy you a drink?" Butler asked. His voice was overly cheerful, loud.

"No, thanks, Butler. I can't stay long," he said.

The cop ignored him, leaned in front of Will to the dark-haired bartender and motioned for a round of drinks. The bartender poured two Irish whiskeys and slid them across the bar.

"Cheers," Butler said, smirking and raising his glass.

Will raised his glass, because it beat the alternative of smashing a fist into the cop's face.

"We should talk," Butler said, pulling a pack of cigarettes from his pocket. "You smoke?"

"No."

He moved away, but Butler gripped his arm. Will paused

and looked down at the other man's hand on his arm, then looked up and into Butler's eyes. "Are you detaining me, Butler?"

Butler released him suddenly and held his hand up. "Hey, no problem. Just wanted to mention that you need to back the hell off your crusade here. No one in this room appreciates what you're doing. Sure would hate for things to get ugly."

Butler had some balls making that statement in a crowded room full of cops, but Will looked around and realized that no one was listening to their conversation. Even the bartender had moved away. The room was too crowded and loud for anyone to have overhead his threat. Still, it wouldn't help him to have Butler announce his suspicions to the entire police force. He moved toward the back of the bar and Butler followed him to the edge of the main room, near the hall that led to the exit.

"What am I doing, Butler?" Will asked, taking a sip of the whiskey.

"You're stirring up trouble," he said. "You're messing up a finely tuned ecosystem. Just leave it alone."

Will met the officer's eyes and downed the last of the drink, then set the glass on an empty table and crossed his arms in front of him.

"Meridian police tried that tactic with me, too. Didn't work then, either."

"Yeah, I have some friends there. They all just got back from paid vacations, courtesy of you," Butler said, leaning against the wall and blocking the hall that led to the exit. "But now that the investigation is closed and no one was found to have acted improperly, they're all back on the job."

"Well, that was my first time running into a fully corrupt police department," Will said, narrowing his eyes. "I've learned better ways of investigating since then."

The detective smirked again. "By fucking the chief's daughter? Don't get me wrong, she's a hot little thing. But Grady's kid isn't going to be your ticket out of here."

He lost it when Butler mentioned Erin. Without a thought, he struck out, hit the detective with a right hook that laid the older man out in the hallway, but only momentarily. Butler scrambled to his feet and threw himself at Will, smashing him against the wall in the narrow hall. Will got in two more good blows, took one, and then the bartender was prying the two of them apart.

"Out!" He pushed them toward the back door and Will found himself in the alley with Butler.

"You think you're going to take me out with fists? Think again, Patton. I've got your girl's future in my hands."

"Stay away from Erin. You don't have anything on her but a fake informant you can't produce," Will snapped.

"Rob Katri will cooperate with me," he said.

"You think you'll be able to beat a statement out of him?"

His hands itched to wipe the cool smile off Butler's face.

"It's enough. Especially when you consider all the pills in her house," Butler said.

That threat made Will's blood go cold. He had no doubt Butler would plant evidence on someone. "You son of a bitch. That's bullshit."

Butler held up his hands. "Hey, just because she's Chief Grady's daughter, we can't ignore the connection. I'm just going where the evidence points me."

"What do you want?"

"Are you asking me to drop an investigation because you're sleeping with the suspect?" Butler asked, and Will's eyes narrowed. He hadn't even hinted at that.

"No, I would never do that," he said. "I just want to know what your end game is here. Why arrest Erin? What do you get out of it?"

"Are you attempting to bribe me, Boy Scout?"

Again, an uneasy feeling simmered inside him. Butler's responses were off. As if he were working from a script. Though he knew he wouldn't see it, Will's eyes went to the detective's chest, searching for a tell-tale bulge from a recording device.

"Maybe I want you out of this town. Out of my department. Out of my evidence room," Butler said. "This could all be over so damn fast. Just do your time here, then get back to the main office. Just leave Lost Coast Harbor. You need a big bust to get out of town, get a federal job in the city? I can help you with that."

"And if I did that? If I just ignore your bad reports and fake informants and perjured testimony? What then?"

Butler shrugged. "Maybe life gets a little easier for poor Erin Grady. She's awfully cute to have to send to prison for a decade."

Will clenched his jaw, flexed his throbbing fist and narrowed his eyes. "The chief?"

"Grady's on his way out. And while I could hand him to you on a platter, it might get messy for me. So you're going to have to find another big case to get yourself out of here.

Play ball, and I can help you with that."

The back door flew open and Chief Grady stormed into the alley, his hand hovering over the weapon on his belt.

"What the hell is going on?"

Will faced Butler, half expecting him to draw his gun, but the detective just scowled and squared his shoulders, barely sparing the chief a glance.

"Nothing, Chief," Butler said, turning and giving the chief a forced smile. "Just a minor disagreement."

Jerry Grady's jaw was clenched so tight, he looked like he was going to break his own teeth.

"If you go near her, I will kill you," Grady said.

For an instant, Will thought the chief was talking to him, but Grady's eyes were focused on Butler.

The detective's eyes narrowed. "I don't have to go near your daughter. I only have to unseal the arrest warrant and her life unravels."

Will clenched his fists, feeling the ache in his knuckles, and barely held himself back from another go at the detective's face. Grady's reaction to the words mirrored his—fists at his side, jaw tense. They were both being held hostage by Butler.

"You both need to let this go," Butler said. He pointed at Grady. "And don't think I can't take you down."

"I won't go alone," Grady said, his voice more of a snarl. "I have evidence—"

He glanced at Will, as if remembering there was a prosecutor present. His mouth softened and a hint of regret shone through his eyes. "And I'll use it."

The detective's cool front slipped a fraction and his eyes

shifted between Will and Grady, but he recovered quickly and gave Grady a cool smile.

"You don't have shit, Grady. You move on me and you'll be out. Hell, you'll be in prison."

Butler turned and walked down the alley, disappearing around the corner, his footsteps fading in the night. Will looked back at the chief.

"What evidence do you have?" he asked. He didn't know what was going on between the two cops, but together, he and Grady could stop Butler.

Grady looked down, his face pale. His lips tightened. "Nothing."

Will closed his eyes and exhaled. Butler hadn't bought Grady's bluff.

"Help me stop him," Will said. "You can't let Erin—"

Grady spun on his heel and went back into the bar, the door slamming behind him.

Son of a bitch.

No wonder Erin didn't trust anyone. Her own father just abandoned her, and not for the first time.

There had to be another way to stop Butler. If he walked away, as Butler wanted, it would all go away. But he didn't trust the crooked detective to stop. He'd still be a thug with a gun and a badge and Erin wouldn't be safe as long as Will or Grady were still around. She'd be the pawn that Butler would use to shut them down.

His investigation into the police department started this mess. But that was barely on Will's mind now. He'd brought this down on Erin, and he was going to make it right.

Chapter Twenty-One

"Say I wanted to break into a safe," Erin said, curling up on Bree's couch and warming her fingers on the mug of tea in her hands.

Bree raised an eyebrow. "Okay."

"How would I go about doing that?"

Erin had thought long and hard about how to fix her predicament. She couldn't just sit around and wait for Will to solve her problems for her. She *wouldn't* just sit around and wait for Butler to arrest her. And she was sick and tired of crying all the damn time.

That meant she had to act. There had to be something she could do to clear her name—ideally, before her name got dirtied up by some corrupt asshole cop. So she called Bree.

"What are you thinking?" her friend asked.

"Jerry has a safe on the boat. I think it's where he keeps important papers. If he had anything that was related to the real estate trust or that company Will is investigating, it would be in there."

Not that she had any insight into how Jerry's mind worked, but he seemed to live there more than at the house.

Bree leaned back in her chair and pulled her feet up under her. "What will you do if you find them?"

"Then I'll be able to figure out what to do. If he has been taking money from criminals, like Will thinks, then I can't take the land. But what if there's an innocent explanation? Maybe I can."

"Are you honestly defending Jerry Grady?"

"No. Not really. He's been a crap father, but he admits that. I don't care about that. I have a great dad in Alan," Erin said. She raked a hand through her hair and stared into the fireplace.

"It doesn't really help you with the other problem."

"There's nothing I can do about that problem." Erin frowned and set down the tea. "Either Butler arrests me or Will gets the charges dropped."

Bree stood and crossed her arms. "God, he's an asshole."

"Which one?" Erin hesitated to ask. Bree's reaction to the news of Will's covert investigation of Jerry had been downright nuclear.

"Both. But right now that district attorney especially deserves my wrath."

Erin's head throbbed. "I don't want to talk about Will."

"You don't need to. Nod silently if you want the bank to repo his car."

Erin had no doubt that Bree could do some serious damage, but she was not in the mood for revenge. Will's abject apology had seemed sincere and she was struggling to hold on to the anger she'd felt at the betrayal.

"Bree, no. Don't do that. He was just doing his job," she said. "I'm fine. I'll be fine."

She would be fine—eventually. One day the hurt would stop and she'd move forward. In the meantime, she had things to do.

"Fucking you was not part of his job," Bree snapped.

"Bree, please." She closed her eyes for a long moment and took a deep breath. "I really don't want to talk about this right now."

Bree looked like she wanted to say more, but at last she nodded. "I'm sorry. I wish there was something I could do."

Erin forced a smile. "If you want to help me, answer my question."

"About safe-cracking?"

Erin nodded, then followed Bree to the bank of computer screens in the dining room. She took the seat next to Bree and watched her friend's fingers fly over the keyboard.

"Yes. About that. And what are you doing?"

"If you're not going to let me ruin Will's life, I'm at least going to fuck up Detective Butler's credit rating. It will make me feel better."

Erin shrugged. "I'm going to pretend I didn't hear that. Now, back to the safe."

"Do you know what kind of safe?"

Erin held up her hands. "About this big," she said with an apologetic smile. "He punched in some buttons, like a code, to open it."

"Do you remember how many digits?"

She shook her head. "Maybe a half dozen?"

"Most people use their birthdays, or the birthdates of their kids or spouse. For a six- or eight-digit code, I'd start with that." She turned in her chair and leveled a hard look at

Erin. "You're serious about this?"

Erin nodded.

"Does he have a security system on the boat?"

"I didn't notice one. But I wasn't looking for one, either. I don't think he has one at the house."

"How about cameras at the harbor? There must be security cameras on the public docks."

"I'm sure there are."

Bree turned back to the computer and brought up a new screen, poking around several websites until she smiled and leaned back in the chair.

"Here we are. The Lost Coast Harbor webcams. Streaming 24/7."

"Those aren't the security cameras, though." Erin frowned. This was the stupidest plan. She had no idea how to break into a boat. He was a paranoid police chief. Of course he'd lock his door.

"Where is his boat?" Bree asked, scanning the half dozen live webcam feeds.

"By the front entrance."

"You're in luck. That camera is out of order."

Erin looked over Bree's shoulder and saw the screen split into six sections, each with a nighttime view of the harbor. "No, it's right there. This is it."

She tapped the screen for emphasis while Bree continued typing, focused on the screen to the left.

"Keep an eye on that," she said, and seconds later, the camera showing the *Winter Solstice* went black.

She didn't know much about what Bree did as a computer consultant, and maybe it was better that way. Her friend was a good person, and she wouldn't do anything evil with her superpowers. Probably.

It wouldn't protect her completely. There were probably other people around, and real surveillance cameras. And Jerry could come home and find her with her hand in his wall safe. That would be awkward.

She stood up before she changed her mind. "Thanks, Bree."

"Wait." Bree stood, too. "You're not going alone."

She grabbed some clothes from the back of the couch and threw them at Erin. "You can't wear that to a break-in."

Erin glanced down at her pale blue sweater and worn jeans. "I'm new at this."

Bree shook her head with a sigh. "You need backup."

She pulled on a dark blue hoodie and a black knit beanie while Erin changed into the borrowed black clothes. "So is Will going to come looking for you? Aren't you supposed to be lying low at his house?"

Erin bent down to tie her shoes. "I just needed to get away for a while. You can drop me off there later so he doesn't have a fit."

"Or you can stay here."

Erin frowned. "Will thinks anyone looking for me will come here."

Bree returned the frown. "Well, thanks for that. I didn't choose to hide out in the woods so I could have surprise visitors."

"Sorry," Erin said, grabbing Bree's bag. "It's dark enough. Let's go."

Bree let her get away with the abrupt change of conversation and Erin appreciated her friend's discretion. She didn't want to talk about Will. As much as she wanted to insist it had been merely sex, that wasn't true. She just wasn't ready to deal with that yet.

Thirty minutes later, Erin stepped onto the *Winter Solstice*, gripping the railing with sweaty hands. The gentle rise and sway of the boat matched the pitching of her stomach. She looked up and down the dock, but the walkways were empty and silent except for the sounds of the boats moving against the ropes.

With a deep breath, she stepped onto the deck and looked back toward the gate. Bree was there, somewhere in the shadows, in case Jerry pulled into the parking lot.

The door was locked, as she suspected it would be, but she remembered her father's penchant for keeping a key hidden outside. She slid her hands around the outside of the door frame, then across and under every other surface near the entrance to the cabin. Finally, her fingers brushed across a square metal box under the console. She dropped to her knees and slid open the lid, and a silver key dropped into her hand.

After one last look up the dock, she unlocked the door and started down the steps. She didn't bother looking around the rest of the cabin, but went straight to the safe on the wall. The picture frame swung open, revealing the keypad. In the dark, she couldn't see the numbers, but as soon as she touched one, the keys lit with an orange glow from behind.

She exhaled a deep breath and pressed in the digits for Jerry's birthday. Nothing happened, so she hit the button marked "clear" and tried it with an eight-digit birthdate, instead. This time, the lights blinked twice, but the door stayed locked.

Jerry hadn't been close with his parents, so Erin didn't think it would be her grandparents' birthdays. But maybe since he had named the boat *Winter Solstice*, her birthday meant something to him. She punched in her birthdate.

The orange lights blinked and she felt the door release under her fingers. Her heart jumped and she opened the door with a trembling hand. Pulling a flashlight from her pocket, she looked around again, but the boat was still silent.

The safe was not huge, maybe six inches tall and twelve wide. Erin pulled out the envelope of papers that she'd given to Jerry, setting them on a nearby chair. Below that was a stack of file folders, which Erin had caught a glimpse of on her prior visit. She pulled those out and glanced at the tabs. They contained paperwork for the boat and various insurance policies.

With a frustrated sigh, she returned to the safe and peered in. In the back was a small stack of CDs in plastic cases. She pulled them out. The CD cases were bound together with a rubber band and a small sticky note on top read simply, "save."

A low beep in her pocket sent Erin's heart racing and she dropped the CDs in her panic. "Shit."

She pulled out the phone and saw Bree's text: *Go.*

Damn it. She put the papers back in, shut the door and then remembered the CDs on the floor. She picked them up, and felt rather than heard the footsteps on the ladder.

Fuck. She swung the picture back into place, stuffed the CDs into the pocket of her sweatshirt, and looked around the cabin for a place to hide.

There was no place where Jerry wouldn't see her. Her panicked gaze fell on the door by the steps and she slid it open. Two tall closets created a short hallway that led to a narrow room, barely more than a two-foot-wide walkway between two twin-sized bunks. She slipped in, hoping that Jerry wouldn't look in the tiny guest room.

Holding her breath, she crouched on the bed and peered at the door, waiting to hear Jerry come down the steps and then turn on a light. Instead, she heard the whisper of footsteps outside the thin door.

A beam of light swept the bottom of the door and Erin stood back against the wall and listened to the sounds of the person in the other room. Still, no light came on, but she could hear the person walking around the cabin, opening doors and drawers.

Drawing a shallow breath, she shifted on the bed so she could peer around the closet at the door.

She pulled her cell phone from her pocket and made sure it was silenced, then texted Bree: *Trapped.*

The reply came fast: *Butler.*

Erin stared at the word and her heartbeat skipped. She had no time to wonder why her father's senior detective was searching his boat in the dark. She just prayed that he wouldn't be thorough.

The sound of a soft chuckle floated through the door and she heard the familiar sound of the safe being opened. She closed her eyes, listening to the quiet rustle of papers, then a sharp curse. It was quiet and it was definitely not her father's voice.

The safe banged shut, the picture frame snapped back against the wall, and heavy footsteps crossed the cabin, growing louder as they neared her. Erin sat back on her heels, crouched on the corner of the bed against the wall and the closet, trying to disappear in the darkness.

But instead of opening the door, the man took the steps up and a second later, she heard the hatch bang shut. The boat rocked slightly as he jumped down on the dock.

She pulled the phone from her pocket and saw that Bree had sent an all-clear. Checking the cabin with the flashlight, everything seemed in place, so she bolted up the steps.

Outside, she took a deep breath, pulled the hood of her sweatshirt over her head, then replaced the hidden key and scrambled down the short ladder to the dock. Walking briskly, she pulled the hoodie around her face. As she passed the gate, Bree stepped out of a darkened doorway and Erin jumped about a foot off the ground.

"Fuck, Erin," Bree said in a low whisper. "Let's get the hell out of here before anyone else decides to board Grady's boat."

Erin bent over and rested her hands on her knees, a year's worth of adrenaline flooding her system. Gulping down the cold air, she tried to calm her nerves. After a moment, she looked up and nodded.

"Yeah, let's go," she said, standing.

Bree's truck was parked around the corner, between two warehouses. They hurried toward it, keeping their faces down and their hoods up. When she reached for the door handle, Erin's hands shook enough that Bree had to open the door for her.

"Good thing I'm driving," she said. "You're a mess."

Erin didn't argue. Her entire body felt jittery.

She climbed into the passenger seat and felt the bump against her stomach from the items in the large pocket on the sweatshirt.

"Oh, fuck it all," she said, pulling the small stack of CDs out of the pocket. "I forgot to put these back."

Bree glanced over and then drove forward. "We're not going back."

Once away from the dock, Erin's breath started to return to normal. "It was Butler?"

Bree nodded. "Yeah. At first I thought he had followed you. What did he do on the boat?"

"I was hiding, I couldn't see. But I think he looked in the safe. Then it sounded like he got angry and he left."

"You didn't find anything about the real estate?" Bree asked.

"No, nothing," Erin said.

"Okay, what's Plan B?"

Erin gave a laugh. "You think there was a Plan A?"

"At least we have something."

"What, these CDs?"

"Maybe. We'll see what's there. But I also got cell phone video of Butler boarding the boat. That's got to help." She tossed her phone to Erin. "Check it out."

It was a twenty-minute drive to Bree's cabin, and as the truck climbed the mountain roads and the distance between her and the docks grew, Erin started to relax. With evidence of Butler's burglary, they had some leverage against him.

Bree navigated the last sharp turn and hit the brakes hard in front of her cabin. The headlights illuminated the dark SUV parked in front of the house, and the tall, very grumpy-looking attorney standing on the porch.

CHAPTER TWENTY-TWO

"It's okay. Bree took care of the cameras," Erin said.

She looked so sweet as she said it, Will thought, her cheeks flushed pink and her eyes wide and staring directly into his. She was dressed in black—from her shoes, all the way up a pair of tight black jeans that hugged every sweet curve, and to the sweatshirt pulled up to her chin. An adorably sexy burglar.

When he'd arrived home to find her gone, he had immediately assumed the worst—that Butler had gotten to her, arrested her. But there was nothing to indicate a struggle in his house, and he'd just seen Butler at Donnelly's. Her house was dark and quiet, as well. That left Bree's remote cabin as the most likely place where she'd be, and he'd once again navigated the dark mountain roads. Then he waited nearly an hour, his mind replaying every possible harm that could come to her.

"Cameras?" he repeated. Both of Will's hands were in his hair now, and he struggled to keep his calm.

Bree unzipped her coat and hung it on a coat rack by the front door. "This isn't my first rodeo, lawyer boy. We were careful."

He turned to her, then looked back at Erin—a pair of black-clad felons who just confessed that they'd broken into the police chief's boat.

"Why?" The word exploded from his mouth and carried all the anger and fear he had been holding in.

"I had to find out if he was connected to those papers you had," Erin said.

"He's your father. You couldn't, I don't know, *knock*?"

"I wasn't sure he'd be welcoming. I mean, the warrant…"

Will sank into the couch and rested his head in his hands. "I don't want to even count all the laws you two just broke."

Bree sat across from him and simply…watched him. Like he was prey, and she was debating the best way to bring him down. "So now doing the right thing matters? You've decided to care about the truth?"

"Bree!" Erin stood and shook her head at her friend, her mouth tight.

"I'm just trying to figure out why I let a self-righteous liar into my house, Erin."

"Bree, can I see you for a moment?" Erin grabbed her friend's arm and dragged Bree to the kitchen, and he heard a very low murmur of voices for a long moment.

He honestly didn't blame Bree one bit for not trusting him. He wouldn't, in her position. Except that Bree didn't understand how he felt about Erin, and how much he regretted hiding the investigation from her.

When the two women returned, Erin was smiling. Bree gave him a suspicious glare, then at Erin's nudge, bared her teeth in what might pass for a smile.

"Just remember I can destroy your entire life in the time it would take you to remember your password."

The words were casual, like she was reminding him to pick up his dry cleaning, but Will's gut flipped at her threat. Someone who could easily tap into the police department's internal network wasn't bluffing. "Understood."

Erin sat next to him, like she was protecting him from Bree's wrath. "Anyway, we didn't break too many laws."

"Well, there's definitely breaking and entering, and some minor destruction of property," Bree said, opening a cabinet and taking out a bottle of bourbon. "I had to knock the surveillance cameras out of position and my aim was a little off."

"And conspiracy and theft," Erin added.

Will rubbed his forehead. "Please. Stop talking."

They both smiled at him and he became very suspicious. "Why are you smiling?"

"Because the chief wasn't there," Bree said, pouring a generous serving.

"But someone else was," Erin chimed in.

Will rubbed his face. Forget how many laws Thelma and Louise had just broken, how about what he'd done? He was guilty of harboring Erin when he knew there was a warrant for her arrest, and now he was listening to them recount their crimes and was at least guilty of accessory after the fact. Because whatever happened, there was no way he'd turn them in.

He sat back against the soft cushions and stared at the troublemaker next to him.

"Do I want to know?"

Bree handed him the tumbler and he accepted the bourbon with gratitude.

"Want to see the video?" she asked.

He choked, and the bourbon burned exiting his nose. Erin patted him on the back as he coughed.

"I think what you meant to ask is if I'd like to see the evidence of your felonies?" he said, wiping his face with his sleeve.

"Not just ours," Erin said.

She pulled the hoodie off her head and smoothed her hair away from her face. She was the picture of innocence, but he knew better.

"I'll do what I can to make sure your prison allows conjugal visits, love."

She laughed. "You'd better."

Bree plopped down on the other side of Will with her smartphone. She tapped the screen and brought up a video. The cell phone video was blurry and dark, and there wasn't any sound.

Then the picture became more clear, though still grainy, and Will recognized the docks behind the Vista del Mar. A man walked away from the camera, his head swiveling as he looked around the dock. He was wearing a black baseball cap pulled low.

The man moved fast, and then took the steps onto a large white boat. Will couldn't see the stern from this angle, but there was no need to see the name. He recognized the *Winter Solstice* without a problem. The camera zoomed in as the man disappeared from view.

Erin sat next to him, barely touching him, and it was enough for his body to react. He wanted nothing more than to hold her close, breathe in her scent, touch her. When he'd seen her earlier, with her eyes the color of a storm at sea, it had nearly broken him. She did so much for others, and he just wanted to make her life a little easier. If she'd just let him do his job, he might be able to do that.

"Nothing happens for a while," Bree said, dragging her finger along the bottom of the screen to fast forward through the scene.

"Here it comes," Erin said.

After a few seconds, the man emerged from the boat and jumped down onto the dock, looking around. The camera zoomed in and the image shook. The man walked closer and kept his head turned toward the water, probably to avoid the surveillance camera.

"Look, here you can see his face," Erin said, nudging him.

Will's neck tensed watching the man's agitated gait. After another moment, the man walked into a more well-lit area at the same time as a car's headlights slowly panned the area. The result was a brief moment of illumination, where Todd Butler's face was captured in crystal clarity.

Then he moved into the dark parking lot and disappeared from view. The camera moved back to the boat and zoomed in and after a brief moment, another figure stumbled off the boat—smaller, but just as furtive and nervous. His heart slammed into his chest at the sight of Erin hurrying down the dock toward the camera. The video ended as she approached the camera operator.

He sent a silent prayer of thanks out to the entity that protected hapless do-gooders, then leaned his head back and studied Bree's ceiling. He ran through everything he'd learned about preservation of the chain of evidence, and all the ways corrupt cops get caught. He calculated prison terms for Erin and Bree if they were charged with trespass, breaking and entry, burglary and God knew what else. If he was lucky, he might be able to find a job as a truck driver when he got fired for this debacle.

"I'm probably going to need that video. Please don't destroy it."

Bree shrugged. "Sure thing, lawman."

Erin reached into the pocket of her sweatshirt and withdrew a bundle of CDs in plastic cases and handed them to Bree.

"What is this?"

"I don't know. Bree's going to see what's on them."

Bree took the CDs to the dining room, where her computers emitted a low hum.

"You stole them?"

"More like borrowed them," Erin said, giving him a smile. "It wasn't intentional."

He touched her cheek, drawing his finger down her soft skin to her chin, tilting her face up toward his. Her eyes met his. The adrenaline from nearly being caught on the boat was fading, and the sadness was starting to creep back in.

"Please don't do that again," he whispered.

"I can't imagine I'll have to," she said.

That wasn't a promise, but it brought a smile to his lips.

Bree coughed from the dining room. "You two should come listen to this."

Will and Erin crossed the small cabin to where Bree was focused on one of her three computer screens.

"This CD has two audio recordings. It's proprietary software that law enforcement uses, but I can convert it," Bree said, queueing up the recording.

The recording started with the loud sound of rustling. Erin strained to hear the sounds filtering past the noise of fabric brushing against a hidden microphone.

"You wanted to see me?" It was familiar voice.

"Yeah, Butler, come in. Close the door," Grady said.

The two men exchanged small talk for a few minutes, and then there was a pause.

"What did you decide to do?" Butler asked.

"I really don't see that I have much of a choice, Todd."

"You really don't, Chief," Butler said. "I'm qualified for Hutchins' job. You recommend me and the council will approve it."

"And if I don't?"

There was another pause. "Then the council will learn about your business with Hastings. I'll look like a hero for bringing it to their attention, and I'll probably get your job."

Jerry was silent except for a long sigh. "Yeah, that's what I figured, too."

"I've set up an account. You can send the down payment here," Butler said, over the sound of paper rustling.

"I told you, I'm not working with Hastings. Peter's in jail and out of business," Grady said.

"But you were. You two were thick as thieves." Butler's voice was cold and Will could easily picture his sneer. "Look, you need me now. If Peter talks, you lose everything. But with me, you get to keep half."

Erin was gripping Will's hand tight enough that he felt his

pulse throbbing in his fingers. Her face was pale.

"Got your retirement papers ready yet?" Butler asked.

"Next summer," Grady said. "Any sooner and you won't have enough experience to get the job."

Butler laughed softly. "I don't know what you're unhappy about. You'll be in Mexico on your boat, fishing and drinking."

"As long as I don't cross you," Grady said.

"You got sloppy. You didn't cover your tracks. If I hadn't caught you with your hand in Hastings' wallet, someone else would have. Probably the FBI. This is better for both of us."

Will put his arm around Erin and kept her close to him as he absorbed the conversation between the two cops. He had been right about Grady, and Valerie's suspicions about Butler were on target. Though neither of them had suspected that Butler was blackmailing Grady, this explained the weird interaction between the two men earlier at the pub.

Will rubbed his forehead. He needed to call Glover, get a copy of the audio files to the FBI for preservation.

"There are seven recordings total on the CDs," Bree said. "I'll burn a copy to my secure server and give you the CDs."

This was what he'd been working for. Depending on what was on the other recordings, he likely had enough evidence to convict the both of them. He could take that to the FBI, to the U.S. Attorney's Office. It was the sort of arrest and trial that made a career.

And he hated it.

A steady drum of pain beat in his head. A year ago, even a few weeks ago, he would have relished bringing down a corrupt police chief and his senior detective. And now all he could think about was what this would mean for Erin.

Chapter Twenty-Three

Will's house had a perpetual chill to it that no furnace or fireplace could remove. Footsteps echoed on the hardwood floors. Rather than helping turn the room into a welcoming space, the single piece of furniture, a long couch facing the fireplace, just emphasized the emptiness and barrenness. Erin sat at one end of the couch, pressed up against the arm, and hugged the thick sweatshirt against herself in a vain attempt to get warm.

It wasn't possible to stop the trembling in her hands and the shivers that occasionally hit her. All it took to start the tremors was recalling her father's voice, confessing to helping Peter Hastings move illegal weapons through Lost Coast Harbor, selling his badge to his old friend. And agreeing to set Butler up in his place when he retired.

"Erin, are you all right?"

Valerie Childs' voice pierced the mental fog that filled Erin's head. The detective took the other end of the sofa, leaving Will and the FBI agent, Shane Glover, to find their own seats. They were all watching her closely. Shane dragged one of the still-packed boxes of books closer to use as a seat.

He looked nearly comical as he tried to get comfortable, his thick body dwarfing the box. He gave up and sat on the wood floor, glaring at Will.

"I'm guessing you don't do a lot of entertaining."

Will ignored him and pulled the box toward Erin, then sat on it, his long legs stretched out in front of him. He was within arm's reach and she wanted to unfold her arms and reach for him, but every muscle in her body was tense and contracted and she wasn't sure if she could manage that small feat.

She smiled at Valerie and nodded, lying to the detective with that simple gesture. She wasn't fine. There was no way she'd be fine for a long time.

"Valerie, what's the status on Rob Katri? Did you find him yet?" Will asked, his voice tense. His body, too, was tightly coiled. He'd barely spoken on the drive from Bree's back to his house. In fact, after he'd stepped out onto Bree's porch and made a call, he'd been uncharacteristically silent.

"Katri is hiding out. His wife says Butler came by looking for him. She wasn't very cooperative, but I think she got the message that it would be better for him to stay hidden for a little longer. She let it slip that her uncle has a hunting cabin about an hour from here. I'll head up there and check it out."

Shane picked up a thin laptop from the floor and opened it. "I have all the information on the trust and that corporation. Will, you're the lawyer. Maybe you can look through that and see what you think. By the way, Spencer Bourne needs you to call him," Shane said. "Said to tell you congratulations."

Will gave him a short nod. "That's probably premature."

Shane shook his head. "Nah, man. You're going to the show. Somewhere in these files is the piece of evidence that will link Grady to both the trust and the corporation, and with those recordings, we've got both of these bastards—"

Erin's heart constricted at the words, even as Shane cut himself off, his face flushed with embarrassment. "Oh, jeez. I'm sorry, Ms. Grady."

She struggled to breathe, but kept her face neutral. There wasn't any denying it. Jerry Grady was a bastard. He was on the take, and had admitted as much on the recordings. When she couldn't find her voice, she just forced a smile and shook her head.

Will laid a hand on her knee and squeezed, as she avoided looking at him. It was nice of him to feel bad for her. He was close to getting what he wanted—that job in San Francisco, working with the United States Attorney's Office. Going after big cases. Really making a difference. And getting the hell out of Lost Coast Harbor and away from her.

All he needed was something that tied Grady to the company on Hastings' payroll. One missing piece. Something that would corroborate the conversations Jerry recorded.

She struggled to get the words out over the lump in her throat.

"They're his."

Her voice sounded strained. No hiding that. She could hardly draw a breath.

"What?" Will asked, turning to her. A furrow appeared in his brow, and his lips turned down slightly. "How do you know that?"

Her hands shook. There would be no taking it back, once

she said the words. But she couldn't see that she had a choice.

"My birthday is December 21st. Which is also the winter solstice," she said.

The room went silent, the only sound the crackling and popping of the fire. When she dared to look up, Will's expression was guarded, cautious.

"Erin," he said, his voice low. "Are you sure you want—"

She nodded. "It's what you need, right? Something that connects him to the 1221 Real Estate Trust and Solstice, Inc."

Shane gave a slow nod. "It's circumstantial, but yeah, it will do."

Sharing the secret she'd been holding back eased the burden, but in its place was a hollowed out feeling. She'd just given Will the last thing he needed to be free.

His hand was still on her leg, the heat seeping through the fabric and warming her.

"Until Butler is in custody, I'm putting you under federal protection, Ms. Grady. He's using you against both your father and Will, and that means you're not safe," Shane said.

"That's not necessary," Will said, jumping up.

"Will, he could arrest her. He threatened her. What—"

"I'll take care of Erin." Will glowered down at the agent, his fists balled at his side.

Shane frowned and shook his head, and Erin had enough. She stood quickly and Will turned to her.

"I'll take care of myself," she said. She'd never been a helpless damsel and she'd be goddamned if she was going to start playing that role now. She didn't need Will's protection, or Glover's. She just needed a car. And hers was in the impound yard, where Butler had towed it.

Fuck.

Will's hands folded around her shoulders and stopped her. "It's not safe."

Neither was standing here, falling into his hazel eyes, and wishing she hadn't just launched Will's career and guaranteed that he'd be moving away.

"This is someone who is desperate to hang on to his job, his standing," Will said. "He'll do what he has to do to keep that."

Erin shook her head. At that moment, she didn't need protection from Butler. But if she didn't put some distance between herself and Will, she was going to fall apart, shatter into a thousand pieces.

Valerie stood and put her hand on Erin's arm. Her dark eyes were kind, but serious. "What he's saying is that Butler's best option now is to kill you."

Erin jerked her head to the left and looked up at Will. He nodded, his jaw tense.

Just to be sure, she looked over at the FBI agent. Tall, bald, and tattooed, he'd be intimidating, except that he had been exceedingly gentle with her.

"That was a bit blunt, but it's true," Shane said, standing. "He must have found out the recordings exist and went there to get them. He's trying to cover his tracks. He screwed up by trying to use you as leverage against your father and Will. He can't back down."

"Oh." Her throat tightened.

"The advantage we have is that Butler doesn't know this is now a federal investigation," Glover said. "I think we have enough to arrest him."

Will shifted on his feet, as if uncomfortable. "Just a couple of nights, okay, Erin? We'll get Butler off the streets. But until then, you can't go home. Not alone."

She nodded, her brain unable to formulate any other plan. She'd go along with their plan until she could think more clearly.

Shane sat on the couch, and patted the cushion next to him, motioning for Erin to sit with him. After a moment, she complied. Shane opened the laptop and she watched as he clicked on a folder and then began opening documents.

The names on the pages were familiar—the 1221 Real Estate Trust, the Solstice Inc., and a long list of properties.

Erin pointed at one of the addresses.

"I lived there, in college," she said. "Jerry found the apartment for me. He paid half my rent."

Shane nodded. "Any other addresses look familiar?"

Erin shook her head. "No, I don't think so. I mean, except for the property that he offered for the clinic."

Will sat on the arm of the couch, one hand on her shoulder.

"Did you find Grady's name on anything?"

Shane shook his head. "No. The trust has been around for twenty years. It bought and sold various commercial properties in Northern California. A strip mall in Novato, a business park in Petaluma. Looks like it was profitable," Shane said. "The parcel he wants to give you for the clinic, it was purchased by the trust about eight years ago and sold to Jerry Grady one month ago. The price is below market, but not by much."

"Is that a tax strategy? If he sold himself the property, and then he donated it, he'd get a tax write-off for the gift, right?" Valerie asked.

"Maybe," Shane said. "There's a property that was transferred from 1221 to Solstice, Inc. about two years ago. We know that Solstice took money from Hastings several times in the last two years."

"I think Jerry and Hastings bought investment properties together, a long time ago," Erin offered. "I don't know any other details."

And she wasn't going to direct them to her mother for more information, either. They'd just have to work with what she gave them.

Will squeezed Erin's shoulder and she looked up at him.

"Shane, can you leave this so I can look at the documents later?" he asked, his eyes still on Erin.

Valerie picked up her coat. "Guess that's a hint. Come on, Glover. You can drive me to my car."

"Yeah, sure." Shane snapped the laptop closed and left it on the couch when he stood. "Let me know if you see anything in there."

The law enforcement officers left Will's house. Will locked the door behind them, then returned to Erin on the couch. He knelt in front of her and took her hands in his.

"Are you all right?" he asked.

"Yes." Her voice was choked. "I'm a little tired."

He nodded, pulling her up and running his hands up her arms. Then he reached for her and she let herself be wrapped in his arms, resting her head against his chest and his solid body.

His hands stroked her hair. "Why did you tell us about the properties, the other connections?"

She exhaled. "If I didn't, I'd be covering up for Jerry."

That wasn't in her. If Jerry wasn't guilty, let him show that these coincidences weren't proof that he'd sold his authority as chief of police. It wasn't her job to defend him. And no matter how much she wanted to think this was all a misunderstanding, his own voice on the recordings confirmed it.

"I know that wasn't easy," Will said.

He was right, but not for the reasons he thought. It had been easier to turn her own father in than it was to let Will go.

He pulled her down onto the couch with her, his arm still around her.

"I'm okay," she said. When he didn't look convinced, she squeezed his hand.

He shook his head. "No, you're not. And that's fine, Erin. You can be not okay with this."

Every muscle in her body ached with tension and sorrow, and she had no coping mechanism for it. Her usual method—action—was useless, unless she could figure out what action to take.

"I'd like to see the rest of the documents Shane left," Erin said. If she could see the full extent of the corruption, that might make it more concrete, and easier to accept.

Will frowned and moved toward her, making her look him in the eye. "I know you're independent and strong and God knows, I love that about you, but please trust me on this. Let me take care of this. Let someone take care of you for once."

Erin gave him a small smile and nodded. A lie, and he knew it.

He sighed, pulled her into his arms and wrapped himself around her. "Goddamn it, Erin. Let me help you."

She closed her eyes. "No."

His body tensed and he pulled back, staring at her. "What?"

"I don't want your help. I don't need it. I can't—"

Will's face hardened. "What? You can't trust me?"

That wasn't what she was going to say, but it would do. She couldn't let him in, couldn't be hurt more than she already was.

His eyes reflected his own pain and she looked away. It was better this way. He got what he wanted—a headline-making bust and new career opportunity—and she'd move forward that much quicker if he weren't there, touching her, reminding her constantly that this was only ever going to be a short-term fling.

Will's hands closed over hers and when she looked up at him, he'd masked any hurt he felt with a stubborn scowl.

"Well, you're stuck with me," he said. "Until Butler is in custody. I'm not going anywhere."

CHAPTER TWENTY-FOUR

Erin sat on the floor with her back against the couch. The room was dark, except for the light from the fire and the glow of the computer that she held in her lap. She reached down and replayed the last recording, adjusting the earbuds so she could again hear her father bargaining with Todd Butler, betraying everything he'd sworn to protect as a police officer.

She'd listened to all of the recordings. No matter how many times she heard the voices, it still seemed unreal.

Behind her, Will shifted and sighed in his sleep. He hadn't been kidding about not going anywhere. He'd refused to go to bed while she was still awake. Eventually, he'd fallen asleep on the couch.

She closed the laptop and set it on the ground next to the piles of papers that she'd reviewed. It all made sense now—how Jerry had money to invest in his estranged daughter, in a monster sport-fishing yacht, in property all over the state.

The recordings left unanswered the most important question—why?

She turned to face Will and brushed a lock of hair that

had fallen onto his forehead. He had been right. When they were together, it never felt like a lie. It felt more real than anything she'd ever experienced. And so did the hurt, knowing that he'd be leaving soon.

His breathing was steady and undisturbed, though his face was still tense, even in sleep. When he didn't stir, Erin sat back down and put on her shoes. She had too many questions and there was just one person who could answer them.

She found her phone plugged in to a borrowed charger in Will's kitchen, and sent Jerry an email. She didn't have his cell phone number, but hopefully he would get her message. She let herself out the front door and eased it shut behind her. Agent Glover had promised that additional agents were en route to Lost Coast Harbor, and not to be alarmed if there was an unmarked car in front of the house in the morning. It was nearing eleven at night, and the curb was still empty.

Erin tugged her hood up for the short walk to the park trail. That would be the safest route to Jerry's house. The streets were empty and silent, but she felt less exposed once she stepped out onto the familiar path. The only illumination on the trail was the pale light of the moon when the scattered clouds parted. The temperature had dropped and every breath puffed in front of her. She pulled the flashlight from her pocket as the trail wound into the trees and kept up a brisk pace.

From the recordings, Butler appeared to have been blackmailing Jerry for years. But Butler should have known enough about his boss to figure out that threatening Erin wasn't going to get him any leverage. They weren't close. Jerry wouldn't care.

Then something had changed. Jerry reached out to her, and they were talking. It might even look to an outsider like they had reconciled. He gave her a valuable piece of property. Now, Butler had more leverage over the chief. He put pressure on Jerry by ginning up false charges against Erin, threatening to get an arrest warrant.

It hadn't worked though. Jerry must have called Butler's bluff, because the detective's plans had escalated.

She was nearing the top of the trail, at the spot where Will had fallen into her life. She slowed and stared up the steep side of the hill, remembering him crashing onto the path, tangled in his bike. It hadn't been that long ago, but now she couldn't imagine her life without him.

The gate came into view and she turned off the flashlight, reaching over the fence to feel for the latch. It let out a groan as she pushed it open. She waited for her eyes to adjust to the darkness before taking a few cautious steps onto the lawn.

The house was dark and she hoped that Jerry had gotten the message to meet her here. Erin walked the length of the back porch, scanning the board until she found what she was looking for. She ran her fingers along the seam between two pieces of wood, found an edge and pulled. It popped out easily, and she reached into the shallow space behind it and pulled out a key. Thank God, Jerry was stuck in his stubborn ways.

She climbed the few steps to the back porch, unlocked the back door and let herself into the silent house. She turned on a small lamp in the hall, but didn't want to draw attention to the house, so she sat at the kitchen table to wait for her father.

It was the least familiar room in the house. Jerry seemed to like to cook, or at least to grill. He'd remodeled the kitchen to a modern gourmet's delight. The wide chrome appliances looked like they belonged in a restaurant.

Erin lay her head down on her arms on the table and closed her eyes. Hopefully, Jerry would talk with her, let her help him get this cleared up. Of course, if Butler was truly blackmailing him, then that meant Jerry wanted to keep something hidden—his relationship with Peter Hastings.

They weren't just friends, but business associates. He had paid Jerry off to look the other way while he trafficked in illegal weapons. That thought made her a little sick.

From the front of the house, Erin heard the sound of a car driving by and she raised her head, waiting to see the headlights pulling into the driveway, but they never came. She started to reach for her phone to see if Jerry had responded to her email. Then she remembered that she had left it charging in Will's kitchen.

Footsteps sounded on the front steps and she sat up straight, waiting for Jerry to let himself into the house. The doorknob rattled, then the door creaked and shut quickly. Faint footsteps echoed down the hall, but no lights came on in the living room. The hair on the back of her neck rose.

Something was wrong.

She started to stand just as Todd Butler walked into the kitchen, his gun drawn.

He couldn't hide the surprise, which quickly turned to glee at finding her. He shook his head and smiled.

"I've been looking for you, Erin," he said. "But I never would have looked here."

Erin stood so fast her chair fell over. She bolted for the back door, but her feet got tangled in the chair legs and Butler grabbed her before she could escape. She struggled to get out of his grasp, but his arms were like steel bands around her.

"Not so fast," he said.

He snapped handcuffs on one of her wrists, the cold metal tight against her skin, then he dragged her to the commercial gas range in the center of the kitchen. Despite her struggles, she found herself secured to the appliance, the handcuffs threaded through the oven door handle.

"That's better," Butler said, stepping back to admire his work. She tugged at the door, but only succeeded in opening the oven a few inches and hurting her wrists.

"Fuck you!" she spat at Butler. "Why are you doing this? Why aren't you just arresting me?"

"I may yet," he said. "But first, I need to talk to your dad."

He walked over to the hall and turned off the small lamp, plunging the house into total darkness.

Oh, shit. Damn. Fuck. She had really surprised him. He was lying in wait for Jerry.

"You son of a bitch," Erin said. "What are you blackmailing him with?"

In the darkness, his laugh sounded even more sinister, but he didn't answer her.

"Is it Hastings?" she asked, figuring she had nothing to lose. But even as she thought that, the image of Will nearly brought her to her knees. That was followed by Hayley, Colin, her parents. Even Jerry. She had so much to lose.

"Shut up."

"Was he taking money from Hastings? Is that it? You found out that he and Hastings were old friends, had invested in properties together. You used that to information to get something for yourself."

His footsteps echoed in the kitchen as he stalked toward her and she crouched down in the dark as they neared her.

Butler's soft laugh came from just feet from her and made her jump, and made her skin crawl.

"You're not hiding from me, Erin," he said. "Just be quiet."

Erin moved as far from him as she could get, the chain linking the handcuffs sliding all the way to the end of the handle.

"You had Jerry transfer you some property. He paid you some money. Hastings paid you, too."

His breathing grew faster and she knew the last piece.

"You were on Hastings' payroll. You tried to make it look like it was Jerry, but it was you. Solstice, Inc. is your company," she said.

He grabbed her by the hair and slammed her head to the countertop and she cried out as pain radiated from her cheekbone to her jaw.

"You need to stop talking," he hissed. Holding her head against the tile, he ran a hand over her body. She squirmed to get away from him, her stomach clenching. "Are you wired? You wearing a wire like your dad?"

"No, you stupid son-of-a-bitch," she snapped. "That's what you need, isn't it. You need the CDs. You need the recordings."

He pushed away from her and she stumbled, catching

herself on the range. Her wrists ached and her head pounded. Instinctively, she retreated as best she could. Butler was pacing the kitchen now and in the shadows, she could barely see his form cross in front of her.

"You've heard them?" he asked, stopping.

"Everyone has heard them."

His breath quickened. "You're lying. I want the recordings your father has."

"He doesn't have them. I do."

"Then things aren't looking good for you, Ms. Grady," he said.

"Those recordings are copied to a server. I couldn't tell you where it was located, and they've been shared with numerous law enforcement professionals," she said.

It was her best protection—let Butler think that there was no point in killing her. She prayed that it would work.

"I don't believe you," he said. "Those recordings are evidence of your father taking bribes. You wouldn't turn him in."

She laughed at him and heard his sharp intake of breath. "How do you know that? My father abandoned me more than twenty years ago. Why would I protect him?"

"To get the property he transferred to you. You're basically blackmailing him, too," Butler said, as if he'd already figured everything out. He shook his head. "Damn, I thought all these men would do anything to protect you, but it turns out, they just don't care that much."

Erin ignored him and tried to work her hand through the metal cuff.

"I told Will all he had to do was drop his investigation

and the charges against you would go away. Guess he wants that job in San Francisco more than he wants you," he said.

The words stung, but she kept her mouth shut. He was just needling her. Torturing her while he killed time.

Headlights shone into the kitchen as a car pulled into the driveway, and Erin's stomach dropped. It was Jerry, and he had no idea what he was getting into. His footsteps on the back porch steps heightened her panic and Erin kicked at the stove and started to yell, but Butler grabbed her and slapped a hand over her mouth.

She bit down on his hand as hard as she could, struggling against him.

"Erin!"

At Jerry's shout, Butler let go of her and reached for his holster.

"Gun!" Erin yelled.

Jerry dropped to the ground as Butler's gun went off and he came back up with his own weapon. Butler grabbed Erin and pressed the barrel against her temple.

"I don't think so, Chief."

Jerry held his hands up, his gun hanging loose from his finger. Slowly, he reached out to the kitchen table to set the gun down.

"What's the plan, Butler?"

"Throw me your keys," he said.

Jerry reached into his pocket and keeping his eyes on Butler, he tossed them across the room.

At the first touch of the metal to her skin, Erin had gone still. A silent calm filled her. This wasn't going to be her last moment on earth. It wasn't. She slowed her breathing, keeping her eyes on Jerry.

"The feds are involved now, Todd," Jerry said, sounding more resigned than angry. "It's over."

Butler gave a harsh laugh. "For you it's over. I'm moving on. Where are the recordings?"

Jerry shook his head. "They're gone. Stolen from my safe."

Butler let go of Erin enough to put the keys in his pocket and she scrambled to get away from him. She could only go about five feet, the length of the kitchen range, but he didn't seem to even notice her now.

"Just let Erin go," Jerry said. "I'm done. We both know that. You don't need to take her down with you."

Butler turned to Erin, his eyes narrowed. Then he swore under his breath and his jaw tightened. He slowly shook his head.

Time slowed as he raised the gun, the barrel tracking her body.

"No!" Jerry yelled, running forward.

Butler whirled and fired, and Jerry fell backward into the dining nook. Erin screamed and tugged at the handcuffs, her wrists stinging from the restraints. On the ground, ten feet away, her father lay in a growing pool of blood.

"Oh God, no!" she cried out, sobbing. She prayed someone heard the shots and called the police, then realized she was looking at the two highest-ranking members of the police department.

"Fuck," Butler swore, stomping out of the kitchen and toward the living room. She could hear him thrashing around, no longer trying to hide his presence.

Through her tears, she watched Jerry's chest heave with

effort as he clutched his abdomen. He needed a hospital, now.

"Jerry, stay with me," she said. His face contracted into a grimace. "I need you to stay focused. Hold the wound. Put pressure on it. Can you hear me?"

His head moved ever so slightly and he pressed his hands to the wound.

"That's good. Really good. Can you use your coat, press it against the wound?"

His fingers moved and gathered the fabric. He groaned at the effort, but did as she instructed. It would help, but it wasn't enough to save him. That would take a surgical team.

A slight whiff of smoke caught Erin's attention and she turned toward the living room, which was filling with white smoke. Butler stalked back into the kitchen, holstered his gun and gave the chief a mocking salute.

"No! You can't leave us here!"

The fire was starting to crackle now and Erin's eyes widened with panic. Her instincts kicked in again and she began pulling at the oven handle, screaming and crying.

Butler ignored her, stepped over her father, and walked out the back door.

Chapter Twenty-Five

"What do you mean, you lost her?" Glover shouted.

Will's jaw tensed and his blood pressure spiked, sending a stabbing pain through his head.

"She was here, then I fell asleep with her. When I woke up, she was gone."

Will's hands clenched and he paced the length of his living room. He lost her. He'd accepted that he'd messed things up with Erin beyond repair, but losing her like this? Letting her walk out, when the stakes were this high? He might not be able to convince her to forgive him, to trust him ever again, to ever love him. But he couldn't let Butler get to her.

"Where would she go? Her friend's house? Her family?" Glover looked at the couch and the floor in front of it, cluttered with papers from the FBI investigation, the laptop with the earbuds still attached. "This yours?"

"No. She was reading everything. I didn't think there was any harm in it. She's been helpful."

Will looked over the papers strewn about the floor, looking for something, anything that might point him in the right direction.

"I don't think she'd go to Bree's. She doesn't have her car," he said. "She wouldn't go to her mom's house because she wouldn't want to bring them trouble."

Her cell phone sat among the papers, plugged into a charger, and Will paused only a second before he picked it up and turned on the screen. She didn't have a password, so he went straight to her text messages. She hadn't sent anything in the last few hours. Then he checked her emails, clicking on the sent mail folder.

"Chief Grady's house," Will said, grabbing his keys. "She asked to meet him but he didn't reply. You go to the boat, I'll take the house."

He made the five-minute drive in half the time, parking on the sidewalk. He was out of his car and halfway across the lawn when he realized the orange glow in the windows wasn't from the house lights. Smoke billowed behind the windows.

"Erin!"

He ran up the steps, found the doorknob too hot to touch, and kicked at the door until it groaned and gave way. The heat that billowed out made him turn away, but he heard the faint reply inside.

"We're in here!"

Covering his mouth and nose, he ran into the house and followed the sound of Erin's voice through the eerie hellscape. His eyes burned and he tried not to breathe. The air in the kitchen was clearer because the backdoor was wide open. Erin was handcuffed to the oven door, which she'd opened all the way so she could lie on the floor. She looked up at him and then to the prone body by the door.

"Oh, God, baby. It's okay, I'm going to get you out of

here," he said, kneeling next to her.

He looked around for something to use to pry the door handle off the oven, settling on a long pair of barbecue tongs. Erin cried out, a desperate sound, as the tongs broke almost immediately.

"Erin, look at me," he said. Her eyes were wide with panic. "If I have to carry that oven out the door, I'm getting you out of here."

Will grabbed the handle and sat on the floor, his feet braced against the oven's base, and yanked backward, pulling with everything he had. The oven door groaned in protest and gave a little, but still held tight.

"Will." Jerry's voice was a low cough, but was just loud enough to hear over the flames. He looked over his shoulder at the chief, who was struggling to move.

He crawled across the floor, glancing up to find that he could no longer see the ceiling through the smoke. They had very little time to get out of the house.

"Keys." The word sounded more like a wet cough.

Jerry's hand fell to his belt and Will saw the glint of metal. He grabbed the keys, crawled back to Erin and with sweating, trembling fingers, unlocked one of the cuffs.

She slipped her wrist free and he pulled the cuffs through the bar, freeing her. As soon as the cuff slipped away, the pressure in his chest let up, as if steel bands had just fallen away.

They crawled toward Jerry. Erin pressed her fingers against his neck, checking for a pulse. Will knelt on the other side of him, by the door, and grabbed Jerry under the arms. He dragged the chief across the floor to the open door, while

Erin crawled along, keeping her hand on his stomach, where blood was steadily flowing out onto the floor.

As they reached the threshold, he finally heard the sirens. He yelled, which set off an aching cough from his chest, and heard an answering shout from a neighbor, who directed the paramedics to the back of the house. The firefighters swarmed them as he pulled Jerry out the door, and he and Erin were helped away from the burning house.

An oxygen mask was slapped over his face and his lungs ached as he tried to breathe it in. Erin was also being treated, but was struggling with the paramedics.

"Let me go see him!" she said, her voice hoarse from the smoke.

Will made his way through the growing crowd of first responders and pulled her into his arms. She looked up at him with wide eyes. Her face was streaked and sooty. And she was alive.

"They won't let me see him." The sob in her voice nearly broke him.

"I'll take you to him," he said, then muscled his way past the firefighters to the ambulance and helped her into the back. The paramedics let her in, but stopped him.

"We're out of room," he said. "Meet us there."

The doors shut and the ambulance sped away. Glover appeared out of nowhere and put a hand on his shoulder. "I'll get you there."

Will filled Glover in on what little he could piece together from Erin's panicked statements on the short drive to the hospital, including the most important piece—that Butler was still out there. They arrived to find Erin arguing with Dr.

Ashette about whether she could go into the surgical ward.

"Erin, you're not sterile. Please. Just wait here," the exasperated doctor begged. "I will take care of your father."

Will came up behind her and held her as she sagged against him. He flagged down the dark-haired nurse he'd met on his first visit to the ER.

"We need to get Erin checked out," he said.

"I'm fine," she whispered, her eyes vacant. "I want to see my dad."

He met Joan's eyes and they both shook their heads.

"You sound like you gargled glass," Joan said.

Will held up her battered and bloodied wrists.

Joan gasped. "You're coming with me, Erin."

After getting Erin cleaned up and checked over, they sat in the ER, stretched out over an empty row of plastic seats. He couldn't take his eyes off her, couldn't stop touching her to reassure himself that she was safe and mostly unharmed—at least physically.

"What happened in there?" he finally whispered, almost to himself. She was still in shock, and he didn't expect an answer.

But after a long moment, she began to tell him how deeply Butler's scheme ran. That Solstice was his company, not Grady's. That both men were taking money from Hastings. And exactly how Butler had trapped her in the house to die in a fire.

Will listened, resisting the urge to ask questions or press her for more details to give the FBI. He merely stroked her hair, still smoky from the fire, and let her talk and tried to tamp down the rage burning inside of him.

After what felt like an eternity before Dr. Ashette emerged to nod at Erin and give a thumbs up.

She rested her head against Will's chest and exhaled.

"Can we go home now?" he whispered.

She gripped his hand and nodded.

CHAPTER TWENTY-SIX

"Will!"

Erin jumped at the sound of the shout from the parking lot, and Will's arm tightened around her shoulders. He hadn't let go of her since they'd arrived at the hospital. Though she'd washed up in the staff bathroom, her skin was still gritty from the soot and she reeked of smoke. If she could just get home, she'd climb into the shower and stay there for a week.

Shane Glover walked toward them, illuminated by the parking lot's security lights. He wore a black flak jacket over his long-sleeved T-shirt and had a large gun strapped to his side.

"We have every road leaving Lost Coast Harbor blocked and are checking cars, searching homes where Butler may be hiding," he said. "But as of now, we don't have him. And I don't need to tell you that he's desperate."

A shiver ran through her body at the thought. Butler's world just crashed and burned and he had nothing to lose. He'd have to get out of town and fast.

"He took the chief's car," Will said.

Shane nodded. "Yeah. It was found abandoned down by the docks."

"The boat," Erin said. Her voice scraped her raw throat and sounded foreign.

"What about the boat?" Shane asked.

"If the roads are blocked, he could take Jerry's boat," she said. "He broke into it once. Why else would he be down there?"

Shane frowned. "We've got a team searching that area. They've been there for a few hours, since the car was found. We'll keep an eye on the *Winter Solstice*, though."

Shane handed Will a set of keys. "Take my car. I'll get yours and bring it to you. You guys heading back to your place?"

Erin shook her head. "I want to go home."

"That's not—"

"I miss my cat."

Will hugged her tighter. "I'll take you home."

Shane shook his head. "Fine. Just be careful. Call me if you see anything." He gave Erin a half-smile. "You're a tough little cookie."

She didn't feel tough. She was fragile, like a thin porcelain shell about to shatter into a thousand pieces. Like if she let go of Will's hand, or left his side, the smallest blow would do her in. Even the five-minute drive to her house set her nerves on edge, and she finally reached over and rested her hand on his leg to maintain contact. He immediately covered her hand with his, and his warmth seeped into her.

He parked the car in the driveway and helped her into the house. She walked straight to the slider and opened it, but the cat wasn't at his usual perch on her patio furniture. An automatic food dispenser was set up next to the water dish and she turned to Will.

He shrugged. "It was getting to be a pain in the ass to come feed him during the day. This seemed like a better solution until things calmed down. John Doe seems to like the regular feeding schedule."

A smile tugged at her lips as she went back to the house. Apparently, she had a cat now. A cat that Will had named and fed for her.

When she'd closed the door, Will locked it and pulled the curtains and then led her to the bathroom off her bedroom, where he started the water in the shower.

He undressed her as the steam started to fill the small room, gently navigating around the wraps covering her wrists. When she stepped under the warm water, he quickly stripped down and joined her.

"You don't have to—" she said, but he cut her off.

"Let me." His voice was gruff, low and reverberated through her.

He poured shampoo into his hand and gently worked the suds into her hair, his fingers massaging her scalp. Then he moved on to her body with a bar of soap, brushing his fingers across every inch of her skin. As the smoke and grime washed away, the numbness in which she'd been wrapped faded, and the horror of that evening filtered into her brain.

Her breath hitched and her body shook at the memory of Jerry on the floor, bleeding out, and the consuming panic of not being able to reach him.

"Shh, baby," Will whispered, and she realized he was

holding her tight against him. And she was sobbing. "It's okay. I've got you."

Through heaving sobs, she tried to explain that Jerry had sacrificed himself to save her, but Will shushed her and held her until the shower went cold. He dried them off and carried her to the bedroom, laying her down and climbing under the covers with her.

Shivers continued to rack her body. Will held her until the shaking slowed, until her body warmed and the only sound was their breathing—his deep and measured and her own ragged and shallow.

"I'm sorry," Erin whispered. Her head was resting on Will's arm, her back against his chest. It felt good having something solid to lean against. "I'm okay. You don't have to stay."

His breath caressed her ear. "Do you want me to leave?"

No. God, never. She wanted his strength and warmth. His touch. His support. For as long as possible.

She shook her head. "No."

"Good, because I didn't want to have to fight you on that," he said, pressing his lips against her temple. "I'm not going anywhere."

It was the last thing she heard before drifting off.

WILL LISTENED TO HER BREATHING UNTIL IT BECAME steady and slow and her body relaxed. When she tensed, he held her tighter and whispered in her ear until the nightmarish images faded from her mind and she slumped again. It didn't seem to matter what he said, as long as he kept talking. Somewhere in Erin's subconscious was a history of his sports achievements dating back to grammar school, a list of failed relationships that she'd learn about eventually anyway, and detailed descriptions of Patton family members.

When he trusted that he wouldn't wake her, he eased out of the bed and slipped on the pants he'd been wearing earlier. The stench of smoke still hung on them, roiling his stomach.

He tucked the blankets around Erin, then took his phone into the living room and checked for any news from Shane. There was nothing from him, and that uncertainty made Will even more tense.

Butler was out there, trapped in Lost Coast Harbor, unless he'd been able to steal a car and get out on a back road. He was a cop, he'd know the terrain. He wouldn't be able to bluff his way through a roadblock. Every uniformed officer in Lost Coast Harbor knew him.

A light tapping on the patio caught his attention and he pulled the curtains aside. John Doe sat in front of the food dish, pawing at the empty tray below the dispenser. Will unlocked the door and stepped out into the dark.

"You hungry, John?"

The black cat rubbed against his legs and purred, as Will bent down to release the dry cat food into the dish.

A larger black shape in his peripheral vision caught his attention and he started to turn, but the force of a blow to the back of his head propelled him forward, onto the concrete patio and into a different darkness.

Chapter Twenty-Seven

A raspy tongue bathed his face and Will reached up to push it away. His head felt like it was being split by a maul, and he had never been so cold. With great effort, he opened his eyes and saw John Doe watching him. It took several seconds for the scene to register.

He was lying on the patio in Erin's backyard, half dressed, and his head was trying to split from the rest of his body. Maneuvering himself to a sitting position, Will blinked to clear his vision, which was slightly doubled.

He'd come out to feed the cat. Then…

Fuck.

He jumped up, his head spinning at the effort, and steadied himself on the furniture until he could walk the few steps to the door.

"Erin," he called.

The house was empty and he staggered toward the bedroom. A heavy, toxic cloud hung in the hall, burning his eyes. Pepper spray.

Fuck.

The bed was empty.

She was gone, but not without a fight.

~

Erin's eyes darted between the road and the gun in Butler's lap. He was scanning the road through swollen eyes and she took some satisfaction that she'd managed to hurt him when he'd pulled her from the bed. She'd also suffered from some of the spray, but he'd taken a hit to the chest and had to abandon his shirt before he wrestled her out to Shane Glover's car and forced her to drive away from the house.

Where was Will?

There had been no sign of him in the house, but he wouldn't have left. Butler wasn't talking to her except for tense orders, and that made her stomach clench in fear. Had he hurt Will? How had he gotten in? She'd finally dropped into an exhausted sleep, only to be awakened by Butler yanking her out of bed and throwing clothes at her. She'd been so disoriented, it had been sheer luck that she saw the pepper spray on the floor.

But not lucky enough.

"Slow down," Butler said, and she eased her foot off the gas, slowly cruising down the dark coastal road that passed the docks. The only other traffic was police cruisers, highway patrol cars, and sheriff's vehicles. The roads out of town were being monitored, Shane had said. Butler was learning that the hard way, directing Erin to take different routes—all heavily patrolled.

Butler fumbled with the wallet in his hand and Erin caught a glimpse of Will's ID, which made her stomach turn over. Butler wiped the card on his pants leg to remove a smear of something that looked like blood from the driver's license. He pulled a baseball cap low, covering as much of his face as possible.

"When we get to the roadblock, you're going to do what I say," he said.

She didn't answer, but watched him pick up the gun. He pushed the barrel into her ribs as the flashing lights directed her to pull to the side. An unfamiliar officer walked up to the driver's side and she rolled down the window.

"I'll need to see your identification, please," he said, flashing a badge that said he was with the FBI.

Erin handed over her license, and Butler did the same, giving the agent Will's ID. The man glanced at both, shone the lights in their faces, and then handed them back.

"You're Chief Grady's daughter?"

Erin nodded as the gun pressed painfully into her side. "Yes."

He gave her a grim smile.

"And Mr. Patton, you're with the district attorney's office, right?"

"That's right," Butler said. "We're getting out of town before the media shows up. I left my contact information with the case agent, so he can reach us."

The agent nodded and waved to the right, where a car was being searched.

"No problem, just pull into the right lane up there and pop the trunk," he said. "They'll get you on your way."

"Why do we have to do that?" Butler asked.

"We're searching every car," he said. "It'll just take a minute."

Her palms damp, she navigated the vehicle to the lane

marked with flashing lights, where two cars were idling. Officers checked the backseat and then the trunk of the first car in line, shining flashlights through the windows and underneath the car, before slamming the trunk and waving it on.

They wouldn't find anyone hiding in this car, she thought. If the officers didn't recognize Butler, whose features were swollen from the pepper spray, they might wave them through, too.

She dropped a hand from the steering wheel to her lap and Butler jabbed at her again.

"If you reach for the door, I will shoot you," he said. His tone was so casual, it could have been mistaken for any other conversation, except for the content of his words. "You saw how fun that was, getting shot in the abdomen. You're a nurse, so you understand what that means. The bullet will pierce several major organs, damaging all of them, most beyond repair. You'll bleed out in minutes."

She swallowed, knowing he was right.

"I'm not going anywhere," she said, irritated.

He just needed to get through the checkpoint, then he wouldn't need her any longer. But that didn't mean he'd let her go.

Her head throbbed and she rubbed her forehead, drawing an impatient poke with the gun again.

"Stop fidgeting," Butler snapped.

The car in front rolled forward and stopped and Erin followed. Butler's leg bounced with nervous energy and he scanned the scene, watching the cops open the trunk and search under the car in front of them.

An officer walked toward the passenger side and Butler's

attention was diverted, so Erin slid her hand to the door handle, grasping it. Slowly, she started to pull it up the handle.

Brake lights flashed on the car in front. Once, twice—and there was a sudden flurry of activity and the car door flew open, jerking her with it. Strong arms encircled her and pulled her to the ground and rolled her away from the vehicle, keeping her shielded from the ring of agents surrounding the car. She inhaled the warm scent and her brain registered it was Will, lying heavily on top of her, his thick flak jacket against her body.

"Drop the gun! Drop the gun!"

Another set of hands helped her up and they were whisked away, her view blocked by more men in black vests. They crouched behind a van, Will pulling her tight against him until the shouting became muted, and radios crackled.

"Suspect in custody."

Will expelled a breath that stirred her hair, and he kept her pinned against him. "Did he hurt you? Are you okay?"

She managed to shake her head and he held her at arm's length, studying her, his jaw tense.

"I'm fine, Will," Erin said, reaching up and putting a hand along his face.

He didn't look like he believed her and ran his hands over her, as if checking for fractures. "Are you sure?"

Shane Glover appeared at their side and reached down, pulling Erin to her feet. Will followed, but slowly and then stumbled.

"You're hurt," she said, trying to determine the source. He swayed and she zeroed in on his head. She reached up and held his face. His eyes were on hers but glassy, and she felt behind his neck, and then gently moved her hands up until he tensed.

"You got hit."

He nodded, giving her a slight smile. "I'm okay now."

She frowned. "You're not okay. Did Butler hit you?"

"I'm fine." He pulled her close, smashing her against the hard vest.

"I thought I lost you," he whispered, and her heart thumped at the words.

"You found me," she said, ignoring the painful crush against the bullet-proof material that separated them. "How did you find me?"

"I would never let him take you from me," he said. "And the car was under surveillance since it dodged the first checkpoint."

Erin squeezed her eyes shut, trying to make the world disappear, make it just her and Will and that promise in his voice.

"Sorry to break this up," Shane said. "I need to take your statement, Erin."

She nodded, still numb, but the adrenaline in her system was starting to rouse her from the shock. Around her was chaos, but as long as Will was touching her, she was fine. Everything would be fine.

"Will, there you are." A man walked out of the crowd, tall and lean and wearing the same vest as the others, but over a dress shirt with the sleeves pushed up. He was about Will's height, but older, with dark hair that was threaded with silver.

"Spencer," Will said, stepping forward to shake his hand.

"Erin, this is Spencer Bourne, from the San Francisco office of the U.S. Attorney."

He shook her hand and smiled. "Ms. Grady, I am very sorry for all you've been through."

She nodded, not sure how to respond, since he knew a lot about her, and she knew nothing about him.

"Spencer is the lead prosecutor on the Hastings case," Will said. "I'm sorry, love. I need to go with him. Shane's going to take care of you."

He turned her so she was facing him. He was leaving? Now?

"It's all right. I'll be back as soon as I can."

He bent down and kissed her, lingering over her lips. When he did that, she could almost forgive him for leaving.

"Will," she whispered.

"Yes, love?"

"Get your head checked," she said.

His smile grew and he nodded, swaying slightly. Her irritation at being left with Shane fell away and she gripped his hand and she smiled. "Promise me."

He brushed her hair from her face and rested his forehead against hers. "I promise."

Then he kissed her again and she didn't care that the entire police force and every other law enforcement agency was watching. His gentle exploration of her lips lit her on fire, made her forget the trauma and terror of the last few hours. Made her believe that everything was going to be okay. Promised her a new life.

And then he was gone.

CHAPTER TWENTY-EIGHT

Another goddamn rainy day. Erin had no idea why she was disappointed at the weather. It just didn't seem right everything looked so dreary after she'd just watched Todd Butler being put in cuffs, had her arrest warrant recalled, and confirmed that she could return to work next week. Things were infinitely better this week than last week. Her mother and Alan had returned last night and she'd gotten to see Leanne settled in at home, among her children and her paintings. She'd be able to continue her recovery at home.

Colin and Hayley were relieved to have the family back together and were up to their usual trouble. Hayley badgered Erin into teaching her how to parallel park, and Colin needed her help on a science project on DNA. It was almost like the last couple of weeks hadn't happened.

She'd gotten what she wanted—a return to her normal life.

And damn if that wasn't disappointing.

It had been four days since she'd seen Will walk off with the federal prosecutor, leaving her behind. Without even a backward glance in her direction. Four days and not a single word from him.

She could take a hint. She gritted her teeth as she pulled the Jeep into the parking space. It wasn't going to kill her or anything. The phantom pain at the thought of his rejection would fade, and she'd move forward. She always did.

Rain gathered on the heavy canvas awning over the shops and then gathered and rolled off, the fat drops hitting Erin's head as she ran from the Jeep and into the shelter of The Sweet Spot. The warm, sweet-scented air inside took the chill off, and she wiped the rain from her face and unfastened her coat.

"Erin!" Annabel waved from the back with a cheerful smile. "I'll be right out."

The bakery was empty and quiet, and Erin took a seat while she waited. When the baker returned, she was carrying a pink bakery box wrapped with string and set it on the counter.

"I didn't order anything," Erin said. "I'm just here to pick up bread. And maybe a cupcake."

Annabel nodded. "I have some fresh-baked sourdough. Will that do?"

At Erin's nod, she bagged the bread, and then put the dessert on a plate and brought it out to her table. She went to the front of the store and flipped the sign, throwing the lock on the door. When she returned, she sat across from Erin, resting her elbows on the table.

"I'm really sorry for everything you've gone through," Annabel said.

Erin smiled. "Thank you, that's really nice of you to say. I guess the worst of it's behind me now."

"Is the Chief going to be okay?"

Erin nodded. "He's recovering."

She didn't want to even think about Jerry's future. He'd be in the hospital for some time, healing from the gunshot wound to the gut. After that, it was anyone's guess. He'd basically confessed to taking bribes. She imagined he would be sent to prison. The thought made her sick. Even though his absence in her life wouldn't be any different than the last twenty years, this felt far worse than that passive rejection.

"And your mother's well?"

"She's fine. She's home now," Erin said, picking up the cupcake. It was topped with a rich chocolate glaze and was one of Annabel's specialties, but today she just wasn't tempted. She set it back down.

"And I heard that Chief Grady was going to give you some land for the clinic before, you know, all this," Annabel said with a gentle wave of her hand.

"Yes, that's true. If he's found guilty, then the government may take the property." Another disappointment that she was just going to have to get over.

Annabel bit her lip, then stood and walked over to the counter and picked up the bakery box.

"Well, I have something that might help you with that," she said.

Erin's heart swelled at the sweet gesture of kindness. Annabel wasn't the only one who had reached out to her in the last few days. Dr. Ashette had raised hell at the hospital until she'd been cleared and reinstated. Maddie and Gabe lured her over for a home-cooked meal. Even Bree suddenly became clingy, insisting on hanging out with Erin, which she knew was simply an excuse to keep an eye on her.

She didn't mind the extra support. Being with her friends had helped her through the last few days.

"That was so thoughtful of you, Annabel," Erin said, untying the string and lifting the lid. She looked into the pastry box and froze.

It was filled with bundles of cash, fat wads of bills secured by rubber bands.

"It's money," Erin said.

"Yes. For the clinic."

"Oh my God, Annabel."

Erin looked up, not bothering to conceal her shock.

"I thought it would help you get the place up and running," Annabel said, her red lips turned up in a warm smile.

"But—I thought it was cake."

"I hope you're not disappointed," Annabel teased.

Erin stared at the pile of cash—bundles of bills of varying denominations. So many. One hand flew up to cover her mouth, as she tried to calculate how many bundles and what that would add up to. She couldn't stop looking at it, as if it would disappear if she looked away.

"How much is in here?"

"Fifty thousand dollars."

All the air in her lungs left in a hurry and Erin leaned back in the chair, finally focusing on Annabel, perched on the chair opposite her.

"It will help you, right?"

Erin managed to nod. "This is so generous. I wasn't expecting— How— Why?"

Annabel shrugged and smiled, then reached across the

table and put her hands on Erin's. "Because I realized I had a bit of money lying around, and I wanted to do something good with it."

Erin blinked back the tears that stung her eyes. *Fuck*. All of sudden she was a crier. This was a change she could do without.

"I don't know what to say," she said. "Thank you so much."

"I'm afraid there's one condition," Annabel said. "Please don't tell anyone where the money came from."

Erin paused, giving Annabel a long look. She took a deep breath, and then one more.

"Is there something I should know?" she asked. "Because I've recently lost two large donations because the donors were arrested and the gifts they promised were illegal."

Annabel shook her head. "I just want to stay anonymous. That's all."

Erin released her pent-up breath. "Good, because I'd really hate to see you go to jail, too."

Annabel blinked at her, taken aback. "Well, of course. That would be awful." She glanced at Erin's plate. "I'll get you a box for the cupcake. You can take it with you."

Annabel packaged up the baked good while Erin stood at the table still staring at the box of cash. It couldn't be legal. But Annabel seemed so nice. She snuck a look at the woman behind the counter—her blonde curls tied back and a dusting of flour on her apron. She made pastries, breads, and soup. Maybe she just sold a whole lot more of it than anyone knew. Erin tried to calculate the profit on a cupcake and how many sales would result in a profit of fifty thousand dollars, but her mind was too rattled to do math.

"I guess you'll want a receipt," Erin said.

Annabel smiled. "When you get around to it."

She brought the bag around and handed it to Erin. "Take care, Erin. Let me know what else I can do."

Erin laughed, though the sound could have been mistaken for a suppressed sob. "I think you've done plenty."

A few minutes later, she found herself sitting in the Jeep, still parked at the curb, just staring at the box on the passenger seat. Her phone beeped, startling her, and she reached for her purse. Disappointment flooded her again when she checked the caller ID.

"Hi, Hayley," she said.

"Mom says dinner is at seven. Can you come early and show me how to drive a stick shift?"

Erin blanched at the thought. "Uh, maybe it would be better to meet on the weekend and do that. We'll go to the high school. The parking lot will be empty."

And there would be nothing for Hayley to smash into.

"Okay. Don't forget the bread," Hayley said.

Erin disconnected the call and glanced at the passenger seat again.

The brief call had been enough to yank her out of her self-pity, at least for now. She ran a finger under her eyes to make sure her mascara hadn't run again. The image in the rearview mirror reflected a pair of tired eyes, skin more pale than usual, and a deep sadness that she could no longer hide from herself. She was a mess. But it wasn't like there was anyone to impress.

Erin started the Jeep and pulled into what passed for traffic in Lost Coast Harbor, heading back to her house. But instead of continuing straight to her street, she found herself turning right a couple of blocks early.

She wasn't driving by Will's house because that would be pathetic. And she was a strong, independent woman. A woman who did not cruise by her ex-lover's house to see if he was there.

And yet, that's exactly where she found herself. Parked across the street from his house, where a moving truck was backed into the driveway.

All the hurt inside, all the heartache, heartbreak, sorrow at her lost chance at love—turned to rage in an instant. Four days after declaring that she was worth fighting for, he was moving out. Back to his old job, maybe. Or to San Francisco, for that federal position he'd been promised if he busted Jerry.

Well, good for him.

She jumped out of the Jeep, slammed the door behind her, and stalked up his driveway. Will walked out of the house and into the empty garage, just as she reached the open garage door.

"Erin," he said, coming to a stop at the sight of her.

She shook her head. "I can't believe you."

He tilted his head slightly, his hazel eyes registering that this wasn't a friendly, casual visit. "I was going to call you…"

If she'd had something in her hands, she would have thrown it at his head.

"Bullshit," she spat out. "From where, your new job? Your new home? Jesus, I didn't even think it was possible to rent a moving van in Lost Coast Harbor that fast. But I guess when you're motivated—"

Will moved so quickly across the last few yards between them that it stunned her.

"Erin, no."

"Oh, my God. I'm such an idiot. I mean, I know, you were just trying to get to my father, but damn it, I trusted you—"

Will's hands were in her hair, on her face, and she tried to pull away, desperate to get back in her car and flee. This was such a mistake. A long series of mistakes.

He wouldn't let her. He wrapped one strong arm around her waist, and kept his other hand at her face. His thumb stroked her bottom lip and sent a tingle through her traitorous body with the soft brush of his skin.

"I was motivated," he said, his voice low. "Very motivated."

His eyes softened as he looked at her. She stilled, her emotions at war. She wanted to believe him. Wanted to trust him. Wanted to put herself in his hands and risk everything.

And yet—he'd lied to her, or at least omitted some damn important information, and then run off without a word when everything fell to hell around her.

Not letting go of her, Will turned her so she was facing the back of the moving van. The door was open and it was packed to the ceiling with furniture and boxes.

"It isn't much easier to get a moving van in Ukiah, let alone pack up my storage unit," he said. "I got back to you as soon as I could."

He was behind her, his arms wrapped around her waist, his head bent down so he was whispering in her ear. Erin's eyes filled with tears that she had to blink away. Still, she had a hard time grasping what he was telling her.

"I have a couple of friends coming over tomorrow to help me unpack," he said, his hot breath stirring the hair by her ear, sending tremors through her.

"You're not leaving?" Erin managed to ask, her voice betraying her dread of the answer.

"Not on your life," Will said, turning her back to him and tilting her face up to his. His expression was serious, his eyes focused on hers. "I'm sorry, Erin. I should have told you everything. You deserved to know what was going on."

She looked down and found herself staring at his chest, the muscles bunched under the tight T-shirt. Erin tried not to think about how it had felt to run her hands over his skin, feel those muscles contract under her touch. That wasn't helping sustain her anger. She could feel the rage slipping away, almost as fast as it rose.

"Your, uh—Jerry is cooperating with the FBI. He's going to plead guilty to a misdemeanor charge of accepting improper payments." Will smoothed her hair away from her face. "He's resigning. May already have submitted his resignation letter."

The news made her unexpectedly sad. Jerry Grady might as well have been a stranger for all she knew of him. Except that he wasn't. She had wanted to believe that he was a good person, just a terrible father and husband. She still did, despite the evidence to the contrary.

"What about Butler?"

"He's facing a lot more charges, and a lot more time. But with your father's recordings and testimony, he doesn't have much of a defense. When you add in the attempted murder charges, he's going to spend the rest of his life in prison."

Erin felt her heart constrict. "And my father?"

Will's arms tightened around her. "Far less. Maybe no prison time. He's agreed to give up the money he made from Hastings, but some of his deals—we can't prove they were in exchange for official acts. They were friends from a long time ago, and they could just be joint investments that benefited Grady as well as Hastings. He was required to disclose all of them, and he didn't. But the statute of limitations on most of the early transactions is long past. He won't be punished for that."

The news that Jerry wouldn't be spending the rest of his life in prison made the tight band of pressure around her chest ease a little.

"When you're ready, if you want, I think he'd like to talk to you," Will said, resting his forehead on hers.

He wiped a tear away and Erin realized she was crying. Damn it. A few weeks ago, had she thought about it, she was pretty sure she would have said she was happy. She wasn't entirely sure that she had been. But at least then, she hadn't felt this vulnerable.

"You don't have to talk to him if you don't want to. As soon as he can, Jerry says he's moving. He's invited us to visit him in Mexico," Will said.

Erin shook her head. "I can't think about that right now."

He pressed his lips to her forehead and the gentle touch was a balm to her raw nerves.

"You don't have to do that, either," he said. "Erin, love, I am sorry. I'm sorry for everything you've been through because of me. I'm sorry I dragged you into this. Butler would have left you alone if I hadn't started digging into his cases."

She shook her head. "You didn't know what he would do, or what he was doing to Jerry."

He held her at arm's length, his hands on her shoulders, staring into her eyes. His expression was pained. "It's not just that. I thought I was going to get in, do my job, and move on."

"I know. To the job in San Francisco."

Will shook his head. "I turned it down."

"Why? You said that was your dream job." Something that felt like happiness started to bubble up inside her. But it was followed closely by worry, a fear that he'd regret his decision to give up his dream.

He shrugged. "I thought it was. But it turns out that there's plenty of work to do here. And I found something—someone, who gives my life meaning, more than any job could."

Erin bit her lip and watched him warily. She opened her mouth to speak, but then closed it, unsure what to say. He hadn't said the words she wanted to hear. The words she just realized that she needed to hear. She wasn't willing to settle for less. Not after Will had convinced her that she deserved more.

"And I hope that she feels the same way about me," Will said, cupping her face in his warm palm, his thumb brushing her cheek.

"How do you feel?" Erin asked, cautiously.

He exhaled. "I've fallen hard for her. She makes me feel like no one else has. And I want to spend my days making her happy. Taking care of her. Waking up with her. Fighting and making up with her. And loving her."

He bent down and kissed her, his lips soft.

"Loving you," he whispered. "I love you, Erin."

"Oh." The breath escaped her lungs in a rush.

His mouth tightened and he started to talk, but then stopped and took a breath.

"I know I screwed this up. But I'm not running away. I'm staying here. I want to be with you. Whatever I have to do to fix this, I'll do it."

"You saved my life. Twice. You saved my father's life."

"That's not—"

She pressed a finger to his lips. "For whatever sins you think you committed, I have long since forgiven you."

She stood on her toes and wrapped her arms around his neck. Will's arms slowly embraced her, his breath on her neck. She closed her eyes and inhaled the clean scent that was unique to him, letting herself relax into him.

He was still here. He wasn't going anywhere.

He loved her.

Roughly, he broke away but kept his hands on her waist. "Do not move. Do not run off. Just stay right here."

He waited until she nodded. When he started to close up the truck, she realized that she hadn't locked the Jeep when she'd stormed off in her temper tantrum, and had left fifty thousand dollars in a bakery box on her passenger seat. She ran across the street, grabbed the bakery boxes and her purse, and locked the doors. When she returned, Will took the boxes from her, and then closed the garage door behind them.

"What's in here?" he asked.

"Cupcakes," she said, and pulled him close to her. Maybe

she should tell him about the cash donation, but then he'd want to talk about it, and that was not what she wanted at that moment.

He ushered her into the house, pulled her through the laundry room and into the living room, now cluttered with boxes.

He dropped the bakery boxes on a dining room table that she'd never seen before and turned to her, taking both her hands in his.

The tension she'd been carrying dissolved as soon as his arms encircled her. She rested her head against his chest.

"I didn't mean it," she said.

"You didn't mean what?"

"When I said I didn't trust you, the other night. I didn't mean that. I didn't trust myself not to fall for you," Erin whispered. "Can we start over?"

His arms tightened. "We could, but I figure we've been through the worst and things can only get easier now."

She smiled and tilted her head back to look at him. "That's a nice way of spinning it. I bet juries love you."

Will grinned. "Speaking of that, my boss is putting me on a committee to look into whether we need to expand the courts in Lost Coast Harbor, since there's been such an uptick in crime here."

"Is that good?" Erin asked. "Would you get to do more of the trials?"

He nodded. "It's very good."

Erin looked around the living room, surprised at how much warmer the dining room table and area rugs made the room. "You have furniture."

"I figured that it was time to unpack, since I'm making Lost Coast Harbor my home," he said. His hands roamed down her back and pressed her against his solid body. "And all that furniture? I intend to break all of it in with you, love."

He turned her, so she was facing the dining room. His arms tightened around her, and his breath brushed her ear. "That table? I am going to devour your body there."

His teeth scraped against her neck and an urgent need grew at his touch.

"And that ottoman? I'm taking you bent over that."

Her knees went weak and she fell back against him.

"Don't forget the kitchen," she whispered.

"God, yes," he said, his voice low. "But right now, I just need you. I don't care where, or how, but I have missed you."

His hands were tugging impatiently at her jacket, then her clothes. Erin grabbed his shirt and pulled it over his head, running her hands up his chest, then down to the button on his jeans. They stumbled down the short hall to the bedroom, a trail of clothes behind them, until they were at the foot of the bed. Erin was wearing only a silver-gray lace bra and panties.

Erin gripped his back, her knees nearly giving out as he lowered the lace and his tongue found her nipple. Her hand moved down his back, roaming over his hot skin and hard muscles.

Will fumbled with the clasp on the back of her bra and then with an impatient sigh, turned her around and unfastened it. He pulled her against his chest and kept her pinned to him, her bare back against his chest, his hands removing the scraps of lace and satin. Long strokes of his hands on her skin, across her stomach, lower, to the lace now wet with her desire. He slipped a hand under the lace, his fingers teasing her.

He groaned into her neck and she arched, rubbing against the bulge in his jeans. "I need you, Erin, now."

He spun her around again and she bit her lip at the sight of him, shirtless, the muscles of his chest and abdomen beckoning her to touch, explore. She pressed her lips against his hot skin, flicked her tongue against his nipple, then reached for the half-undone fly. Slowly, she moved down his body, pushing his jeans and boxers down, until she was kneeling in front of him, his cock in her hands.

So warm, so hard, and so thick. She touched her tongue to him, tasting, teasing. The muscles in his thighs bunched and she slid her lips over the head, swirled her tongue, and heard him exhale, as if in pain. His hands were in her hair, but she controlled the movement, easing him into her mouth, taking as much as she could. She gripped him, using her hand to stroke him. He jerked and groaned, the sound making her sex clench with anticipation.

"Too much," he gasped, pulling her to her feet and kissing her. "I need to be inside you. I need you around me. Now."

The silvery lace panties were the only piece of clothing left between them and Will hooked his fingers in the waistband and slid them over her hips, letting them drop to the floor. She stepped out of them and he pulled her close, running a hand over her hair and then down her body with long, light strokes that made her tingle and ache.

"So beautiful," he murmured, his hands stopping at her waist, lifting her onto the bed and following her down. "I missed you. Missed tasting you. Hearing you say my name."

He bent his head and kissed her, a sweet kiss that made her insides quiver. And then it deepened, and she pulled him closer, her hands in his hair. The quiver grew to a quake when his tongue glided against hers and his fingers tweaked her nipple.

"I'm not going anywhere," he whispered, his hands continuing a path down her body.

His hand cupped her sex, pressing against her gently, then slowly, he began to stroke her, teasing her until she arched against him with a ragged cry.

"I'm home," he whispered in her ear.

He pulled away long enough to find a condom and roll it on, with Erin's shaky hands helping him.

The first thrust lit her nerves afire. Every bit of her came alive. She took his face in her hands and kissed him, her nerves firing again with the warm slide of his tongue against hers.

When he met her gaze, her heart leapt.

"I love you, too," she said.

His eyes softened with relief and he took one of her hands, twining their fingers together. He drove into her and she arched, her hips rising to meet him.

"It doesn't count if you say it when I'm inside you," he said.

"Then I'll tell you again later," she gasped. "Now kiss me again."

He growled and grabbed her other hand, stretching both of them above her head, his full weight resting on her. His lips, his tongue, his teeth teasing her neck, moving up to her lips.

When he brushed his lips across hers, a spark lit within her. And when he slipped his tongue between her lips, sweeping her mouth, the spark grew into a flame.

"More," she whispered.

His hands tightened on hers, their fingers tangled, and their bodies moved together. She wrapped her legs tighter around him, taking him deeper.

"Always, love," he said, his words floating on a breath that brushed her neck.

He released her hands and pushed himself up, pulled her hips off the mattress, filling her with a thrust that made her cry out. The release hit her like a wave, rolling her and consuming her and pinning her down. Will's body shuddered. At his hoarse moan, another wave hit her. When she came up for air, panting, gasping, he was there, his arms around her, holding her tight against him.

He buried his face in her neck. "I want to take care of you, love."

Her heart swelled at his words. "I don't need you to take care of me. I just need you to love me."

"I can do that," he said, raising his face to kiss her. "Just ignore all the times I'm taking care of you."

She smiled. "I can do that."

Chapter Twenty-Nine

Erin sat on the picnic table, rested her feet on the bench, and sipped her latte. She was a safe distance away from the Jeep that bucked like a championship bull at a rodeo. As the vehicle lurched across the empty church parking lot, she could see Will's hand gripping the dash as he instructed Hayley on using a clutch.

It was his penance, he said, for keeping her from her family's dinner. When it was clear they weren't going to make it out of the bedroom, Erin had called and made her excuses. And her failure to make the family obligation was met with no dire consequences—her parents merely shrugged and told her to come by the house when she had time. Then she and Will shared the cupcake for dinner and went back to the bedroom. And they stayed there for the next twenty-four hours, until it was clear they'd have to put on clothes and leave the house or risk starvation.

If Hayley hadn't called at six in the morning to beg her for a driving lesson, Erin would have been just fine locking herself in the house with Will for the foreseeable future. Eventually, of course, they would have to rejoin the rest of the world. Will had taken the rest of the week off. Erin wasn't scheduled to return to work until Monday. It was too much to hope that by then some other scandal would have erupted to eclipse the spectacular drama in her life, and she wasn't looking forward to that part.

The Jeep hopped across the parking lot again and Erin cringed at the sound of the gears grinding. She checked the time on her phone, and saw a text from Valerie Childs.

Rob Katri is checked in at rehab.

She smiled and sent a reply, thanking Valerie for the update. Erin had pressed hard for an alternative to jailing Rob after Valerie had arrested him. To her surprise, the detective agreed and had found a residential facility in the Bay Area, where he'd get medical help for his addiction and treatment for his mental health issues while his burglary case wound through the system.

The Jeep made a stuttering roll back to where Erin sat, and she stood and walked to the driver's side.

"You've got to be in class in fifteen minutes," she said, helping her sister out and then herding her into the back seat.

"Did you see? I made it to second gear!"

"You did great, Hayley," Will said, and hardly even sounded like he was lying.

"Next time, can we go out on the road?"

"Hmm-mm," Erin said, desperately trying not to commit to anything. "So, when does softball season start?"

"We start conditioning next week. I'm playing shortstop again. Coach Dyer says my arm isn't controlled enough to be pitcher. I think he's wrong, but I like playing shortstop, so it's okay," Hayley said, and then launched into a rapid-fire monologue about her teammates. With luck, she'd be distracted enough to drop the subject of taking Erin's Jeep anywhere near a road.

Will reached across the seats and squeezed her hands in a silent thank you for the diversion. She returned the squeeze and smiled, then pulled over in front of the high school to let Hayley out.

"Thanks, Erin," Hayley said and gave Erin a hug. She waved through the open door. "Thank you for the lesson, Will. Nice meeting you. You coming to dinner Sunday? It's Colin's turn to cook and he's making lasagna. You should come."

She was gone with a toss of her long hair before Will do more than wave.

"Wow. She has a lot of energy," he said as Erin climbed into the driver's seat. She pulled away from the curb and started toward the town square.

"Did she talk the whole time she was driving?"

"Yes, when she wasn't screaming in abject terror. Oh, wait, that was me."

Erin laughed and leaned over to kiss him. "Thank you. That was far beyond the call of duty."

"You're welcome. Can we go back to bed now?"

She bit her lip. "Ah, actually, I told Bree and Maddie that we'd meet them for breakfast at the diner. Is that okay?"

"Is Bree going to try and kill me?"

"No. She likes you now. Saving me from a homicidal madman got you a lot of brownie points," Erin said. "And then I need to meet with Barney Minton about the clinic."

He smoothed a hand across her hair. "I'm sorry you lost the property."

Erin shook her head. "It's okay. I think things are going to work out."

She hadn't told him about the bakery box full of cash, which was currently stashed in his freezer. He might be a little suspicious about such a large anonymous donation, so it seemed a better idea to keep that to herself. But with Annabel's gift, Erin figured she had enough to move forward and lease a building. There was an empty space in the medical complex across from the hospital that she thought might work, with a little renovation.

"Let me know what I can do," Will said. "I want to help you with this project."

Erin spied an open parking space and pulled in, already distracted by the epic to-do list she was constructing in her mind.

"I'm going to need painters," she said. "And help finding furniture, moving it in, and I guess I need to order signs, and probably a thousand other things I haven't even thought of yet."

"Make a list. I'm all yours," Will said.

Through the diner's window, she saw Maddie and Gabe were already in the corner booth. She reached over and took his hand.

"You'll like Gabe and Maddie. Gabe's preparing for law school."

Will unfastened his seatbelt and reached for her, cupping her neck and then drawing her close and kissing her, and her insides got all warm and melty at the touch.

"I'm sure I'll like your friends," he said. "You're sure I don't have anything to fear from Bree?"

She shook her head. "No, once I told her that I was in love with you, you didn't have anything to fear from her. All her threats about messing with your life were just a bluff."

"When did you tell her that?" he asked.

Heat crept up her cheeks. "At her cabin. After we broke into the boat, when you and Bree were at each other's throats."

He tilted his head. "When you pulled her into the kitchen?"

"I saw you on the porch, and you were so angry and worried and I was so happy to see you, even though I was still mad at you," she said, with a small shrug. "I knew."

Will's eyes softened and he kissed her again, like he was savoring her. "I don't know how I deserve someone who could love me at that moment, but I'm not letting you go."

She smiled and raised her chin to answer him, but was interrupted by a knock on the window behind her. She turned and saw Bree, arms crossed and eyes narrowed.

"Pancakes now. Kissing later."

Then she grinned and waved at Will before walking into the restaurant.

"Nothing to fear, huh?" he asked.

"Not with me at your side," Erin said.

"Then I'm definitely keeping you around."

Erin placed a hand along his face and stared into his warm hazel eyes, in no hurry to venture out into the real world just yet. But when she did, it would be with this man, who loved her.

Acknowledgments

I have a long list of people to thank for helping me to get to The End in this book.

At the very top of that list is Lily Danes—my co-conspirator, aider, abettor, creative force, and very patient listener. She kept me sane during the drafting of *A Kiss in the Shadows*, or at least she made a valiant effort to do so. Creating the world of Lost Coast Harbor with her has been more fun than I could have imagined. I love this world we're building and am excited to hang out here with our imaginary friends for many more books to come. Thanks also, Lily, for lending me Bree Rogers. I can't wait to read her story in *Sins of Her Past*.

Thank you to my editors, who made this book so much better. Jodi Henley always provides thoughtful editorial guidance and insight into my characters' journeys. Kaari Busick made sure I was saying what I meant to say, and I'm grateful for her brilliant copy-editing skills. If there are any errors, that's on me.

Lily and I want to also thank the Divas community for its support and encouragement as we launched this venture. In particular, thanks to Zoe York for so generously sharing her experience and advice in planning a series.

About the Author

Eve Kincaid is a lapsed lawyer who decided that fictional crime was more fun than the real deal. When she's not writing about mysterious women and the men who love them, she's probably shopping for books, lipstick, or imported cheeses to complement a nice California pinot noir.

You can keep up with Eve's new releases by signing up for her reader newsletter at evekincaid.com. She'd love to hear from you. Just don't be creepy about it.